HIGH-STAKES BOUNTY HUNTER

Melinda Di Lorenzo

HARLEQUIN

ROMANTIC
SUSPENSE

If you purchased this book without a cover you should be aware that this book is stolen property. It was reported as "unsold and destroyed" to the publisher, and neither the author nor the publisher has received any payment for this "stripped book."

HARLEQUIN® ROMANTIC SUSPENSE™

Recycling programs for this product may not exist in your area.

ISBN-13: 978-1-335-62880-0

High-Stakes Bounty Hunter

Copyright © 2021 by Melinda A. Di Lorenzo

All rights reserved. No part of this book may be used or reproduced in any manner whatsoever without written permission except in the case of brief quotations embodied in critical articles and reviews.

This is a work of fiction. Names, characters, places and incidents are either the product of the author's imagination or are used fictitiously. Any resemblance to actual persons, living or dead, businesses, companies, events or locales is entirely coincidental.

This edition published by arrangement with Harlequin Books S.A.

For questions and comments about the quality of this book, please contact us at CustomerService@Harlequin.com.

Harlequin Enterprises ULC
22 Adelaide St. West, 40th Floor
Toronto, Ontario M5H 4E3, Canada
www.Harlequin.com

Printed in U.S.A.

"And he's the one who took Katie."

"You know I'm going to ask why," Noah replied softly.

"Do you always ask your clients personal questions like that?"

Elle pulled her hands out of his, and the cool air hit his skin, making the loss of contact more acute than it ought to have been. Noah looked down at his empty palms before raising his gaze to her face again.

"I always ask the questions that need to be asked so that I can do my job effectively."

"You don't need to know why he took Katie. You just need to know that he did. And that he had no right to do it."

There was a defensiveness in her tone that spiked Noah's concern. Why tell him the kidnapper's name if she wasn't going to give him a reason? Why hold back? What was she holding back? He opened his mouth to ask her as much, but a knock at the door cut him short. He almost stayed put so he could demand an answer. Then he remembered that the little girl's life depended on time as well as information, so he pushed to his feet and moved to the door with worry clouding his mind.

* * *

Amazon bestselling author **Melinda Di Lorenzo** writes in her spare time—at soccer practices, when she should be doing laundry and in place of sleep. She lives on the beautiful west coast of British Columbia, Canada, with her handsome husband and her noisy kids. When she's not writing, she can be found curled up with someone else's good book.

Chapter 1

It was ten in the morning, and already the sun beat down so hard that Elle Charger regretted her clothing choice. Come noon, she'd be dying. Her top was sleeveless and light, but it was also black, and the dark color drew in the heat, making the fabric stick to her skin. She'd had the foresight to put on shorts, but they didn't do much to cool her off, either. In fact, they might even be making things worse. Sweat was pooling at the cuffs, and her legs itched from the quick shave job she'd done. Even her hastily pony-tailed hair—blond and barely shoulder length—felt sticky.

And you've been walking for only five minutes, pointed out a voice in her head. *Imagine how much worse it's going to get.*

She groaned and wished she was sitting in front of the portable A/C unit back in the first-floor apartment she'd rented for the month. But she'd promised Katie a day out. And breaking promises was something she didn't do. She'd assured the kid that there'd be swings and slides and possibly ice cream, if they could find a shop nearby.

And speaking of Katie…

Elle squinted against the unforgivingly bright light. The dark-haired girl was barely half a block ahead, but it was still a bit of an effort to keep her petite six-year-old body in perfect view. She darted in between trees and benches, seemingly unaffected by the all-around swelter. Katie was like that. Almost impervious to the seasons. She forgot her mittens in the winter, and never grabbed a raincoat no matter how hard it rained.

Smiling, Elle watched as Katie grabbed hold of a lamp standard and did a spin, then let out a noisy giggle. A moment later, she jumped down and bent over, momentarily disappearing from view before immediately popping back up again. Elle swiped a bit of sweat off her brow, and fought an urge to call the little girl to come closer. She wasn't really that far ahead. And Elle knew that any second, Katie would stand up, spin and run back. It was a game the kid was overly fond of—sprinting ahead, sprinting back, and then calling Elle a slowpoke. For no good reason, Katie thought it was hilarious. And as nervous as the separation made Elle, she still indulged. As always.

I just want a normal life for you, kiddo, she thought.

And right now, outward appearances made it seem like she was succeeding. Katie looked utterly carefree. Her French braids whipped with her spinning, and an older woman with a cane paused on the other side of the street to smile indulgently at her visible zest for life. No one would be able to tell from looking at her that they'd spent the last week on the road, making their way from Toronto to Vancouver, or that Katie had been through six schools over the course of her kindergarten career. They wouldn't suspect the agony Elle had gone through in deciding to enroll her in the first place, and they'd probably be shocked to hear about the danger that hung over their lives.

A sharp sting of familiar worry slid in under the heat and gave her a chill that was anything but pleasant. But Elle was quick to stow it when she saw Katie turn and bound back.

"Did you see him, Momma?" she called out excitedly as she approached.

Elle resisted a need to jerk Katie out of view and forced a small smile and a light tone. "See who, little love?"

"There was a big fluffy cat up there!"

Elle exhaled. "A big fluffy cat?"

Katie nodded and bounced a little. "He was just lying beside that bench, and when I said hello, he purred. Guess what his name was?"

"Mr. Fluffy Pants?"

"No."

"Linda?"

"That's a girl's name!"

"Well, are you sure he was a boy?"

Katie nodded. "I read his nametag."

"Hmm. Maybe you'd better just tell me then."

"Three more guesses, Momma. Please?" Katie begged.

Elle conceded. "Okay. Was it… Lyle?"

"No."

"Erik the Great?"

"No."

"Hmm. Final guess. How about… Kidney Bean?"

"Momma!"

Elle grinned. "My guesses are up. You have to tell me now."

"It was Billy Boddington," Katie announced proudly. "That's a weird name for a cat, right?"

Elle fought a laugh. "It sure is."

Katie's little forehead wrinkled in a way that made her look like a worried old lady. "It also said he lived on Greenburn Street. But the sign up there says Redburn Avenue." She pointed to the street sign in question. "Do you think he's lost, Momma?"

Elle's heart squeezed. "No, little love. I don't think he's lost. He's probably just visiting."

Katie's forehead smoothed out. "Well, that's a relief."

This time, Elle couldn't contain her chuckle. "How old are you again?"

"I'm six, silly Momma. You know that!"

She scampered ahead again, and as Elle watched her go, she felt her own forehead wrinkle. Katie was only six. Just barely. Her birthday had passed only a little over a week ago. But her heart and mind often seemed much older. And her ability to read so well was just the tip of the development iceberg. At her last school—the one they'd just left—the kindergarten teacher had called Elle in for a parent-teacher conference. Elle had been worried. So much so that she'd seriously considered taking Katie and running right then and there. But there'd been only a month left in the school year, and she'd made the kid another unbreakable promise—that Katie could go to her kindergarten graduation.

So she'd sucked it up and gone in. And when she'd arrived at the classroom and sat down for the discussion, she'd literally been aching with tension. But Ms. Lisa had jumped right in, explaining that she felt Katie was gifted. She wanted to put her name forward for a special program. One not just based on academic accomplishment—though Katie did excel there as well—but one for kids who shone in other ways.

And Elle has that shine, the teacher had said, sounding utterly delighted.

Elle had been overwhelmed. And deeply torn. On the one hand, she knew in her heart that Katie deserved the benefit of the very best school. And if she was gifted—which Elle had no trouble believing—then she also deserved to be challenged. But on the other hand, standing out meant unwanted attention. It meant more carefully kept records. And though the little girl's name had been changed so long ago that she never knew herself as anyone but Katie Marie Pearl, one glance at her little face, and her father would recognize her in an instant. There was far too much of him in her features. And there was the little scar over her eyebrow. The wickedly curved mark that her dad had left her with on the day that Elle took her away for good.

Elle exhaled, thinking of how the teacher's eyes had widened with surprise when Elle asked how long she had to decide about the enrichment program. The other woman flat out said that no one had ever declined, so she wasn't sure if there was a cutoff. And Elle had mumbled an excuse about a possible move that summer, then got out of the classroom as fast as humanly possible. At home, she'd automatically started packing. Stuffing what few items they kept permanently into the well-worn, well-traveled suitcase they'd shared. But the rare look of disappointment on Katie's face, and her whisper—"you promised"—had stopped Elle from going through with it. She'd stuck it out. Stayed on until just last week, praying the whole time that it wasn't a mistake.

And it wasn't, she told herself now, watching as Katie paused at the crosswalk ahead, then turned and sprinted back.

"Come on, Momma!" she said. "I saw the park! The slide is huge!"

Stuffing away her melancholy, Elle laughed and let

Katie grab her fingers and tug her along faster. Together, they looked both ways, then crossed the road. On the other side, Katie dropped Elle's hand, then bolted into the playground. In spite of the heat, it was full of moms and kids, and in seconds, Katie was pushing a little boy on a swing, chattering away happily.

It's going to be fine, Elle thought.

Low River was the perfect town to spend the summer in. Nestled between a riverside campground and an out-of-the-way hiking area, it was just touristy enough that they wouldn't stand out, and just small enough that Elle wasn't worried about who was lurking around every corner.

She watched as the boy and Katie traded places.

"Excuse me," said a feminine voice.

Startled in spite of the friendly tone, Elle jumped a little, then turned her head. A woman with a baby carrier on her chest smiled and pointed down.

"Sorry," said the woman. "I didn't mean to scare you. I just noticed your shoelace was undone. Thought you might want to know."

Elle managed to smile back. "Thanks."

She bent down, tightened the lace and secured a new bow—double knotting it for good measure—then stood up again, ready to add a more genuine expression of gratitude. But the woman was gone. And so was Katie.

Noah Loblaw paused at the end of the road and glared up the street. He was already in a foul mood, and his current view was just the metaphorical icing on the cake from hell. Which had been served up in stages. Unpleasant ones. It started this morning when his truck had chosen—on the hottest day of the year so far—to blow a gasket. He'd waited an hour for a tow truck before the company finally called him back to tell him their primary driver was out sick and that their backup driver's wife had just gone into labor. Then Noah's phone had died. So he'd walked for thirty-eight minutes—and yeah, he'd counted them—to get to the mechanic, then found a closed sign on the door. He'd taken it as a hint to just go home. Except that hadn't worked out either. Fifteen more minutes of walking, and he'd run into yet another problem. A detour. Multiple intersections closed for underground utility repairs.

With a wordless mutter, he gave the button for the walk signal a third tap. The stupid thing hadn't changed yet. He supposed he could've just run across. He was a grown man, and if he chose to jaywalk, the consequences were on him. It wasn't like shooting up a bank. Except if he was being honest, he wasn't exactly in a hurry to cross. He could see the top of the twisty slide in the playground just ahead. He could already hear the children's laughs and squeals and the mothers calling out to be careful. He knew he was dreading walking past.

Noah ground his teeth together.

The sounds themselves weren't unpleasant. They didn't actually grate on him. Maybe they evoked more emotion than he would've liked, but it'd be a lie to say it bothered him on some negative level. But he had rules, and cutting past the playground violated one of them.

No kids.

He kept to it obsessively in regard to his work. It only made sense to let it spill into his day-to-day life. Staying away from parks and school zones and pretty much everywhere that appealed to the twelve-and-under crowd just made it easier. If it weren't for the three-way road closure and the fact that the heel of his left boot had come loose and started to flop up and down, he would've taken a longer route. As it was, making his way past the kids and their moms would get him home in two minutes.

Assuming I don't get hit by a bus while I cross the road, Noah thought grimly as the light finally changed.

On cue, a car came whipping around the corner, too fast and too hard. He just barely managed to pull back in time. The driver laid on his horn, too. Like it was Noah who didn't have the right of way. He reined in an urge to lift his middle finger.

No unnecessary attention.

It was another rule. He needed to be able to blend in with a crowd when the occasion called for it. Or at least not be too memorable. And his two-hundred pound six-foot-four-inch frame already made that hard enough.

He watched the rear of the car disappear around the corner, then breathed out and stepped into the crosswalk. He moved quickly over the hot pavement. But by the time he'd reached the other side, his speed and his posture had already changed. He'd unconsciously jammed his hands into his pockets, hunched his wide shoulders, and dipped his head low. His feet had slowed, his broken size thirteen boots smacking rhythmically against the ground.

C'mon, Noah, he silently chided himself. *If you don't want to draw attention to yourself, you probably shouldn't stalk by a playground looking like a creep.*

He knew it was true. He could picture exactly how he'd appear to the moms in the park. Unkempt hair, dirty blond and a little too long to be called anything but shaggy. A couple of days' worth of beard on his chin. Long jeans, ripped in the knee, white tank top, sweat-soaked to his chest and speckled with dirt from the overly long trek from the highway. Like he'd just been released from prison, spent three days on a bender in a biker bar, then emerged into the sun, ready to steal away their children.

The irony of the thought—juxtaposed against his past—was almost enough to elicit a dark laugh. Not quite, though.

Noah's bad mood wouldn't let the chuckle pass through his lips.

Grimacing instead, he made a concentrated effort to give off less of a kidnapper vibe. He couldn't do anything about his clothes, but he did his best to adjust where he could. He rolled his shoulders and straightened them. He forced his hands out of his pockets and held them loose at his sides, then tried to relax his face into some semblance of normalcy. Indifference to the nearness of the park and its inhabitants.

You gonna pull out a razor and shave, too? asked a sardonic voice in his head.

He snorted at the sarcasm, but he also grabbed the thick rubber band from his wrist and twisted it into his hair, just at the top of his neck. The art of creating a ponytail was still new to him. Something he'd done in desperation once while trying to unlock a coded safe, and which he'd been doing with increasing frequency as of late. Each time, he reminded himself that he needed to take a half hour and get a haircut. Something he wished he'd actually done as he got closer to the park.

The layout of the street was such that Noah had a choice. He could either stay the course, remain on the sidewalk and go directly past the playground. Or he could step across the cobblestone, pedestrian-only pathway under the cover of the large trees on the other side. The latter had more appeal, but he suspected it would also be more likely to draw suspicion.

Nothing like a man lurking in the bushes to motivate a hasty 9-1-1 call, he thought.

He flexed his hands, unclenched his jaw, and made his way over the cobblestone. On the sidewalk, he concentrated on looking natural. He walked at a reasonable pace. Tried to look like he wasn't overthinking the whole thing.

Which, of course, was exactly what he was doing. Over-thinking his walk. The way he held himself. The correct side of the damn road. The fact that his efforts to look natural probably had just the opposite effect.

Exhaling, he rolled his shoulders again.

A man who's trying too damned hard to look like he doesn't care just ends up looking like he does care.

The thought had a proverbial ring to it, but Noah knew it was just because it was true. For the third time in as many minutes, he brought his shoulders up, moved them back, then dropped them down again. This time, he lifted his eyes for good measure. Just a cursory glance in the direction of the park, because the kids' shouts and laughter had reached a crescendo, and it would've been odder not to look. When his gaze came up, though, it didn't find the source of the fun. Instead, his attention landed on a twenty-something blonde. And it stayed there.

Noah was so engrossed that he just about tripped over his own boots.

It wasn't so much that she was too pretty to look away from. Though really, in another setting—even in the slightly worn clothes and the battered-looking shoes—she might've been. Probably more than pretty, actually. Stunning in a girl-next-door way. Her hair was a perfect shade. Honey. Sunshine. All the good stuff. She was curvy, but short. Just the right height for pressing her head into the chest of a six-foot-four man. Makeup free, full pink lips, high cheekbones… Noah noted all of it. He even had a fleeting moment of wishing he could see the color of her eyes. But it was secondary, because every instinct in his body screamed something more important.

The look on her face.

The tilt of her head.

The quick back and forth of her eyes.

She's looking for her kid.

The realization hit Noah hard. Old panic—*personal* panic—rolled through him, and this time, he did trip over his boots. He had to grab hold of the low fence around the playground to steady himself, and a curse nearly slipped out before he could stop it.

An unusual urge to break both his "no kids" and "no unnecessary attention" rules surged up. With that went a need to dash away a third edict—no freebies. Noah held the fence a little tighter, and he was pretty sure his grip was the only thing keeping him from rushing into the park.

Rein it in, Loblaw, he ordered silently. Action over emotion, like always.

It was the code by which he lived. The personal mantra he'd adopted in his teens and held fast to ever since. Except at the current moment, he not only couldn't act; he couldn't move at all. His gaze hung on the pretty blonde. He willed the kid to come running out from one of the covered playhouses. Thirty seconds passed. Then forty-five. Except for the odd flick of her eyes, the woman didn't move. She didn't even speak.

Why?

Noah knew from experience what an average mom did when she couldn't find her kid. She called out for her. She asked the other moms in the park if they'd seen her. She gave a panicked description. Checked every child that came even close to matching. Ran around like a crazy person, desperately searching. Not this woman, though.

An explanation popped to the front of his mind. The blonde didn't want anyone to know she was looking for her kid.

Why? Noah thought again.

Not shame at losing sight of her own child. Not doubt that the kid was missing, either. He could read her face.

So something else.

With his gut churning and his spine tingling, Noah took a slow, subtle look around. Eight moms. Two dads. Two dozen kids, and three dogs. Nothing amiss.

He widened the frame of his search, and that's when he spotted it. Spotted *him*. On the next street over—the one behind the park—was a dark-colored sedan. In its passenger seat was a bald-headed man staring far too intently at a newspaper.

In his head, a warning bell rang to life. The long-buried questions floated to the surface.

Did you see anything unusual?

Anyone dressed not for the weather?

Someone who just felt wrong?

A man alone?

Please, Noah. You must have seen something.

Noah couldn't shake the memories off. He breathed out, and—against both his better judgment and his rules—he let go of the fence and strode right into the playground and straight up to the pretty blonde.

Chapter 2

This isn't happening. There has to be a logical explanation.

The same two thoughts kept running through Elle's mind, each time followed by an excuse for Katie's continued absence.

She's in that little green house over there.

But even from where she stood, Elle could see that a solitary boy in a blue ball cap was the only person seated at the table inside the structure.

She went to the bathroom.

But Katie would never, ever leave without saying something.

The excuses came faster.

She's playing with those kids under the trees. She joined the baseball game over there. She's playing hide-and-seek.

With each new theory, Elle swung her gaze and found no evidence to support her idea. Hope was sliding from view. And yet her brain argued. Pleaded. Insisted.

This.

Isn't.

Happening.

But her body knew the truth. Panic was a wave under her skin. Fear clouded her vision, and her lips tingled with the terrible reality. She swayed. And she braced for a collapse. Her feet, though, were rooted to the spot, as though someone had poured concrete around her shoes.

She knew what she was supposed to be doing. Calling Katie's name. Then yelling it. Darting through the park. Flipping from mom to mom to mom, asking if they'd seen her. Finally, acknowledging that she really was gone, then calling the police.

Except she couldn't do any of that. In her head, she could hear a voice, telling her—low and deadly—what would happen. It was his voice—the man she wouldn't name, even to herself—and the words were seared into her memory.

I'll find you both, and when I do, I'll take her. She's mine. Rightfully. And you'll have a choice. You can forget her. Leave her. Or you can come looking...and I'll kill her. A pause. A light crackle on the phone. *But not you. You... I'll leave alive. That way, you'll always know whose fault it is that she's dead.*

It was the one time in six years that he'd nearly caught up to them. And it was only a phone call. One that came in the middle of the afternoon, right during Katie's naptime. Elle had answered quickly, hoping that the unexpected interruption wouldn't wake the little girl in her toddler bed. She'd anticipated a telemarketer or a wrong number. Anything—anyone—but him. The moment she'd heard his voice, she'd wanted to hang up. But she'd needed to know just how close he was to locating them. The relief that all he'd tracked down was her phone number had been a physical thing. So had the realization that she hadn't been careful enough.

Elle had grabbed two-year-old Katie, the diaper bag, and nothing else. Not her car, nor a single item of clothing. She'd taken the bus. Seventeen hours. And on the long trip, she'd come up with a new plan. Never stay anywhere longer than three months. Cash jobs, burner phones and no community connections. Nothing traceable. And it had worked.

Until now.

Her head swiveled again. A small part of her brain asked if maybe she should do all those things any normal mother would be doing. The yelling. The police. But a bigger part of her knew that his words had been more than a threat. She had the memories to prove it. There was the singular most terrifying one—the time he'd pulled out his knife and slit a man's throat, right in front of her. And there were the longer-term scars, too. Mental and physical. The poorly healed broken rib. The burn marks under her left arm. The nightmares that she fought on a nightly basis.

Except it wasn't herself she was really worried about. She'd endured the abuse for years, and while she'd sworn never to be under his thumb again, she knew just how much she could suffer through. It was Katie she cared about. Katie she had to protect.

Oh, God. Katie.

Elle's throat constricted with fear and worry and all the feelings that hovered under the surface during her day-to-day life. And beside those…the terror that this was her moment of failure. What was she going to do? She truly didn't know.

She let herself have a moment. She spun, eyes searching the playground for what she knew would turn out to be one more fruitless time. But as she turned in her slow circle, a hand suddenly landed on her arm. It paralyzed her. Not because the grip was hard or rough. If anything, it was gentle. But fright stilled her. And she braced for a threat. A marching order that would undoubtedly lead to her death. And a masculine voice did immediately fill her ear. Only it held a warning instead of a threat.

"You should turn around and pretend you know me," the strange man said quietly. "Be excited to see me, even. I have a feeling that if you don't, the gentleman in the car over there—just to your left—is going to follow through on some unpleasant plans for you." He paused. "If I'm wrong, feel free to kick me in the shins. If I'm right…my name is Noah."

Elle had no real reason to trust the man attached to the voice. But a quick look to her left told her that he—Noah—was right. About the car, anyway. It was dark colored and out of place.

Is Katie inside?

As soon as she wondered it, Elle knew that the answer was a resounding no. The man who wanted Katie was far too clever for that. Whoever sat in the vehicle was simply there to find her. And to observe her reaction.

Exhaling, she plastered her biggest, most winning smile onto her face. Then she spun, an equally enthusiastic greeting on her tongue.

"Noah! Is that seriously you?" she said. "It feels like it's been forever!"

She barely had time to process his looks—intimidatingly tall, shaggy, biker-esque hair pulled into a ponytail, and a very attractive, stubble-peppered face—before he yanked her into a thorough hug. He even lifted her off the ground and pressed his lips to her cheekbone.

"Your name?" he murmured.

"Elle," she whispered back, her voice surprisingly breathless.

"Elle!" he said as he set her down and pulled away. "You look fantastic."

His eyes did roam over her for a second, but she caught the way they flicked toward the car again before settling on his face. He dragged her in for another hug, his lips brushing her cheek in a second light kiss.

"In case you were wondering… The thing you're looking for?" he whispered in her ear. "It's not in that car."

"Yes," she breathed back, disturbed to hear Katie referred to as an object, even though she understood that it was a logical precaution. "I figured."

Noah released her again, his face dominated by a wide smile that didn't come even close to touching his eyes. "I only have a minute. Work break. But I saw you standing over here, and I couldn't pass by without saying something. Sit with me to catch up for a few seconds?"

He nodded toward a nearby bench, and as much as Elle wanted to scream that the last thing she wanted to do was to sit still, she nodded. "Sure. I'd love that."

He guided her to the bench, gestured for her to sit first, then settled in beside her, his denim-clad knee resting against hers as if they knew each other well enough to sit like this often. As he turned his head her way, his mouth stayed easy, his jaw relaxed, his forehead smooth. But when he met her eyes, his near-black irises were so intense that Elle felt physically immobilized by their stare. So, when he leaned forward and brushed back a loose strand of hair from her face, she didn't move at all. Not even when he stayed so close that she could feel the light heat of his lips as he spoke again.

"I don't know what the hell's going on," he said, his cheerful tone at odds with his words. "And honestly, I don't want to. But if you're not going to call the police, I have to assume you have a damn good reason."

She nodded and managed a smile. "I do."

"Then here's what I'll tell you. Your friend in the car? He's a lookout of some kind. The person who took your… property…is long gone. Car dude is waiting to see what you'll do. Understand?"

Every one of his words caused another little stab of fear, but Elle managed—just barely—to hold it in. "Yes."

"Good. Have you got a phone?"

"Yes," she repeated.

"Okay," Noah replied. "You're going to pretend like I'm giving you my number."

Elle swallowed, leaned back enough that she could drag out her cell from her pocket, then held out the slim device expectantly. The rough-looking man took it, flipped it his way, and typed into the screen, then handed it back. Elle looked down, and she was surprised to see he'd put an actual phone number into the address book. She'd been anticipating a coded message.

"That's the number of a friend," Noah stated. "He's good at locating stolen property."

Her pulse jumped, and she bit back another thrum of fright. "Thank you."

He nodded once, then slung an arm around her shoulders and pulled her close, raising his voice as he did it. "It was fantastic seeing you again, Elle. You've got my number now. Don't forget to use it."

She blinked up at him, hearing the emphasis behind his last statement. And before she could muster up a response—or even a falsely cheerful goodbye—Noah gave her shoulder a squeeze, then turned and strode away, leaving her alone. With no Katie. A strange man watching her from a car. And an insurmountable fear in her heart.

* * *

Noah could've kicked himself. What was he thinking, violating his own rules like that? The park. The kid. Both a recipe for trouble. That wasn't even factoring in the fresh-faced woman and her palpable fear. Stupid mistake to jump into what was obviously a complicated personal situation. Probably a custody thing.

Yeah, yeah, said an annoying voice in his head. *That's probably all true. But what's worse? Breaking your arbitrary rules, or leaving that pretty blonde alone back there?*

For a second, her big blue eyes hung at the front of his mind. Oddly haunted. Afraid for her kid. And with no one to help her. Yet somehow trusting, too.

You're being melodramatic, he told himself. *You gave her Kirk's number, and he's the best there is in the kid-retrieval business.*

Although that wasn't quite true. Noah's twin sister, Norah, was the actual best in the business. Hell. She ran a real-life reputable hostage negotiation firm. She often worked closely with the police. Her cases were sometimes worked on behalf of high-profile figures. Celebrities. Politicians. Her success rate was phenomenal, too. She was also pricey, rarely took pro bono work and didn't do parental rights disputes. Oh, and she hadn't spoken to Noah in close to a year. All in all, offering a referral her way would probably have done more harm than good.

Didn't make you help the blonde personally, though, did it?

He scoffed at the self-directed guilt trip. It wasn't that Noah himself didn't care what happened to the kid or the kid's mom. Just the opposite, really. He wanted them to be safe. Hence, the referral. Maybe the man was only second best, but he was still a better option than Noah himself. A bounty hunter was not a lawyer or a family counselor.

"And Kirk does a damn fine job," he muttered.

The weirdest thing about it, though, was that he felt no relief at having handed off the woman to his acquaintance. *Elle.* Her name—simple but pretty—rolled over a few times in his head. Pleasantly. Worriedly. Was her kid a boy, or a girl? Was this actually a custody thing? Was she on the run from an ex? And most of all…what kind of jerk was he that he knew what'd happened, yet still took off?

Not my circus, not my monkeys, he insisted as he crossed the road.

Still. He had to walk a little faster to resist the urge to turn back. Determined to shake off the unusual—and unwanted—surge of conscience, he dug his hands into his pockets and focused on forward momentum. He took the next couple of streets at random, hoping that it would give his mind time to settle. Instead, it seemed to have the opposite effect. With no clear destination in mind, his brain churned even harder.

Living by a code mattered to Noah. His morals were sound, even if his chosen career sometimes took him into more gray areas than straight-up black-and-white. It was just that allowing his emotions to overrule his own code opened the door to weakness. Softness. A tendency toward feeling instead of doing. And with all that came something else—a hell of a lot of room for hesitation. Which he didn't have time for in his work or in his day-to-day existence.

He rolled his shoulders a little, mentally reaffirming that he knew what he'd just done was right. A good deed. After all, he could've kept going when he realized what was happening. He could've told the woman what he'd seen, then not shared Kirk's number. He sure as hell came in contact with enough shady characters to know there were many people who would've ignored the situation altogether, kid or no kid.

His mind wandered back to Elle, wondering if she still sat where he'd left her, or if she'd moved to a quiet place to make the call. Out of sight of the man in the car. *The man in the car.* Thinking about him gave Noah another stab of guilt, this one more forceful than the last.

Yeah, Loblaw. That's because you can tell yourself whatever you want, but inside, you know that any normal dude would've made sure the creep wasn't going after her directly.

Noah tried to brush off the thought as he'd done with all the others he'd had so far. He failed. With a sigh, he stopped abruptly, wondering if it was even possible to win an argument with his own, blunt conscience. He suspected not.

Sure, he wasn't the blonde's personal bodyguard. And yeah, whatever was going on with her and her missing kid and her lack of calling the police was really none of his concern. But everyday decency did kind of dictate that he make sure someone wasn't going to jump out of a car and kill her right then and there, though, didn't it? Even the minuscule shred of chivalry that Noah considered himself to possess hollered that he ought to have stuck around for a minute or two. So—dropping a curse under his breath— he started to turn around. And he immediately realized he didn't have to. The random streets he'd traversed hadn't been quite so random at all. All he'd done was circle to the other side of the park. Like he'd unconsciously known what he'd decide anyway.

Sighing, he swung a look toward the spot where he knew the car should be sitting. He didn't quite complete the glance, though, because when he swiveled his head, he caught a flash of unidentifiable color disappearing behind a building just a ways up the block. Noah's spine tingled.

It looked as though someone had been following him, seen that he'd been about to catch them, then hidden.

What the hell?

His gut wavered between wanting to duck out of sight and wanting to initiate an angry confrontation. Assuming someone was actually there, and he wasn't just being paranoid. He held still and waited, his eyes on the now-empty spot, his mind on Elle and the man who'd been watching her. The two things had to be connected. A random tail, right at this moment, would be too coincidental, and while Noah's job might bring him in contact with unsavory people now and then, he was careful enough that disgruntled clients weren't an issue.

And that's what I get for breaking my own rules.

He stared for another few seconds, but the street remained still, and Noah knew he had to make a choice. If someone was following him, they were unlikely to reappear while he watched. Growling wordlessly—and damning his spontaneous decision to approach the blonde in the first place—he opted to steal a quick look at the park. First, he sought the car, and his relief at finding it in the same spot was oddly deep. Next, he brought his attention to the park itself, scanning for the blonde. When he didn't find her, his heart did an unusual thing—it squeezed hard in his chest with concern. He tried to tamp it down, but the effort only made it spike.

Where was she?

Momentarily forgetting about his own potential stalker, he slowed his perusal of the playground and surrounding area and told himself not to assume the worst. She could've taken off in search of her kid. Or maybe found somewhere quiet to call Kirk. Either made sense. Except as he mentally posited the theories, the sudden squeal of tires made him dismiss them altogether.

Crap.

His eyes flicked to the dark-colored sedan just in time to see it peel away. Rules and codes and excuses all disappeared with the taillights. Automatically, Noah's attention dropped to the license plate, trying to memorize it before the car slipped completely out of sight. He caught only the last three digits, and he took three steps before remembering that he couldn't chase down a vehicle while on foot. His brain went into analytical mode, slamming quickly through his options, and dismissing them twice as fast as they came. The first and only one that stuck was to call a business associate who had an uncanny ability to digitally stalk vehicles. The man came with a hefty price tag, though, and was questionable as hell in the ethics department.

Only option, Noah thought grimly.

He dragged his phone from his pocket, spun with the intention of placing the call and making his way home—where his resources were—at the same time. Except the turn yielded him another flash of moving color. His stalker was still there. Closer, even.

Unusual tension rolled through Noah. He was accustomed to being in control. Now he had a missing woman, missing kid and missing car. Someone was tailing him, and he genuinely didn't know which thing to shove to the top of his priority list.

"Seriously," he muttered. "I don't have time for this garbage."

A voice on the other end of the phone spoke up then, making him jump.

"You called me, man," said his acquaintance. "No need to be so salty."

Noah grunted and started to pass off the call as a pocket

dial, but then changed his mind. "Sorry, Spud. It's Loblaw here."

"Yeah, man. I know who it is. I have call display. Like about six billion other people."

"Funny. You got time for a quick trace with a partial plate?"

"No such thing as a quick trace with a partial."

Noah gritted his teeth. "How much?"

"How fast you want it?" the other man replied.

"Fast." He didn't mention the woman or her kid; it would only drive up the price.

The other man paused, then said, "Double my standard fee."

Noah wanted to ask if he really expected to get that much, but Elle's blue eyes filled his mind again, and he opted for not quibbling. "Fine. I'll pay you in the usual way. But I'm gonna need to do it post job this time."

"You're kidding, right?"

"Time's ticking by, Spud."

There was another pause. "Triple."

"Holy— Fine." Noah ran his finger over his stubble and did his best to keep his voice level. "I need GPS coordinates pinged to this phone. Preferably."

"I'm not a flipping magician."

"You saying you're incapable?" When he got no reply but a grunt, he continued. "Dark sedan. No make or model markings. Last three numbers are four-five-nine."

"That's all you're gonna give me? You can't be—"

Noah tapped the phone off before the other man could finish—and before he could ask for quadruple his rate—then pocketed the device. It wasn't an ideal situation, and he far would've preferred to have gone after the car and the woman himself. But he was sure Spud would come through. He always had in the past. Knowing that a small bit of reassurance was in place, Noah narrowed his eyes in the direction of the flash of movement. Whoever was following him could probably answer a question or two about the rest of what was going on. It'd give him something to focus on, too, while he waited for Spud.

"All right," he said. "Let's see if you can outmaneuver me."

He spun quickly, darted a quick look back and forth, then jogged across the road. Once on the other side, he pivoted again, and took off to his left. He passed two squat houses, then cut up a path that acted as a shortcut to the next block. Picking up his pace, he hurried past another three homes, around a corner, then straight through a yard.

Noah wasn't being particularly stealthy, but he wasn't being elephant-esque, either. Too-subtle movements might mean losing the stalker for real. Too-obvious ones would give away his game.

He kept going for a short while longer. Up the alley behind the yard. Between a truck and a camper van. Around a large shrub. Finally, he paused behind a six-foot fence, ducked down, and waited. It took only a few seconds before the light tap of approaching feet hit his ears.

He tensed as they got closer. He prepared for a fight. Except when the person following him rounded the wooden slats, it wasn't the hooded bandit he'd pictured. Instead, a petite body slammed into his chest, and a blond ponytail whacked him straight in face.

Chapter 3

For several panicked moments, Elle assumed the worst—that her plan to ditch the man in the car had failed. That he'd intercepted her attempt to catch up with the strange biker-type guy and that she was going to be hauled off and made to relive the nightmares of her past. And worse, she was going to have to watch Katie suffer through the same. Blackness hovered around her vision, and she thought she might faint.

No! her mind protested. *No, I can't let this happen!*

She hadn't run this far and protected Katie for this long to just lose it all because she was scared. Drawing on thoughts of saving the little girl, she forced herself to lift a fist in an attempt to fight off the attack. But a strong hand immediately closed on her wrist, stopping her before she could start. She lifted the other hand. Her assailant did the same. He held both her arms and said something she couldn't hear over the frantic thrum of her pulse.

A desperate scream built up in the back of her throat. But a heartbeat before it released, her sight cleared long enough for her to realize that her assumption was off. It wasn't the man from the car. It was the one from the park. *Noah.* And he was looking down at her with the strangest mix of emotions on his stubble-dotted face. Confusion. Relief. Concern. Irritation. Under other circumstances, it might've been comical. But there was nothing funny about the last fifteen minutes of her life. Nothing at all.

Her body sagged a little. He dropped her wrists. And she stared up at the big man, her voice breaking more than she would've liked when she spoke to him.

"Please," she said. "You have to help me."

He blinked a slow blink, and Elle noted vaguely that his eyelashes were enviably long, and that his irises were the deepest shade of hazel she'd ever seen. She could see hesitation in them. A guardedness that she could relate to. One she thought was going to make him send her on her way. But after a second, even slower blink, he asked a question. Growled it, really.

"Why the hell are you following me?"

Elle exhaled. It was better than being told to leave.

"I need your help," she told him.

He shook his head. "I don't do what you need."

She lifted her chin. "What do you do?"

His hazel eyes flicked pointedly up and down the alley. "What I don't do is discuss my personal business in the middle of the street with women who're chasing me."

She didn't let his snappish tone deter her. She needed to be firm and strong. For Katie's sake. At the thought of the little girl's name, Elle's throat burned.

No, she told herself. *Don't cry. That'll just make things worse.*

"I'm not interested in your personal business," she replied in as even a tone as she could muster up. "I'm interested in your *business* business."

"I already told you I don't do what you need."

"I heard you. But I don't believe you."

His face darkened. "Calling me a liar isn't going to help you plead your case."

"What will help me, then?" she countered. "Threats? Screams? Because whatever it is, I'll do it. Katie is six. She'll be terrified for good reason. And I'd throw myself in front of a bus to save her."

He ran a hand over his head in an exasperated way. "Call Kirk. Hire him. That's what'll help."

"I don't want to hire him."

"Why the hell not?"

For a second, Elle wasn't sure what to say. When Noah had slipped away, she'd tried to call the number he'd given her. But as she'd punched in the last digit, she'd frozen. In all the years that she'd been on the run, she'd never told a soul her story. She'd never asked for help. But God knew she needed it then. For Katie's sake, she'd willed herself to hit the final number. To have the strength to explain that she knew who had her kid. To admit that trying to find her was going to mean risking lives. Like, really risking. But that she'd take the chance. And then she'd have to hope like crazy that when she was done explaining it all, the unknown person on the other end of the line might still say yes.

But as she'd stood there, staring down at the phone, she'd realized she didn't have to go through those motions. Not if she was able to use the resource that had just tumbled into her life. Noah. Who was clearly competent. Who had to have some kind of know-how in the current kind of situation.

Of course, standing here now, it seemed a little crazy

to have run after him. Because as reassuring as his presence might've been in the park, he was a complete stranger. And intimidating.

A complete stranger whom you're asking for help.

It was true. But Elle had to take the best option she had. And he was it. If she had to trust anyone with any of it, this was the man she was going to pick. So she opted for a bit of honesty.

"Because I want to hire you," she admitted.

"I just told you this isn't what I do."

"I don't care what it is you normally do."

"Look. Even if I made an exception…you can't afford my services."

"You have no idea what I can afford," she said.

He grimaced. "You already owe me three thousand dollars, and I haven't even agreed to work for you yet."

She ignored the imaginary bill he was sending her way—she'd probably have to sell a kidney to come close to meeting his price—and latched onto the "yet," and pushed herself for even more honesty. "The truth is…you officially know more about my life than anyone else. So it doesn't matter what the cost is, and that's all the résumé you need."

His brows knit together. "I don't know a single damn thing about you."

Elle swallowed. "You know about Katie."

There was an extra heartbeat before his reply, and when he did speak, his voice had dropped timber and was gruffer, too. "We can't have this conversation here."

Did that mean they could have it somewhere else? Elle thought it was an opening. Almost. Or at least not a complete shutdown. But she didn't let the bubbling hope carry her away.

"I have to get to Katie," she said firmly.

"I heard you."

"You might've heard me. But I don't know if you understood what I meant. I need to get to Katie."

Something indefinable crossed his rough features. "I do understand."

The three words weren't a promise to help. They weren't even close. In fact, the statement and the tone in which he spoke it begged more questions than they offered any answers. But Elle wasn't there to get to know Noah. She'd followed him on a strange, unpredictable path through the streets for the sole purpose of soliciting his assistance. Her singlemindedness in getting Katie back wouldn't allow for questions about anything else.

She lifted her chin. "Help me."

His expression was the very definition of stormy. And she braced for him to shut her down with a finality she wouldn't be able to fight. But then he did something completely unexpected. He grabbed her hand, slid his fingers between hers, and a moment later, he was pulling her along the street. Striding along with her in tow like they were lovers in a hurry to get a tryst somewhere rather than two people who'd just met at a park.

At a park where Katie was taken. And met because Katie was taken. Her heart slammed painfully against her ribcage. *Oh, God. She's really gone.*

So Elle let this man take *her.* Even though she knew the action should've made her more worried. More scared. After all, he was leading her farther away from where she'd last seen Katie. And with no explanation. But all she felt was mild relief. It just blurred the edges of the fear. The quick speed helped, too. It meant that she didn't have time to focus on her dread.

The streets seemed to whip by, and in a little over five minutes, Noah slowed their pace enough that Elle could take a better look at her surroundings. It surprised her to see that they weren't in a commercial area. Even though she hadn't consciously thought about it, she guessed that she'd been subconsciously anticipating an office building of some kind. But what lay out on the street in front of them wasn't even close to that. And it wasn't residential, either. What they were approaching was most definitely a seedy motel.

Abruptly, Elle stopped. So hard, in fact, that she jerked the shaggy-haired man to a halt as well. Which was really saying something, considering his size and strength. Noah spun back, and the surprise was evident on his face, too.

"Thought this was urgent," he said.

Her gaze flicked to the motel. Then to Noah. He was looking at her…expectantly. And her brain did a weird analysis. A contradictory one. First, it pointed out the big man's intimidation factors. His size, obviously. The way the corded muscles stood out on his forearms. His ripped jeans and thick stubble and hair in need of a cut. Running into him in a dark alley would have sent most people high-tailing it in the other direction. And yet…he was undeniably attractive. Strong jaw. Perfect cheekbones, and soft lips. His skin was golden brown, like he spent a lot of time outside. There was no doubt that he probably drew a fair amount of female attention.

"Elle?" he prodded, making her start.

She felt her face heat up. "When I said I'd throw myself in front of bus to save Katie, and you said I couldn't afford you, this isn't really what I was thinking."

His brows knit together for a second. Then his face cleared, and he did something even more unexpected than grabbing her hand; he burst out laughing. The sound was a booming bass-filled one. It was pleasant, too.

"C'mon," he said as his chuckles tapered off. "Let's go inside. Before someone sees us together and thinks the same damn thing."

* * *

If someone had asked Noah ten minutes earlier if he'd be laughing his butt off about anything in the present situation, he would've vehemently denied the possibility. How could there be anything funny about a missing kid and her distraught mother? Yet somehow, Elle had managed to fill him with amusement. The look on her face as she concluded that he wanted her "services" as payment had been priceless. The head-to-toe glance that had puzzled him. The pink in her cheeks. The way she bit her lip like she was really considering it.

Noah was still grinning as he led her through the squeaky gate past the pool—devoid of water and full of leaves—and through the so-called garden—which was really just a mess of vines wrapped around someone's old bike—and straight up to his door. He grabbed the handle and turned, and the thin panel opened easily. He never locked it. With the exception of his laptop, his gun and some necessary ID, there was nothing of value in the room. Since those three things were in a military-grade safe that he'd taken the liberty of bolting to the floor in his closet, he was never too worried about his questionable neighbors walking in uninvited.

"Welcome to one-oh-five," he said, gesturing to Elle to go in first.

He forehead creased. "The number on the door says ten."

"Yeah. Apparently the five fell off a few years ago. Very confusing for pizza delivery dudes."

"Why don't you just get it fixed?" she asked, stepping through the door frame.

He followed her into the room, oddly conscious of the tiny bit of mess that he didn't normally care about. "Apparently replacement door numbers aren't included in the rent. I'm not gonna pay for it myself. On principle."

"Okay, then. I guess it's good to take a stand about the important things in life."

His mouth twitched. "Indeed it is."

As he tossed his keys into the unused ashtray on the dresser, then flicked on the air conditioner—the one good feature in an otherwise dismally bare-bones room—he pretended not to watch as Elle curiously perused the space. There was a solitary Chinese food box sitting on the edge of the trash can, and an array of local newspapers on the armchair in the corner. A stack of recently folded T-shirts sat on the nightstand, waiting to be put away. Cold coffee waited in a pot, and the hot plate needed a good wipe down. Noah had left the bed unmade this morning because he'd left in a hurry, and the pile of blankets lay scrunched up in the middle of the mattress, while a dog-eared copy of Stephen King's *The Stand* rested on his pillow. He couldn't help but note the way Elle's eyes hung on the bed for an extra second, and his earlier entertainment at her assumption of what he wanted from her faded away.

Would she really have done it?

The question—and the possible answer—had a dark undertone that rubbed Noah the wrong way. What had Elle and her kid been through, that it was even in the realm of plausible options? An unusual flash of protectiveness surged up under Noah's skin. He hated the idea of someone hurting the fresh-faced blonde and the daughter she clearly loved. Uncomfortable with the unexpected sensation, he cleared his throat and decided it was best to attempt to treat this like any other job.

Elle beat him to it. "About Katie… I've heard that the first twenty-four hours are critical."

"True in most cases, but let's not get ahead of ourselves,

all right?" he replied. "First things first. I want to make it clear that missing kids are outside my normal realm of—" He cut himself off before he could say expertise—because it would've been a lie—and smoothly changed it to "work."

Her expression became curious. "What *is* your realm of work?"

"I find and retrieve people who'd rather not be found and retrieved."

"For money."

"Couldn't pay for this lovely place without it." He swept his hand over the run-down space.

She met his gaze. "So you're basically a bounty hunter."

"More or less."

"And you don't work with kids. You live in a crappy motel. And you charge three thousand dollars for a single job?"

"Yes. Yes. And no." He cleared his throat again, feeling more than a bit awkward about what he had to admit. "That three K is a direct payment to the man I hired to find your stalker in the car."

"You hired someone to find the guy at the park?"

"Yeah. Surprised myself, too."

"I don't understand."

"Guilty conscience," Noah muttered, and then he sighed. "Look. If your ex is so determined to get his kid back that he's got something this elaborate—"

"You can stop right there," Elle said, her voice sharp. "The man who took Katie isn't my ex."

"Bull," he replied immediately.

Blue eyes blinked up at him, visibly startled. "Excuse me?"

"Are you particularly wealthy?" he asked.

He already knew the answer. In fact, he didn't doubt that she couldn't afford to pay him at all. A big part of

Noah's job was noticing the details, and Elle's details told him she wasn't in a position to be throwing cash around. Her shirt and shorts were worn-out in a way that wasn't designer, her hair had blunt ends that told him she probably used a one-hour, drop-in hairdresser rather than a real stylist, and her tennis shoes were a hundred percent knockoffs. He waited for her own answer anyway, wondering if she'd tell a lie. Or maybe avoid the question in an evasive maneuver of words.

After a second, though, she just shook her head. "No. I'm not particularly wealthy."

"And we both know this wasn't a random thing. The guy in the car. The fact that you didn't immediately start calling the police. It adds up to this being planned, and you knowing it was a possibility. I'm good at what I do, Elle, but you can go ahead and correct me if I'm wrong."

"No," she said softly. "You're not wrong."

"So. I don't buy it. People take kids for three reasons." He ticked them off on his fingers as he went on. "One. For things I'd prefer not to talk about. Two. To extort their parents for cash. Or three…because they have a parental rights issue."

Elle's gaze was unwavering, and so was her response. "All of that might be true. But I promise you, the person who took Katie from the park is nowhere near an ex of any kind. I have nothing to gain by lying about it. So please. Can we just get the details out of the way and move on to finding my kid?"

Noah yanked out the single wooden chair from his tiny table. "Have a seat."

For a second, he thought she was going to argue, but she just exhaled and sank down, her face weary and vulnerable and worldly all at the same time. "This is something you don't want to do. I'm not ignoring what you've said. But be honest with me. Is it something you *can* do?"

It was a chance to opt out. To simply say no. He was sure that if she believed he couldn't retrieve her daughter, that she'd walk out. But some reason, Noah couldn't make the lie come.

"Yes," he admitted instead. "Finding people is my job."

Her face stayed pinched. "And your success rate?"

"Very, very high."

"How high?"

"You know that term 'the one that got away'?"

"Yes."

"Applies perfectly to my track record. I've only had one miss."

Her eyes closed, then opened, and her relief was audible as she said, "Hit me with the price tag. Whatever it is, Katie is worth it."

Noah had to steel himself against the sudden need to reach out and take her hand, and he silently recited his mantra. Action over emotion.

"My flat rate is ten thousand dollars," he made himself say. "I typically take five up front, and the other five when I find the subject in question. The fee doesn't include expenses, which I keep track of and bill you for at the end. If I'm going to go over five hundred dollars at any one time—except in the case of emergency—I'll let you know ahead of time. If I ever think I can't complete the job, I'll refund you half of the five grand, minus the expenses." He paused, knowing she wasn't going to be pleased with what he said next. "I work alone, Elle."

As expected, her head shook vehemently. "No."

"Yes."

"I need to be there."

"That's not how this goes. I move quickly. I'm careful,

but I sometimes have to do things that seem irrational. On top of which, I can't take care of you and be effective at the same time."

Her eyes flashed with a mix of irritation and stubbornness. "You won't have to take care of me. I've been doing just fine on my own for the last six years."

"Until someone walked off with your kid," he snapped before he could stop himself.

Elle flinched, but to her credit, she kept her head high. "If you knew what kind of man he was, you'd know just how much skill it took to last this long."

"Why don't you tell me what kind of man he is, then? Or better yet, just tell me his name. It's going to be a hell of a lot easier if I have a good place to start."

"I'll do my best to explain. But I'm not going to sit on my hands while you look for Katie. I can be helpful. I know this guy. I know what he wants and what he's capable of."

"If you know all of that, then why're you bothering with me?"

She didn't flinch. "He'll be expecting me. And he knows my weaknesses."

"Which makes you a liability," Noah countered.

"My knowledge is an asset. But I don't have the skills to track where he'll take her. If I did, we wouldn't be having this conversation."

Frustration crept in. He felt like he was losing a battle he shouldn't have been fighting in the first place.

"Then let me ask you something else," he said. "Can you put aside that pit that's sitting in your stomach? The one that'll remind you over and over that you let her be taken? That you failed? That makes you feel sad and hard and scared and furious all at the same time?"

She blinked at him, and he realized he'd probably said far too much. He didn't give her a chance to respond. Very quickly, he added a question that he was sure would make her beg to stay in the background as he did what he was best at.

"Can you obey orders?"

Her blink became a frown. "You're kidding, right?"

"Dead serious. I can't stop and have an argument like this with every move I make. Some of your knowledge might be an asset, but that's not as important as knowing that you'd be able to do what I say, no questions asked. So if—"

He stopped short as a familiar noise carried through the thin walls from outside—the squeak of the front gate.

"What's wrong?" Elle asked right away.

"Someone's out there," Noah murmured.

She opened her mouth again, and he shook his head, waving off any further questions with a gesture to be quiet, then took a few careful steps toward the drawn curtain.

The sound wasn't odd in and of itself. What was weird was the protraction. People who lived in the motel tended to push the gate hard and fast to get it over with. People who were passing through as temporary guests tended to be startled by the grating noise. They usually paused when they heard the squeal, then started again a second later.

But this…

It sounded like someone trying desperately not to be heard.

Noah inched along the window, careful not to disturb the heavy fabric that hung over it. Though he hadn't made an effort to make the place his own, one thing he had done was invest in some drapes that blocked the room from prying eyes. Holding his breath, he took a hold of one corner of the curtain, moved it just wide enough to reveal a narrow view of the courtyard, and peered out through the diaphanous shade. A shadow of movement right by his door caught his eye, and he dropped a mental curse. He started to pull himself back, his mind on grabbing his gun, then getting himself and Elle out safely. Except as he reached up to flick the curtain shut again, something else drew his attention. Sitting across the street, just in sight, was the same dark sedan from the park.

How did he find us? Noah wondered. *We sure as hell hadn't taken the direct route home.*

Mulling it over, he watched for several more seconds. What he saw surprised him. The shadow flashed again, then solidified into a person—a skinny teenaged boy in a dark tank top and faded black jeans. The boy cast a slow look back and forth, visibly nervous. When he was surveying the empty courtyard, he ducked low, loped over the pavement and exited the gate with another noisy squeak. For a moment, he disappeared from view. When he popped up again, he was right behind the sedan. He walked past it quickly, but the move didn't fool Noah. He saw the kid's hand come out sideways just as he reached the window. He also caught the size and shape of the item that the teenager palmed, and he'd bet his left arm that it was a wad of cash.

But for what?

His mind churned. An idea slipped to the surface, and he dropped the curtain and grabbed his phone. With another quick motion to Elle to stay quiet, he slipped to the bathroom to place a call to his neighbor. After some specific instructions, he moved back into the main room. Ten seconds went by, and a shuffle sounded from outside. It was quickly followed by the crack of breaking plastic. Satisfied, Noah spoke over his shoulder.

"All right," he said. "You're gonna need to strip."

He snapped the curtain shut and swung to face a pair of startled blue eyes.

Chapter 4

Elle stared at Noah, sure she had to have misunderstood. "What?"

"You're going to need to take off your clothes," he said, a hint of impatience entering his voice.

Unconsciously, Elle's gaze slid to the bed. It was a rumpled mess. Cream sheets tangled with a navy comforter. An unexpected vision filled her head. Noah, sprawled out, one hand on the back of his head, the other on the tattered book that currently lay on his pillow. And even weirder than that was the fact that the mental picture didn't make her feel like running. If anything, she liked the way imaginary him looked up and smiled at her. But then non-imaginary him spoke, jerking Elle—with her face flaming—back to the moment.

"Not like that," he said, obviously reading the way her thoughts had gone, and dismissing them with a wave.

And for no good reason, the gesture and words were

somehow worse than if he had meant it like that. Which was ridiculous. Elle stood still, trying to compose herself as the rough-around-the-edges man ran his eyes over her in a way that wasn't sexy, but that still made her feel exposed. When he finished his head-to-toe perusal, he lifted his attention to her face, his expression far grimmer than any man checking out a woman's assets should be.

"On your way out of the park, did you bump into anyone?" he asked. "Talk to someone you didn't know?"

"I don't think so, but what does that have to do with—" She cut herself off, her mind latching onto a detail that she'd forgotten until right that second. "Wait. There was a woman who told me my shoelace was undone. But that was before I left the park."

"Did she touch you?"

"I'm not sure."

"Could she have?"

"Maybe. Why are you asking? What's going on? What happened outside just a second ago?" She deliberately left out a query about why any of it meant she had to take her clothes off, but it was on her mind just the same, and she still couldn't shake the heat from her cheeks.

"That was my neighbor, destroying a listening device some punk stuck to my exterior wall," he replied. "And I owe him fifty bucks for it, so remind me to add that to your tab."

She ignored the latter comment in favor of the former. "A listening device?"

He gave her another appraising look. "Someone is pretty damn determined to get to you."

His tone wasn't accusatory, and it had no edge, but it made Elle want to shake a little anyway. She knew exactly who had the desire and the resources to stalk her. The same man who would enjoy driving fear into her heart more than he'd enjoy straight up killing her. The one who'd taken Katie. And she needed to get to him. Which currently meant listening to Noah. Doing what he'd asked and obeying orders, no questions asked. Because while he might be right about not being able to shed herself of those thick, horrible feelings in her gut, she could at least fight them. Or use them. She had to prove that she could. Even if Noah needed her to take her clothes off for some insane reason.

Meeting his eyes for one second before she did it, Elle reached down and grabbed the hem of her shirt. She tugged it up and over her head, shivering as the artificially cooled air blasted over her skin. She only got the shirt as high as her face, though, before Noah made a choked noise and issued a protest.

"Whoa!" he said. "What're you doing?"

She stopped with her arms raised. "You told me to take off my clothes."

"I—" He muttered something incomprehensible, then added, "I didn't mean strip for *me*."

She lowered her arms a little and peeked over the hem of her shirt. "You literally said strip."

"Not here." He cleared his throat. "You can do it in the bathroom. I'll tell you what to look for."

"I don't understand."

"That makes two of us."

He shifted from foot to foot, looking for all the world like a little boy caught doing something he shouldn't have been doing. Surprised by his outward awkwardness, Elle rested her eyes on him for another second. He seemed to be straining to keep his gaze off her. When his eyes betrayed him a little—flicking from a spot over her shoulder to her midriff to her face, then quickly over her shoulder again—it actually made her feel a little pleased for some reason. It was certainly better than that analytical, all-over visual examination he'd done of her a minute earlier. Maybe it was silly to even care, but she felt it all the same.

Noah cleared his throat. "Could you, uh, pull that down?"

Stowing the poorly placed bit of satisfaction at his obvious effort to not check her out, Elle moved to reposition her shirt. But as she started to yank it down, the tiny, silver ring she wore on her right forefinger got stuck to the fabric. She pulled a little harder. The motion made the shirt bunch up even more. And another tug—Elle was getting embarrassed now—sent her elbow up so that her entire chest was exposed. The heat in her face flared so high that she didn't know how the shirt didn't just burst into flames. And she was afraid to make any more effort in getting herself free for fear of creating further issues. But just when she thought she was going to have no choice but to take it all the way off, Noah's hands landed on her—one on her arm, the other on her stuck finger.

The contact was utterly unexpected and thoroughly pleasant. As rough as the man might appear, his touch was gentle. She'd noted it in the park when he'd closed his hand on her upper arm. But the feel of him was doubly careful now. His fingers were warm and deft, and in just a couple of seconds, he'd freed her from the mild humiliation of being held hostage by her own clothing. And when he was done, he didn't immediately pull away. Instead, he held her hand for another moment, examining her ring before bringing his eyes up to hers.

"Pretty," he said softly.

She knew he meant the jewelry, but she tingled as if it were a compliment for her directly. "Thanks."

He still didn't release her hand. "Just so we're clear… I'm not in the habit of forcing women to take off their clothes."

"No?" Elle's voice was slightly breathless.

"Definitely not. And while we're on the subject, I would never, ever ask for anything other than good, old-fashioned cash for payment," he said.

The pointedness in his statement was clear, but this time, it wasn't embarrassment that warmed Elle. It was a surge of forceful attraction. It prickled along her skin, settled in her chest, and made her feel a little reckless. Her gaze dropped to his lips. And for a moment, her brain scrolled through a series of crazy things. Like wondering whether the full feel of his mouth would be as warm as his hands. His lips had touched her cheek back at the playground. Twice. But Elle couldn't recall their heat well enough. And she wanted to. She considered, also, what would happen if she leaned forward to find out. She inched closer. Would he pull away? Jump back? Or sink in and kiss her with unbridled thoroughness?

Elle's own lips tingled with anticipation of the possible answers. And she might actually have followed through on the urge, too, if Noah hadn't abruptly dropped her hand and taken a small step back. She stared at him, watching as his Adam's apple bobbed up and down in his throat. Her mind seemed to bob with it.

Were you seriously about to kiss a man you just met? While Katie is missing? While you've barely scratched the surface of what needs to be done to find her?

Except as incredulous as her conscience might be, there was no denying that the resounding answer was yes.

Like her body couldn't quite believe it either, her hand tried to come up to her mouth. She had to order it to stay down. But she couldn't quite tear her gaze away from Noah.

She couldn't recall the last time she'd thought about pressing her lips to a man's. Before Katie, for sure. Possibly longer. And at just twenty-six years old, Elle knew it was unusual. Maybe even unreal. But how could she take a moment to even look at a man when her whole life was spent protecting Katie?

She breathed out, wondering if the half-surprised, slightly puzzled look on her face matched the one she saw on Noah's. She suspected it did. Maybe he felt the same, magnetic pull. And maybe it caught him off guard, too. The thought made her want to smile in an uncharacteristically dreamy way.

Noah's mouth opened, and Elle anticipated a confession of some kind. Instead, his light cough—and the words that followed it—swept the fantasy away.

"You've, uh, got a rip," he said.

He took another step away, gestured to her top, and she looked down, following the direction of his finger. Sure enough, the struggle with the ring had left a gaping, jagged hole in her top. It curved from her stomach all the way to her side. As if to emphasize the size of it, a blast from the air conditioner ruffled the fabric and made goose bumps rise along her skin.

"Hang on," said Noah. "I'll grab you something."

Elle watched him turn to his dresser, her mind attempting to find a rational reason for her desire to kiss Noah.

Yes, he was a stranger. Last name, unknown. Backstory, unmentioned. Yet the setting was intimate. They were in his space. A motel room that screamed of illicit things. She was depending on him in a way she hadn't depended on anyone since her mother's death more than a decade earlier. It made perfect sense to have some kind of misguided feelings for him, even in this short space of time. There was even a word for it. Transference. But as he swung back and tossed a T-shirt her way, and her hands closed on the cotton, and Noah's light, masculine scent filled her nose, the word *misguided* seemed wrong. In fact, the attraction itself was what felt right. So when he suddenly let out a curse and told her to hold still in a rough, angry voice, it wasn't worry that made her freeze. It was disappointment that the hand he reached out was all business.

As Noah tried to pluck the thumbnail-sized tracking device from a spot just above Elle's hip, it took a surprising amount of willpower not to simply toss the electronic dot aside, then drag the blond woman close and bury his mouth against hers. It was an irrational want. One he'd almost given in to just moments earlier. One that was spurred by the silky softness of her skin under the pads of his fingers as he pressed in and finally managed to pull the flat round object free.

Get ahold of yourself, he ordered silently as he stepped a safe distance away and held up the tiny tracker for better examination. *Scared moms with missing kids aren't looking for make-out sessions with strangers.*

Except he no sooner created the physical gap between them than Elle moved closer and eliminated it. She put a hand on his wrist, pulled it down, and drew in a sharp breath as she looked at the object pinched between his thumb and forefinger.

"Is that another listening device?" she asked, unease evident in her voice.

Noah shook his head, his reply grim. "No. It's a GPS tracker. Pretty damn sophisticated, too, judging by its size."

She inhaled again. "I'm sorry."

He tipped his head her way, surprised by the apology. "Sorry?"

"You said I'd be a hindrance. I promised you it wasn't true. But I let someone put that on me, and I didn't even notice." Now she exhaled, and it was shaky. "Now he knows where you live, and that's a very bad thing."

"I'm not worried about anyone knowing where I am," Noah said.

It was almost true. One of the reasons he opted for only a semipermanent home was the ease of uprooting at a moment's notice. He'd had his share of shady people after him before. But none of that was his most pressing concern at that moment. What he wanted was to know more about the mystery man who made Elle's eyes pinch every time she mentioned him. Whose name she hadn't said even once, in spite of her daughter's status. Who was she to him? Who was *he* to the missing girl? How was the man as well equipped as an undercover police unit? Palming the tracker, Noah started to ask those questions, plus a few other pointed ones as well. Except she spoke before he could.

"Aren't you going to destroy that?" she asked.

He opened his hand again. "Kinda pointless. They already know where we are. Besides which, if the signal suddenly stops transmitting, they'll also know we found it. Better not to let on that we figured out their little trick."

Elle's gaze hovered on the offending object, and Noah realized it was truly making her even more upset than she'd been already. Another prick of protectiveness surged up. The woman was dealing with enough. If he could do a small thing to ease her mind, then he'd do it.

"You know what?" he said. "You're right. I'll crush the damn thing into oblivion."

He tipped his hand, let the device bounce to the floor, then lifted his foot. At the last second, though, he diverted the sole of his boot away.

"I've got a better idea," he said, bending to snag the tracker up again. "We're going to enlist the help of Gus-

Gus to throw your stalker for a loop so we can concentrate on getting your kid back."

"Who's Gus-Gus?" she replied. "Your neighbor?"

Noah's mouth tipped up. "Of a sort. Why don't you get changed in the bathroom while I make another call? I'll meet you in there in a minute."

"You'll meet me in the bathroom?"

"Yeah. Trust me. This'll be worth it. Plus, it'll help us get out of here undetected."

Her expression was equal parts curious and puzzled, but she didn't argue. As she moved to follow his suggestion, Noah took his phone out and dialed once more.

"Hey, Rog," he greeted. "Feel like doing me another favor?"

"Twice in one day?" croaked his two-pack-a-day neighbor. "Getting needier than my dead wife, God rest her soul."

"Didn't you tell me the other night that you'd give your left kidney to have her back?"

"Yeah, well. Might've been the whiskey talking. What're you needing now? Want me to break something else? A leg. Tell me it's a leg."

"Ha-ha. No. But actually, I've got something weirder. I was hoping you could bring Gus-Gus to my bathroom window."

"You serious?" said the other man.

"Mmm," Noah acknowledged. "I'm also going to order you a pizza, but I want you to bring it to my front door when it gets to your place."

"This is getting weird."

"You're a peach, Rog. See you in a minute."

Noah tapped off the phone, scrolled down to the number for the pizza place that probably knew him better than they should, then quickly placed the bare minimum order for delivery. He was careful to make sure they knew not to come to him but to his neighbor's door instead. When he was satisfied that they understood, he hung up and stepped toward the bathroom. He made it only a single step before the door swung open and Elle stepped out. She held Rog's one-eared twenty-three-pound tabby in her arms, and she had an understandably amused look on her face. The cat was purring so loudly that the noise practically filled the room.

"So…" Elle said. "Your neighbor seems nice. Gave me a 'little' something through the window. I think my arms might fall off."

Noah chuckled. "You can put him on the bed."

She complied, and the behemoth feline turned in a single circle, let out a meow, then plopped down and closed his eyes. Smiling, Noah got to work on the first part of his plan. He moved to the night stand, dragged open the drawer and pulled out a roll of Scotch tape. With swift hands, he snapped off a piece, rolled it up, then stuck it to the miniature bugging device. Next, he stepped to the bed and took a gentle hold of the oversized beast's collar. He rolled the tag over, pressed the electronic item to the metal, and squeezed.

Then he met Elle's eyes. "Aaaaand. Our decoy is good to go."

She shot him a dubious look. "Good to go where? And what makes you so sure he'll make it as far as the door?"

"Now, now," he replied lightly. "We're not here to body shame the cat."

She made a face. "I don't think he got this lumpy from chasing birds."

"Nope. Gus-Gus is actually an indoor boy. But every time he gets out, he takes the same path. Down the block. Around the corner. Through a patch of overgrown shrubs and past this big boarded up house. Then he sits at the koi pond. Takes his time, too. Should lead our friend in the car on a nice little chase." Noah sank down onto the bed and gave the animal a good scratch behind the ear.

"So…we just set him free?"

"Not quite. First we wait for pizza."

"We what?"

"The second half of our decoy." Noah glanced toward the generic digital clock that sat on the dresser. "They like me over there. Delivery shouldn't be much more than seven minutes. Which gives us time to talk."

"Good. Because I do have something to ask you."

"Ask away."

"How much does a borrowed cat run?"

"What?"

"Just trying to keep a running total," she said. "Three thousand dollars to track a car. Fifty bucks for a neighbor to smash a wire. So…how much to borrow a cat?"

He knew she was stalling—diverting the conversation from where it should be going—but his lips twitched anyway. "Gus-Gus works for treats."

"Uh-uh," said Elle. "You said nothing but cash."

"I wasn't thinking in terms of hired pets."

"Well then, how much does a bag of treats run? Like, brand name ones."

"I dunno. Under ten bucks?"

"Then we'll round it up. So I owe you three thousand, sixty dollars in expenses."

"Hmm."

"What?"

"You're forgetting the pizza," he told her. "Better make it three thousand, seventy-three dollars."

"Noted."

Elle inhaled and closed her hands into fists. The combative pose made Noah think she might be preparing to dig in her heels and say nothing else. Instead, she spoke in a low, worry-tinged voice.

"If I tell you anything more, you might change your mind about helping me," she said.

This time, he gave in to the urge to reach out. He put his hands on her wrists and put pressure on the exposed lower half of her palms. When her fingers unfurled, he closed his over them The contact was distracting. Oddly familiar, yet completely new.

Noah brought his gaze up, and Elle's expression seemed to hold an electric charge. He wanted to help her, dammit, even though his mind cautioned him that it might take him into dangerous territory.

"I won't change my mind," he promised, his voice thick with far more emotion than should've been there.

Elle breathed out again. "Trey Charger."

A lick of true unease flared up. If Noah had been expecting any name at all, it wouldn't have been one he'd heard before. Let alone that one. A decade or so earlier, the business mogul had featured prominently in the news. A longtime partner of his had died under questionable circumstances, and Charger was under investigation. Then the media stories had dried up quickly. A key witness retracted his story. A high-profile politician stepped in. The details were foggy, but what Noah did remember was the man's eyes. He could vividly recall flicking on the TV, right in the middle of a feature. Trey Charger, thirty-something and dressed in a pinstripe suit, appearing on TV to give a brief statement. His gaze was cold, dark and utterly superior. Noah had turned the TV off before the man spoke a word. The idea that he was somehow connected to Elle and her daughter made Noah's gut twist.

"What about him?" he asked, keeping his tone neutral.

"You know who he is." It wasn't a question.

"I haven't crossed paths with him personally, but it'd be a lie to say I'd never heard the news stories about him."

"The news stories…" It was barely more than a whisper, and her eyes sank shut. "Everything you heard? He's worse. He's got deep pockets, and the only two things he cares about are filling them a little more and making sure everyone knows he can keep filling them." Her eyes opened again. "And he's the one who took Katie."

"You know I'm going to ask why," he replied softly.

"Do you always ask your clients personal questions like that?"

Elle pulled her hands out of his, and the cool air hit his skin, making the loss of contact more acute than it ought to have been. Noah looked down at his empty palms before raising his gaze to her face again.

"I always ask the questions that need to be asked so that I can do my job effectively."

"You don't need to know why he took Katie. You just need to know that he did. And that he had no right to do it."

There was a defensiveness in her tone that spiked Noah's concern. Why tell him the kidnapper's name, if she wasn't going to give him a reason? Why hold back? What was she holding back? He opened his mouth to ask her as much, but a knock at the door cut him short. He almost stayed put so he could demand an answer. Then he remembered that the little girl's life depended on time as well as information, and he pushed to his feet and moved to the door with worry clouding his mind.

Chapter 5

Ella's heart bounced so hard in her chest that it hurt. She could barely breathe as Noah took a swift look through the peephole, then swung open the door. It wasn't that she was concerned about who was on the other side. She didn't even care when a short wrinkle-covered man with no more than a tuft of gray hair came into the room, a pizza box balanced on his hand and a curious look on his face. What set her lungs burning was the way Trey's name had come out of her lips.

She hadn't said it aloud once since she'd managed to escape him. Even on the solitary call—the single time he'd tracked her down—she hadn't offered him any kind of greeting. In fact, she hadn't let herself think his name, or even picture his face. Her only consideration of him had been involuntary. Unwanted. In nightmares, most often. Or in sudden, breath-stealing memories at odd moments of time. Like when she'd once spied his preferred wine in a shop window. She'd stopped abruptly, recalling the smell

of it emanating from his pores. The memory was so strong
that it made her queasy, even then. She hadn't been able to
pull herself out of it until Katie had given her hand a little
tug and said, *What's wrong, Momma?*

Elle shuddered again, thinking of it now. Disliking how
his hold crept up like that, and how it threatened to drag
her under. Saying his name was like a violation. An oil
slick on her tongue. She could barely believe she'd managed to let it free. And when Noah had asked why, the rest
had almost spilled out, too. She'd had to physically restrain
herself from not adding more.

Trey Charger.

Entrepreneur was what he called himself. But really, he
was a glorified mobster. One who'd attempted to destroy
her life. Tried to control her in the worst way possible.
And for a time, he'd succeeded. But Elle had broken away.
Saved both herself and the helpless baby who'd grown into
the vibrant little girl she loved more than life.

And now he has her again.

She didn't realize that she was swaying on her feet until
Noah took ahold of her elbow.

"Elle?" he prodded. "Are you all right?"

She started to nod, but her head spun, and the wizened man—who still hadn't been introduced—spoke more
quickly.

"She's clearly not okay, you numbskull," he said, his
voice gravelly with age. "What kind of gentleman doesn't
recognize the way a lady looks when she's about to faint?"

"Hey, now. Watch it with the name calling," Noah replied, his tone lighter than his expression. "You know perfectly well I dislike being referred to as a gentleman."

His eyes hung on Elle, his concern evident, and he
opened his mouth again, clearly intending to address her.
But for the second time, the older man was faster. He

stepped closer to Elle, put a hand on her shoulder, and guided her away from Noah. Then—with a firmness that contrasted sharply with his frail looks—he pressed her to a seated position on the bed.

"That's how it's done," he said. "Now. You want a glass of water? A slice of pizza? It's actually a damn fine restaurant, even if it is practically inside a laundromat."

Slightly overwhelmed, Elle met the stranger's kind gaze. "I don't think I could eat if I tried."

"You might surprise yourself." He spun away, retrieved a slice from the box, then spun back. "I'm Roget Moreau, by the way. Neighbor. Cat-for-hire owner. And pizza delivery guy, apparently."

He held the slice out, and Elle eyed it dubiously, sure that just the sight of the gooey cheese should make her throat close up. Instead, her stomach rumbled. A little embarrassed, she accepted the proffered food and took a bite. The lightheaded feeling eased almost as soon as she finished chewing.

"Better?" asked Noah.

"Much," she admitted.

"See?" interjected Roget. "Might be nothing but an old man, but I'm still good for a thing or two." He swung to face Noah. "As per our usual understanding, I have zero interest in knowing what you're up to. If I'm captured and tortured, I want a clean mind."

Noah's reply was dry. "As per our usual understanding, I wouldn't tell you even if you did want to know."

"So you keep saying. But here Gus-Gus and I are, serving pizza to a beautiful girl in your crappy room." Roget grinned, revealing an enormous gap between his front teeth. "And I assume you need something else from us, or you would've sent us packing already."

"As a matter of fact…" Noah strode across the room,

snapped a hooded sweatshirt from the closet, then held it out toward the older man. "I'm gonna need you to put this on, take off your pants and pretend to be the beautiful girl for about five minutes."

Elle just about choked on her pizza, but Roget just raised a nearly nonexistent eyebrow.

"Can't say that's not gonna cost you," he stated.

"How much?" Noah replied.

"A hundred bucks."

"Done."

"Dammit," Roget muttered. "Should've shot higher."

But in spite of his grumble, he kicked off the slippers he wore, then snapped off his belt and dropped his pants to reveal a pair of plaid boxers that hit his knees. He grabbed the hoodie from Noah's hands, zipped it up, and covered his head.

"How do I look?" he asked. "I feel more like a rapper than a woman."

Elle could see that Noah's mouth was trying not to curve up.

"What do you think?" he asked, directing the question her way. "Can this guy and his knobby knees and hairy legs pass for you?"

She had a hard time containing her own amusement. "I don't know whether saying yes is a compliment or an insult."

Noah let out a chuckle. "Either way, it'll have to do. Pass me the cat."

Elle stood up and scooped the big guy off the bed, but as she started to hand him off, she had second thoughts about using the purring feline. "He's going to be fine, right?"

Roget snorted, then peeked out from under his hood. "Gus-Gus will outlive us all."

Noah gently took the cat from her hands. "Rog and I

are going to sneak around back. We'll release our pudgy friend out there. I'll follow Gus-Gus from a distance to make sure that your stalker takes the bait. The second after I've done that, Rog'll head out. When he catches up to the beast, he'll dump the GPS tracker right into that koi pond I mentioned. I'll come back for you."

"You're leaving me here alone?" she asked.

But as soon as the words were out, Elle realized how ridiculous they were. She was entirely capable of being alone. She'd fought hard for self-sufficiency, and she had zero interest in giving it up. On top of which, she'd met Noah all of an hour ago. And she'd hired him to do a job. So even if the other bits weren't true, she had to let him do what she'd asked him to do. But she didn't get a chance to retract her question. Noah pressed the cat into Roget's arms, then stepped directly in front of her and closed his hands around her wrists. And the contact made it harder to regret asking the question in the first place. His hands were warm, his gaze reassuring.

"Eleven minutes," he promised. "Twelve, tops."

"You don't want to round that up to an even fifteen?"

"Pretty sure fifteen is still an odd number," he said teasingly.

She rolled her eyes. "You know what I mean."

He smiled, gently squeezed her wrists and replied, "Yeah. I do."

For a strange moment, Elle thought he might lean in and kiss her. She tensed, expecting the light brush of his lips. Maybe on her cheek again. But maybe more. A long moment hung between them. Weighted with oddly heavy anticipation. And when Roget interrupted and broke the spell, more than a small part of her was disappointed.

"Okay, okay," said the pants-less man. "Let's get outta here before I keel over from old age."

Noah released Elle's hands. "Eleven to twelve minutes," he repeated. "Don't forget to stay out of sight. We don't need our friend in the car to get suspicious before he gives chase, okay?"

Elle nodded, but didn't quite trust her voice to not come out with a little crack, so she watched silently as the two men and their accompanying cat slipped out the door. When the latch clicked shut, she expelled a stinging breath. And she realized something. It wasn't that she didn't want to be alone—it was that she didn't want to be alone with her fear for Katie. As little as she might know the big bounty hunter, he had been an undeniable buffer between her and her fright-filled thoughts since the moment his hand first found her elbow. Without him, the questions crowded in.

Was her little girl too scared to act brave?

Had she fought back when she was taken?

Had she been physically harmed?

How far away was Trey, right at that very second?

The last question sent a chill through Elle as something else occurred to her. Trey could be there. He could be somewhere in town. Maybe renting a room at the quaint B and B near the highway turnoff. Or he could've leased the top floor of the only apartment building in town. The same place where she and Katie had rented a suite at the bottom.

No, Elle told herself. *If he'd known we were there, he wouldn't have bothered with the park. He likes to play games, but he prefers a guaranteed win.*

She paced the room a few times, trying to keep her mind from taking a darker turn. She eyed the door several times, wondering just how long eleven to twelve minutes could feel. Her gaze swept the room in search of a distraction. The book on Noah's bed caught her attention, and she paused in her restless striding to pick it up. The spine was cracked to the point of floppiness, and some of the pages were just barely hanging on. It was obviously a favorite, and it made Elle curious about why. It also made her wonder what other personal things were hidden throughout the space.

Glad of something else to think about, she let herself peruse the room in a soft search. She didn't want to open any drawers or rifle through any belongings, but she figured anything in sight was fair game. Her first scan left her disappointed. There were no trinkets or souvenirs. Even Noah's wardrobe—on display in all its folded glory—was nothing more than basic. Jeans and T-shirts. Denim and black or white cotton. But as Elle took a second look, a flap of paper sticking out from under the bottom of the nightstand drawer made her pause. What was it?

She threw a slightly guilty glance back to the door, but she didn't really waste time hemming and hawing about taking a closer look. As her fingers found the edge, she realized it wasn't paper at all; it was a photograph. Any protests her conscience might've continued to make were swept away by curiosity. And she grew only more interested once she'd pulled the picture free.

The shot was of a pair of kids, one a boy with a buzz cut and the other a girl with a shoulder-length mop of strawberry blond curls. Seeking an explanation, she quickly flipped over the picture.

"Baby Greta, three years old," read the back.

Intrigued and puzzled, Elle ran her finger over the words, then turned it right side up again. She studied the picture a little more. There was clearly no baby in the picture. The older girl was grinning at the camera, a visibly mischievous look in her eyes. The boy, on the other hand, had his attention angled down.

Strange.

Elle tried to follow his sightline. But he just seemed to be looking at nothing. Thoughtfully—with an idea bubbling up—she slid her thumb along the edge of the photograph. The material was just jagged enough to not feel right. Someone had cut off the bottom half of the picture. Her spine tingled unpleasantly as her musings solidified. Someone hadn't just cut off the bottom of the picture. They'd cut out Baby Greta, age three. And the words that would've identified Noah and the other girl, too.

"Why?" she murmured.

She couldn't think of any good reason for the hack job. And she wasn't sure she wanted to consider any of the bad reasons that tried to spring to mind. Resolving to find some way of asking Noah directly—and sure that she had to be nearing the eleven-minute mark now—Elle slid the photo back into the skinny space under the nightstand drawer and turned to the door once more. And sure enough, the moment her eyes landed on it, it opened. She started to let out a relieved breath. But it was sucked away quicker than it could be expelled. Because instead of Noah standing on the other side, it was a three-hundred-pound man with a barbed wire tattoo wrapping around his neck and a gun in his hand.

As Noah approached the street that ran along behind the motel he called home, he found himself having to force his feet to keep from breaking into a run. Not because he didn't still feel an urgency to get back to Elle, but because he was questioning the source of the urgency. His job often required him to work under a tight deadline. He knew how to hurry, and when. A missing kid was definitely a reason to rush. Even if the case in question hadn't involved a dubious character like Trey Charger.

But that's not it, is it?

It wasn't thoughts of getting the job done that had propelled him to tuck his smart-mouthed neighbor under his arm and drag the old guy out to the path behind their mutually crappy accommodations. It sure as hell hadn't been the promised paycheck that made him lift Rog through his bathroom window to get back into his room, either. There wasn't enough money in the world to make it worth gripping the skinny butt of a ninety-year-old man. Especially when that very same man chortled about getting more action today than in the last two decades. So, yeah. There was definitely something more going on in Noah's head.

You sure it's your head that's interfering here, Loblaw?

He wanted to argue against the thought. To point out that any body part other than his brain had zero business getting involved in his interactions with a new client. Even if that client was particularly attractive. And yes, he could acknowledge that fact without losing any professionalism. Because really, professionalism was all he did.

Noah put in long hours whenever possible. Took jobs that ate up days at a time. By design, relaxation wasn't a big part of his life. Leisure activities left too much room for mulling over the past. Yeah, that also meant sacrificing some of the more pleasurable bits of life that free time afforded. Like pretty women with blue eyes, soft hands and a hint of steel under their perfect lips.

Uh-huh, said that same obnoxious voice. *When was the last time you went on a date, anyway?*

He tried to brush off the question as irrelevant, but he couldn't quite manage it. Mostly because there was no denying that his dating life could only be described as desolate. At best. He didn't do the online stuff. He didn't frequent bars. When he grocery shopped, it was for the sole purpose of—get this—buying groceries. His friends were few, and Rog could hardly be counted on for introductions to potential women. The thing was, though, Noah didn't normally care. He enjoyed solitude. When he encountered female clients, he noticed only in the most surface-level way whether they were plump or thin, old or young, tall or short. Yet when the word *date* had cropped up in his mind just a few moments earlier, he pictured one.

Elle, across from him in a simple black dress. Hair in a tidier ponytail, still makeup-free, but with no pinch of worry around her blue eyes.

It was ridiculous to even think about it. Possibly idiotic. The current situation couldn't be less of a call for romance. He didn't know anything about the woman. Not even a last name. Yet somehow, he was sure that what pushed his feet to move faster again was the want of the vision to come true.

Frustrated with the way his mind refused to cooperate and not go there, Noah scrubbed a hand over his stubble and sighed. He'd reached the rear corner of the motel property now, and he honestly wasn't sure if his deliberately slowed pace had done any good. In fact, it might've made things worse. It'd given him some extra time to mull it over and get halfway to admitting that he was tempted to let go of the ever-present professionalism. Either way, he'd run out of the allotted eleven to twelve minutes.

He paused for just long enough to double-check that the stalker's car was still gone—it was—then hurried around the building toward the front gate. Except as he approached it, his hackles rose, and his gut told him something was off. For the first time since turning around from the koi pond, his pace eased up on its own.

What was it that caught his attention and filtered in a drum of worry? Noah flicked his gaze over the courtyard, searching for an answer.

The gate was shut. So was the door to his unit. A light

breeze tossed a prematurely dropped leaf into the air. No one was in sight. Most rooms had the blinds drawn. Then he heard a faint groan, and he realized he wasn't looking for something; he was listening for it.

Moving quickly again—but infusing his steps with caution, too—Noah made himself as small as possible and edged along the fence. The metal slats were spread apart, and only four feet high. They offered little coverage, but he took what he could get. When he reached the gate, he unlatched it and gave it a push, then waited. There was no responding movement or sound from the other side, so he stepped the rest of the way through.

What he spied next was like a shot to the gut. Rog was sprawled out on the concrete, his already shrunken form looking frail and broken. His eyes were closed, his mouth open, a gash marring one cheek. How the hell had the man managed to get into that state in under ten minutes? Noah rushed to his neighbor's side, and he was relieved when Rog opened his eyes and greeted him with a clear gaze.

"The girl," he croaked.

For a second, Noah thought the old man meant Elle had done this to him. Then he clued in that Rog's words were an expression of concern. *No.* With his heart pumping hard with worry, Noah lifted his eyes back to his own door. It was still closed. *Thank God.* He dropped his attention back to his neighbor.

"She'll be okay for another minute or two," he said. "We need to take care of you. Why did you come back out here? I thought we agreed that you'd wait in the room until Elle and I were gone."

"Because I had no choice, dummy." Rog rolled to his side and managed to sit up. "The girl is gone. Don't think she wanted to, but she left with some big guy—even bigger than your ridiculous self. Had a stupid tattoo, too.

Tried to stop them, slipped on the damn concrete before I made it three steps."

Noah's mind and gut both churned. *Damn, damn, damn!*

He knew exactly who his neighbor meant. The "stupid tattoo" description gave it away. A need to chase after them like a madman pushed him to his feet before he realized he couldn't just leave Rog lying there bleeding. His legs practically itched with a desire to bolt.

"I'll get the EMTs lined up," Noah said, pulling out his phone to call an ambulance. "Which direction did they head? How long ago?"

"Two minutes, maybe. Headed out the gate. Don't know what direction, but I'm guessing the opposite of where you came from. And don't you dare place that call," replied Rog. "Paramedics'll want an explanation. I'm a terrible liar, which is why I never ask about your business. The police'll wind up here, and you know them and me don't mix."

Noah's impatience to get to Elle battled with his need to help the old man. "You need medical attention, my friend."

"So I'll call Nancy. You know that old kook is always looking for an excuse to check up on me. You're wasting time with me when you could be going after the girl."

Noah tapped his thumb against his thigh. Rog was right. On both counts. The retired nurse who lived a block over doted on the man and would be pleased to come over and patch him up. And time was most definitely wasting.

"Fine," he said, pressing his phone into Rog's hands. "I promise I'll be following up to make sure you actually placed the call."

"No interest in dying out here by myself," his neighbor replied, pushing a finger to the cell. "See? Already dialing."

As satisfied as he could be under the circumstances, Noah nodded, swung south, and started to move. He paused again, midstep. Then he spun back and bolted toward his room. Trying not to think about losing precious seconds, he flung open the door and dashed in. He yanked open his closet so hard that one of the hinges on the top came free. Splinters flew, and Noah ignored them. He sank down, slid away the laundry hamper and punched the sequenced code into his safe. The unlocking mechanism buzzed an error.

"C'mon, c'mon," he said under his breath.

He tried again, punching the numbers with frustrating slowness. Thankfully, the second effort paid off. The safe clicked, and the door opened so that Noah could reach in and grab his gun. The moment he had it in his grip, he was on his feet and running again.

He darted past Rog, noting absently that his neighbor's phone conversation had become animated—which he thought was a good thing. He leaped over the corner of the pool, slammed through the gate once more, and thumped to the curb. There, he stopped just long enough to swing his head back and forth.

Which way?

Not the direction he'd come—his neighbor was right about that. Unlikely to have headed into town, too.

"South," he muttered.

Then he hit the pavement again, his boots slapping the concrete with the effort. In seconds, he was at the other end of the motel. A heartbeat later, he was rounding the corner. And just a moment after that, he was wishing that he'd exercised a little more of his usual caution. Because the inked-up man—who was exactly who Noah had thought it would be—stood waiting.

The six-foot-five man had his back pressed to a tree, looking more like he was holding it up than the other way around. The tattoo in question added an unnecessarily dangerous element to his already intimidating presence. His stance was also designed to be daunting. One meaty hand rested on a weapon, and a scowl covered his features, and the sheen of sun on his shaved head seemed designed to dare anyone to approach. None of that was unexpected. None of it—not even the gun—was a deterrent for Noah. What made him stop dead was the position of the man's other hand. It was wrapped firmly around Elle's ponytail.

Chapter 6

Noah very nearly took a step toward Elle. He could see that the enormous man's grip was causing her pain. Her mouth was set in a line, but she was drawing in quick, short breaths between her narrowed lips. Dots of tears marked the corners of her eyes. Her hands were clenched into fists, too. She was the picture of silent suffering.

It pained Noah in an oddly sharp way to see it, and it was the little stab in his ribcage that made him realize it would be a terrible idea to go to her. The last thing he needed was for her captor to see that he might have some leverage.

Action over emotion, he told himself firmly.

Careful not to meet Elle's eyes again—or even look at her—he instead tucked his gun into the rear of his pants, then greeted the big man as if it were just the two of them grabbing a coffee. "Afternoon, Dez."

The big man's bald head bobbed, his tone equally friendly. "Loblaw."

Noah could feel Elle's surprise at the casual exchange of names, but he still didn't turn his attention her way. "You're pretty far from home."

"I go where the cases take me. Can't help it if that lands me in your backyard."

"True enough. But it does look like you've got something that belongs to me."

Dez spat sideways. "C'mon, man. You know how this works. You abandoned a target—I snatched her up. Fair game."

Noah layered his reply with a careful mix of disbelief and surprise. "Putting aside the fact that leaving her in my home is hardly abandonment, and not bothering to point out that it'd be equally hard to describe breaking and entering as fair game... Sorry, dude. You've got it wrong. She's not a target."

Dez tipped his head in Elle's direction. "You walking around under the name Elle O'Malley?"

She let out a whimper that could've been either a denial or an affirmation, and Noah fought a growl. He wanted to tell the other man to loosen his damn grip, but he kept it in.

"Doesn't matter what her name is," he said dismissively. "She's a client."

Dez didn't budge. "I think we can both agree that sometimes in our business, the lines on these things get crossed. She's a big ticket, friend. I'm not turning her over to you just because she's trying to use you to buy her own way out of a debt."

Noah's jaw ached from holding it so stiffly. "She's a bigger ticket on my end."

For the first time, the big man looked interested. "Is that right? You know, I *have* always been curious about your rates."

Noah sidestepped the implied question about his earnings, and instead said, "What's the price on her head? I'll pay it."

"I wouldn't be able to stay in business if I sold out my clients whenever the opportunity came up. You know how many times a target offers to pay me off?"

"I do. And I don't care. I'll add half again to your usual fee as a show of good faith. Call it solidarity."

"You're saying you'd give me four and half K, just to get this girl back?"

Noah almost laughed. Both at how much lower the man's fee was than his own, and at the probability that even with the gap, he was probably exaggerating the price.

"I'm not saying I would. I'm saying I will. That 'girl' owes me three thousand, one hundred and seventy-three dollars in expenses," he stated. "So I'm just gonna tack your fee to that, bill her for the whole thing, and call it a day."

Both of Dez's eyebrows went up. "Who the hell is she to you?"

Noah kept an utterly neutral tone as he offered a shrug. "Like you said… Elle O'Malley. This month's paycheck."

The other man studied him like he was considering the validity of the claim. "Tell me the truth, Loblaw. What's your going rate? Fess up, and I'll think about giving up my target."

"How about I make you a deal instead, Dez? You let her go first. Then you answer a few questions for me, and instead of telling you my going rate, I'll give it to you."

"Give it to me?"

"I'll pay you my usual retrieval fee."

"Interesting proposal."

From the corner of his eye, Noah saw the slightest bit of tension slip from Elle's face, and he was sure his fellow bounty hunter had eased his hold.

Good.

"You're a man who knows which risks to take," Noah added. "Guess it's up to you whether you'd rather engage in a physical fight with me or whether you want to take a chance at making some money."

Dez's gaze turned shrewd. "What makes you think I won't just kill her instead of fighting you?"

"Because you're not a 'dead-or-alive' guy to start with, and also because whoever's paying for the retrieval wants her in one piece."

There was a long pause, and then Elle stumbled forward a little. Noah exhaled, but he didn't let himself reach out like his instincts told him to. In fact, he really had to fight to keep from doing it. A big part of him expected her to jump into his arms anyway. To her credit, though, she just drew in a deep breath, stabilized herself, and stepped to his side. Noah's fingers twitched with a need to brush against her elbow, and he wanted to gently ask if she was okay. He stayed both urges, promising silently that he'd follow up once they were alone.

He bent his head down just long enough to say, "Let me do the talking," then lifted his attention to the big man once more.

"Okay…" said Dez, his demeanor abruptly easier. "Now that that's out of the way…ask whatever it is you'd like to know. I'm all yours."

Noah nodded brusquely. "First and foremost, I want to know who hired you, and how you got wind of the job."

"Can't answer the former too well," the other man admitted. "It was a company name of some kind. Iris International."

Elle stiffened in a barely perceptible way, and Noah knew she recognized the organization. He didn't comment on it, and instead remained focused on getting more information.

"And the latter part?" he prodded.

Dez scratched at his temple with his weapon. "You gotta know already that some of us operate outside the…uh… usual channels. Folks who don't ask a ton of questions about retrieval."

Impatience crept up. "Yeah, buddy. I'm aware that very few of us like to color inside the lines."

"No need to get defensive. Just saying. There's a forum online. Coded and stuff. This came up just this morning."

Noah's fingers drummed against his thigh. He had zero interest in becoming involved with the seedier side of his chosen profession. He was, however, curious about how it worked, and whether there was some advantage to be had in knowing about it.

"So what do you do?" he wondered aloud. "Answer an ad?"

"More or less. Usually it goes to tender. Best offer gets it. But in this case…" Dez trailed off, scratching his temple again.

"Whatever it is…" Noah said. "Just spit it out."

"The client said he had his own guys on this, too, but wanted some insurance. Offered a thousand-dollar bonus and called it a contest."

"Classy."

The other man lifted his shoulders. "Gotta pay the bills. A grand is a grand is a grand."

Noah felt his lip curl in distaste, and he forced himself to push past it. "Tell me about the info you were given."

"Name. Description. Approximate location. Once I got close, I got pinged some GPS coordinates, which is how I found you." Dez paused, eyed Elle, then added, "And all of that came with a warning."

"What kind of warning?"

"That she killed the last guy who tried to bring her in."

The statement gave Noah a start that he couldn't quite cover. His head swiveled in Elle's direction, seeking an explanation. She met his eyes. Her gaze was controlled, her face pale.

"No one has tried to bring me anywhere," she told him.

He couldn't help but note that response was just vague enough to not be a real answer to his unasked question. He pretended like it had been anyway.

"There you have it, Dez," he said. "No one tried to take her in."

"Whatever you say, man. Anything else you wanna know?"

"Just a couple more things."

"Hit me."

"Any idea how many people picked up the job?" Noah asked.

The inked-up man shook his head. "No way of finding out. All done electronically. Those messages that disappear after a few seconds. So you could have ten guys headed this way, or you could just have me and your buddy in the car."

"Speaking of which…know anything about him?"

"Nothing except that he's a high roller in a crappy car. Assumed he was the client's personal guy. Had a sweet cell phone and some fancier-than-average gadgets. Nice work with the cat, by the way."

Noah shot him an even look. "You spying on me, now, Dez?"

His acquaintance let out a chortle. "I knew I was right. I was hanging around back, biding my time, and I saw it all go down."

Noah raised an eyebrow, and Dez coughed.

"Sorry, man," said the other bounty hunter. "But again…"

"Bills. I heard you."

"Anyway, I saw the cat stuff happen. Was completely clueless until the GPS coordinates changed. Then I figured it out. Saw you take off, too, with the old man in the sweater. Placed my bets on finding the target—er…your client—in the room."

"Glad that worked out for you," Noah replied with more than a hint of sarcasm.

"Easy, man. I didn't have all the info," Dez protested.

"That's what you get for not asking questions."

"Not all of us can afford to live by your code or whatever, Loblaw."

Noah sighed. "Forget it. I'll transfer you your cash within twelve hours."

"I know you're good for it."

"I'd say thank you, but you kidnapped my client, so…"

The other man gave him a little salute and pushed away from the tree, then took off up the road far faster than his size should've allowed. As Dez slipped out of sight, Noah turned to tell Elle they should hurry back, but when he spun, he found her staring at him with an incredulous look on her face.

For a good ten seconds, Elle was speechless. And not only that…she was also hearing-less. She could see Noah's mouth moving. His urgency was clear on his face. But she had no clue what he was saying. It was like she'd been sucked in a vacuum. She stared at him, unblinking. The frightening minutes of being pulled forcibly through the streets were already a blur, fading to unimportance. So was the exchange between her captor and the man who she was relying on to help her. What was sticking out was what the two *hadn't* said. The question that *hadn't* been asked. And it was making her head spin while also rendering her immobile at the same time. Then—finally—when concern replaced Noah's harried expression, and his hand came out to touch her forearm, Elle's mouth at last jolted to life.

"Katie!" she gasped.

And her hearing resurfaced, too.

"We're going to get her," Noah assured her. "But first, we need to go back to my place."

"But you let him leave!"

"He didn't have any info about your little girl. Trust me on that."

"How do you know?" she demanded. "You didn't even mention her."

He ran a hand over his too-long hair, his face full of frustration. And for a second, Elle was sure he was just going to grab her and pull her along like the big man— Dez—had done. Instead, he muttered something, then lifted his free hand and placed it on her other forearm.

"Listen to me," he said, his voice low and intense. "If I'd thought there were any chance that he knew something about where Katie was, I wouldn't have let him walk away. In fact, I would've led with questions about her and physically restrained him if he tried to leave. But I'm a hundred percent sure he didn't have a clue. And I need you to give me a bit of trust, because we're running into a borrowed time situation now."

She stared up at him, measuring the sincerity in his hazel gaze. She wondered if he'd still expect her to say yes if he knew the whole truth. And even more than that, she wondered why she felt like telling him. It wasn't like she was more than a client. Or even like she knew enough about him to say he'd understand or sympathize. And that kind of closeness would take years, Elle was sure. In fact, she'd never imagined herself telling anyone. Even when she imagined the future, she couldn't wrap her head around the idea of explaining it properly to Katie. Yet it was still on the tip of her tongue to blurt it out to Noah.

"Please," he added, the word at odds with his rough looks and gruff voice.

He released her arms and held out his palm. And Elle couldn't help but note how it sharply contrasted with the way he'd grabbed her hand just a short while ago when they'd made the rush to his motel. Then, it had been an insistent demand. Now, it was a request. An offer. And she wanted to take it.

Without even realizing that she was doing it, she nodded and slid her hand into his. Warmth permeated her skin. But as quickly as she looked down in surprise, Noah gave her the slightest tug, and they were on the move.

For some reason, Elle expected silence on their trek back. Instead, as Noah carefully scanned the street and kept them going, he also filled the air with his rumbling voice. And what he talked about was Dez. About meeting the man ten years earlier during a job, and everything that followed.

At the time, Dez hadn't been a bounty hunter. He'd been a thug. Selling the odd bit of drugs. Ripping off convenience stores and doing something described as "collections for less-than-reputable organizations"—a euphemism that Elle took to mean retrieving cash for gangs. But before all that, he'd been a father. A husband. When an accident took his wife and left his daughter in a coma—which eventually pulled her from the world as well—Dez had been left devastated, unemployed and deeply in debt. So he'd slid into a rapidly self-destructive pattern.

But by the end of Noah and Dez's short meeting, Dez was on a new path. Not a perfect one. But certainly one that was better than the violent law-breaking one he'd had before.

The story was heartbreaking. And in spite of the fact that the man in question had taken her at gunpoint, Elle felt more than a little sympathy for him. She understood loss. She understood grief. She'd spent six years fearing that she'd turn around and find that Katie wasn't there. That Trey would catch up and rip away the life they'd created. Now he was halfway to being successful at doing so. And if Elle was being honest, the only thing that was keeping her from falling into her own pit of despair was the pace at which things had been happening since the park. From Noah showing up and warning her that she was being watched to this very moment, she hadn't had more than a short time to dwell. Even for the ten or so minutes she'd been alone in the motel room, her mind had been occupied. But what if it hadn't been? What if she'd been alone to deal with it? Would she have persevered, for Katie's sake? Or would she have slid over the edge? Would she eventually become like Dez?

"Hey," said Noah. "I didn't tell you that story to make you sadder than you already were. I just wanted you to know the reason I was so sure he would've mentioned it if he knew anything about your daughter."

They'd reached the motel again, and they paused just a few feet from the gate.

"I'm not sadder," Elle said.

"No? Looks that way to me."

"What do you mean?"

Noah lifted their still-clasped hands to her cheek, and when his knuckles brushed her face, she realized she was crying. Embarrassed, she tried to pull back so she could wipe away the rest of her free-fallen tears. But he didn't let her. His grip tightened, and instead of easing back, she actually fell forward a bit. Her chest met his torso, her head tipped up and her breath caught. Those hazel eyes of his were locked on her mouth. And the need to kiss him came back with a vengeance, even harder to resist this time. Especially when a little voice in her head piped up with what could only be called a terribly valid question.

How many times can the perfect moment come and go before it goes completely?

But her mouth had different ideas than her brain, and even as she pressed to her tiptoes and neared Noah's lips, she spoke without meaning to, breaking the spell.

"How did you change him?" she asked.

Noah blinked like he was coming out of a fog, flicked his attention to her mouth once more, then stepped back. "Change Dez?"

"Yes. With everything he had going on, you must've said something that made him become a bounty hunter instead?"

Noah's mouth twisted into a not-so-amused smile. "I'm hardly a psychiatrist."

The guarded look was back in his eyes, and Elle found herself wondering if he even knew it was there. His statement was vague. Undoubtedly an avoidance of some kind. But she was half sure that the wary expression was unconscious. How could someone deliberately hide something yet not seem aware that he was giving himself away? Elle's curiosity over that won out over the battle to kiss and be kissed, and she frowned up at him.

"I'm not suggesting you cured him," she said. "But you must've had some kind of discussion that swayed him away from the life he was living."

Noah averted his eyes and gave his stubble a scratch. "I dunno. Dez was a damn big hot mess that day. We talked about a lot of stuff."

Elle opened her mouth to insist that he had to have some clue—and she was certain he did—but her words were abruptly chased away by the crack of a gunshot ringing through the air.

Chapter 7

Noah knew the nearby blast was related to Elle and her missing daughter. It had to be. The small town where he'd taken up residence might not be perfectly crime-free, but a gunshot wasn't even close to a common occurrence.

For a second, he was torn. He wanted to chase down the noise. Figure out its source. Who it was aimed at. Know for sure whether or not it had hit its mark and demand a few answers. All of that. Except what he wanted more was to ensure Elle's safety.

"C'mon," he said. "Let's get inside before someone aims that our way."

He started to swing toward the motel. Elle, on the other hand, stayed completely still. The color had drained from her face, and her eyes were fixed in the direction of the gunshot. It was the same blank expression that had plagued her features when Noah let Dez walk away. But this time, he recognized the brief, silent horror for what it was—direct fear on her daughter's behalf.

"It's not her," he said firmly.

Her attention refocused. "How can you be so sure?"

"Think about it. They wouldn't be going to all this trouble if they were just going to shoot her," he told her, not adding that they would've been smarter about it, too. "And you're supposed to be giving me a little trust, remember?"

"Right." She said it like she didn't quite believe it or mean it, but a moment later, she breathed out, eyed the space where the shot had seemed to come from, then stretched out her arm and pressed her palm to his.

The move surprised Noah. Partly because she was the one to reach for him. Mostly, though, what surprised him was the way her small, slightly cool fingers felt so natural in his grip. Like the moments of separation had been the less normal state.

Which is ridiculous, Noah thought as they started moving toward the motel again.

Except the silent chastisement didn't make it any less true. Her hand felt good and right in his. Like it was supposed to be there. It reminded him, also, that just a heartbeat before the bang of the gun, he'd been pretty damn sure he was about to blab out his life story. The same life story that had made Dez think there could be a little light in the world. Or at least a place to hide from the shadows. And right before that moment had been another. One where their lips were about to meet. Hell. Noah wished they had met. In fact, he kind of wanted to stop again right then, take her face in his hands, and finish the kiss that he'd never even started. It was probably a good thing that he had a few seconds to regroup as they moved from the street to the gate, then across the patio to his front door.

Clearly I need it.

Noah was also glad to see that Rog appeared to have

gone inside and doubly relieved that the older man had left Noah's phone in easy sight and grabbing distance, too, saving a knock on the door. Because he honestly wasn't sure he could make up some believable reason for the way his hand refused to loosen its grip on Elle. He somehow doubted that telling his aged neighbor that it just "felt right" would be met with anything but embarrassing hilarity. In spite of that, Noah probably would've kept holding on, even as he reached out to twist the doorknob, if Elle hadn't given a sudden, slight tug back. He swiveled around to see what the issue was, already half dreading what he'd find. But instead of another problem, he saw that Elle was smiling.

"Look at that!" she said, lifting one of the fingers she'd just freed. "Gus-Gus made it home."

Noah followed the direction she'd pointed in, and he spied the humungous cat lounging in his favorite spot on the inside of the other man's window. For no good reason, his throat tightened, and he had to clear it a little before answering.

"Fat old thing always does," he managed to say gruffly, pushing open his door. "Let's go inside."

He fought a flash of disappointment as she simply followed him in rather than taking his hand again.

Not where your focus should be, he reminded himself. *Plenty to do, and none of it requires you to be holding your client's hand.*

He forced a businesslike tone. "Slide the lock shut. That'll slow down any other visitors. It'll help them think we're still in here, too, even after we're gone."

"What do you mean?" She frowned at him. "Won't we have to unlock it, then relock it from the outside when we go?"

He shook his head. "Nope. We're not going out the front."

"I don't get it."

"You will."

He stepped to the bed, lifted the mattress, and grabbed a flattened backpack from underneath. Next, he removed his gun from his waistband and dropped it onto the unmade bed. He could feel Elle's curious gaze follow him, but he didn't take the time to explain. If nothing else, the bit of time they'd spent together had taught him that it was far too easy to get sucked into a conversation with her. And far too hard to keep from saying things he didn't want to say. Time was slipping by too quickly to risk it.

With speed on his mind, Noah moved to the still-open, now partially damaged closet. There, he bent down and yanked out the few remaining items from the safe. He dropped the first two—some ID and a thick wad of cash—into the backpack. The third was his shoulder holster, and that, he tossed on the bed alongside his weapon. As the sheets settled again, he strode back to the dresser and yanked open a drawer to retrieve a fresh T-shirt. He grabbed one at random and draped it over the corner of the dresser. Thinking he would've loved time to wash off the grit of the day, he pulled off his tank top and turned to throw it toward the corner where his dirty laundry tended to pile. Then he froze as he remembered abruptly—belatedly—that he had an audience.

You forgot about her? said an amused voice in his head. *Yeah, right.*

It was true, though. Despite the fact that his current actions were directly related to Elle, and even though he'd literally just been thinking about her, his urgency had momentarily robbed him of common sense. Now it was robbing him of movement, too. Except for his eyes, of course, which lifted to the blond woman who stood just a few feet away.

Her gaze was on his chest, her lower lip quivering as she drew in a breath. She didn't say anything. She didn't look away. Instead, her stare traveled over his body in a way that would've made Noah blush if he were the kind of man who was prone to it.

Chest to extended arm, then back.

Along his torso.

Down to his stomach.

Skimming over the spot where his jeans hung on his hips.

Then up, up, painfully slow, pausing to trace the line of his clavicle.

The exploration was as explosive as a touch, but far more of a torment.

When her stare finally reached his face, every part of Noah felt seared. Almost branded. His breathing was practically ragged, and he couldn't help but wonder what would happen if she actually touched him in that moment. Would he ignite? Melt? Or just drag her to the bed and pour all that extra heat from his own body into hers?

Get a freakin' grip, Loblaw.

But he wasn't sure he could comply. Desperate to break the hold of her simple, visual exploration, Noah covered a growl—which might actually have been closer to a moan—with a muttered apology for the display, then forced himself to grab the fresh T-shirt. It took two tries to actually get ahold of the cotton, and the second attempt sent the item to the floor. Growling again, he yanked it up and viciously yanked it on.

Ultra-conscious of Elle's attention now, he pulled another shirt from the drawer—this one a short-sleeved button-up in charcoal gray. With that in hand, he strode to the bed, pretended he hadn't pictured her there just a moment earlier and snagged his holster. He slid on the straps and buckled his weapon into the appropriate slot. Then he slipped on the dress shirt so as to cover the gun and spun back to face Elle once more.

"Ready?" he said, glad that his one-word question came out sounding damn close to normal.

"Sure. I'm not sure what I'm supposed to be ready for, but if it brings us closer to getting Katie, then…yes. A hundred percent." She spoke casually—like she hadn't just given his bare chest a thorough perusal—but as Noah turn away, he caught the way her throat worked in a silent swallow, and he knew she'd felt the heat, too.

He kept his thoughts to himself, though, opting instead for a thumb jerk toward his closet. "C'mon."

Elle tipped her head to look past him. "C'mon…where?"

In response, he shoved aside the clothes on the hangers and stepped over the safe. He pressed his hands to the rear wall, lifting at the same time as putting pressure on the cool surface. The drywall barely protested as it rose from the floor to reveal a dark, narrow space. He quickly stepped inside, then called to Elle.

"Good to go," he said. "And shut the closet door behind you."

"Is that a secret passage?" Her reply had a nervous quake that made Noah pause and stick his head back out.

"More of a structural anomaly." He studied her face, noting that she sucked in her lower lip, then released it again before answering.

"A structural anomaly that you just happened to know was there?"

"That. Or one I created myself for an eventuality such as this one."

"And you want me to get inside?"

"Pretty much our best chance of getting out of here in one piece."

He saw her throat work in a second swallow, only this time, it was pure worry.

"I don't do all that well with small dark spaces," she admitted.

"I'll be right there with you," he promised.

Her eyes closed. "Trust and Katie, right?"

"Trust, Katie and me," he corrected without thinking about it.

The comment made her eyes open, and when her blue gaze found him, it was both sharp and unsure at the same time. Like she was trying hard to decipher if he meant it. Or maybe what he meant. Something he wasn't all that sure of himself. Whatever it was she was searching for, she seemed to find it. She turned away and dragged the closet door shut. Then she took a breath and a few steps at the same time, setting one foot beside him, then another. And Noah was thankful for the move in his direction, because as he reached for the panel that would close them in, the light, almost imperceptible rattle of someone trying the door handle carried to his ears.

Startled by the sound, Elle went from cautiously entering the space to practically diving in. She smacked into Noah, and he stumbled back. His body thumped the wall behind, and Elle cringed as she saw the concerned way his eyes flicked to the opening in the closet.

Crap.

She tried to breath out an apology, but he vehemently shook his head and made a keep-quiet gesture. Then he pushed off the wall and slid past her—the space was just barely wide enough to allow it—so he could grab hold of the panel on the other side. As he lifted it into place, more panic tried to rise in Elle's chest. She beat it back.

You'll be okay, she told herself.

But it was a hard thought to believe. Even harder when Noah succeeded in his task, because the darkness closed in completely, cutting off the last of the already minuscule amount of light. Her heart rate surged. She ordered it to slow.

C'mon, Elle. You've got this.

But then the wide-shouldered man leaned back, his body brushing hers, and she almost jumped.

"You good?" he murmured.

"I'm fine," Elle lied in a whisper.

"Good. We're just going to wait here for a short bit to see if anyone breaks down the door."

"Breaks down the door? Don't you think we should keep moving?"

"They won't find us in here, and their conversation might give us a hint on what direction to take once we're out of here."

"Right. Okay."

"Just a minute or two. I promise."

"All right."

I can do this.

She let her eyes sink shut, then breathed in through her nose and out through her mouth in an exercise meant to calm.

It wasn't that she was claustrophobic. She just had bad memories of a small dark space that she never wanted to revisit. And climbing into a secret passageway—or whatever Noah wanted to call it—was a sure-fire way to stir up the parts of her past that she kept locked firmly away. Add the potential threat on the other side of the wall, and it was a recipe for a full-fledged panic attack.

Think about anything else.

But when her mind slid around in search of a topic, it did the inevitable; it latched onto Katie. The same questions that had plagued Elle since the moment of realization in the park jumped to the forefront again. Where was she? Was she okay? Was she locked in a place that was dark and oppressive like this one? Or somewhere worse?

An image of her little face—framed by her dark locks and full of a fear—slammed forcefully into Elle. It cut away the measured breaths she was trying to maintain. It made her heart want to burst. And she knew that if she didn't channel her brain elsewhere, the worry would overtake her.

Elle shifted her attention to the physical world. Behind her, the wall was cool and rough, and her right hand had unconsciously clasped around what had to be a wooden beam. Her fingers flexed on it, feeling the myriad of imperfections under her skin. It was a good feeling. A solid one. And it grounded her enough that she was able to gain control of her breathing again.

As she inhaled slowly and deeply, she noted that the air had a slightly musty, slightly chalky scent. It wasn't exactly awful, but it brought to mind attics full of old clothes, and it was accompanied by a need to pull out some lemon-scented cleaner and wash it away. Elle exhaled, then drew another breath, noticing that on top of the mustiness was another smell.

Noah's.

There wasn't more than a hint of cologne emanating from him—and maybe it was just aftershave or even deodorant—but it still begged another breath. Elle sucked one in, enjoying the way the scent intensified, and how it mingled with a trace of sweat. The latter addition to the smell wasn't at all odorous; it reminded her of long hot summer days on the beach. A place she'd far rather be. Soaking up the rays and building sandcastles with Katie.

Her stomach dropped again, and she had to really work to stop from letting the fear seep back to the surface.

Shift your focus, Elle. You can do it.

She squeezed the beam again, drew yet another breath and tried to seek out a small amount of good in the situation. It was an old trick she used when things were at their worst. And after just a moment, she realized there was something pleasurable in the midst of the fear and chaos. Her hand snaked out to find it, and even in the dark, she had no trouble seeking what she wanted. In a heartbeat, she had her fingers threaded through Noah's, and he immediately squeezed back. The contact was exactly what Elle needed. It didn't completely rid her of the hard pit of worry in her stomach, but it anchored her to the current moment. And that was enough.

Breathing out a perfectly calm breath, she pulled her eyes open and found Noah's increasingly familiar gaze fixed on her.

"Hi," he said, his voice low and somehow full of intimacy.

"Hi," she said back, feeling oddly shy.

"Still doing okay over there?" he asked.

"All things considered," Elle replied.

"All things considered…" he echoed. "You're holding it together in a pretty damn impressive way, actually."

"Am I?" She shook her head. "Because this is the worst day of my life. And I've had some doozies. I feel like I'm falling apart at the seams."

He freed his fingers, palmed the back of her hand, then dragged his thumb up her arm. When he reached her shoulder, he slid the tips of his other four digits over her clavicle, up her throat, then cupped her cheek. For a moment, his hand stayed there. Then it reversed its path. Slowly. So slowly. And the heat in the small space doubled. Tripled, maybe. Electric attraction zapped through Elle, but a little part of her protested the timing yet again. Except a bigger part of her pointed out that they were stuck where they were. They weren't moving until Noah was sure that the intruders were either coming or going. What was the sense in fighting the heavy air and the need to let him sink his mouth into hers? So when Noah pulled his hand back, his expression unreadable in the dark, there was no part of Elle that wasn't disappointed.

Why had he stopped? Was he worried about the timing, too? Did he need a sign that she wanted him to keep going? Elle was too out of practice to know how to be subtle. She opened her mouth to do the only thing she could think of and ask him directly to kiss her. But her lips barely parted before he spoke first.

"See?" he said.

Puzzlement made her frown. "See what?"

"All of your seams are perfectly intact. At least from my perspective." His mouth twitched up into a wide grin, revealing his perfectly even teeth.

Elle stared at him for a second, connecting the dots between her minute-earlier comment and his exploration of her body and the terrible joke. And something unexpected happened. A laugh built up in her chest. It was a foreign feeling. Like she hadn't laughed in a year. It bubbled out all the same. And the fact that Noah had managed to make it happen only made Elle want to kiss him even more. But as she leaned forward a little more—with the giggles not quite subsiding—and pressed up in anticipation of lip-to-lip contact, Noah's visible amusement wiped abruptly off his face. His hand came up to clamp over her mouth. But the move was unnecessary. The look in his eyes was enough to kill her laughter all on its own. For several seconds, she was confused by his tense expression. But right when she was about to assume it had been for naught, Elle figured out what had sparked the sudden change.

From outside the small space, a man's one-sided conversation carried in.

Chapter 8

A string of curses coursed through Noah's head. Some-where in the back of his mind, he'd been assuming that if—when—someone burst in to his motel room, they'd literally burst in. Smash through the door with enough force to send the crappy wood flying and enough noise to alert him to the entry.

Stupid assumption.

A less experienced bounty hunter might've had a good excuse for thinking everyone on the chasing end of things was a mindless thug. Noah knew better. Caution and subtlety were what got the marks caught, not smashing through doors. He was just thankful that his floorboards had creaked right as Elle's laughter had started to taper off. Much like the squeak of the courtyard gate, it was a sound only a resident would recognize. The protest of the weakened floor came from a spot two steps into the room, and he knew it well enough to know that someone over two hundred pounds had triggered it.

Peeling his hand from Elle's mouth—certain she'd stay still and silent now—he mouthed an apology, then strained to hear what was happening on the other side of the wall. Words trickled in, muffled by both the drywall and the man's position in the room.

"Empty." *Pause.* "I know what I…" Indistinguishable. "No." *Pause again.* "Yes." *Heavy feet thumping on the carpet.* "Hang on." *The rattle of the closet door.* "Call you back." *The shuffle of someone coming closer.*

Even though he was certain that there was no way to know they were there, Noah tensed. Beside him, he felt Elle do the same. He immediately had to fight an urge to reach out and draw her in close. But as the need to keep her safe hit him, Noah realized something. It was the growing softness toward the woman he barely knew that had left them vulnerable. He'd been thinking about her, when the man out there had managed to sneak in. He'd been wanting to see her smile. To make her feel as okay as possible in a very not-okay situation. To kiss away the suffering that played out over her features every single time she thought of her daughter. He knew that's what was happening when her eyes grew tight and her lips pressed together like she was holding her breath. Maybe she thought she was hiding it, but it was too late. Noah could already read her. He'd let the emotion creep in, dammit, and it was backfiring as it was always guaranteed to do. What he needed now was to get back into professional mode, and to pretend like there was no bubbling need to be or do more than that.

Under the guise of trying to hear what the man in his room was doing, he took the tiniest step away from Elle. Instead of relief, Noah just felt an unexpected sense of wrongness. Growling silently at himself, he forcibly turned his attention to the shuffling noises still going on in the closet. He pictured a vague figure—above-average height, above-average built, features made indistinct by a hood covering his face—searching methodically for clues. Digging through the clothes. Opening the two shoeboxes full of miscellaneous papers that gave away nothing aside from Noah's preference for Vietnamese food. Bending to look into the empty safe, then realizing his search was futile. What Noah didn't do was take any satisfaction in being sure that his subterfuge had worked; he was too aware of how cockiness could lead to a downfall. He just waited. And after another few moments of stuff moving around, the unseen man spoke up again, obviously resuming his call.

"They're gone," he announced, pausing for a response. "Yeah, I'm damn sure. Cleared out whatever valuables he had." The stranger's feet hit the ground again, signaling his move away from the closet, but his speech was agitated now, and loud enough to hear. "The door was locked from the inside." Another pause. "How the hell would I know? Through a window?" There was a muttered curse, clearly not intended for his phone audience, and then he said, "No, don't tell Trey that. I'll call him myself as soon as I figure out who the hell this guy is and why he's suddenly so involved." There was a final moment of silence before the man signed off with some chilling words, then his feet tapped away and the door slammed behind him. "Okay. You need something to say to him? Then go ahead and let him know the first of his backup hunters is dead."

Noah's eyes sank shut as a name floated up, then stuck to the front of his mind. Dez.

Intuitively, he knew that his colleague was the backup hunter in question. From that, it was easy enough to infer that what had killed him was the shot that he and Elle had heard, and Noah's gut twisted at the dark conclusion. His mind shot back to that first night when he'd met the other man. The story he'd recounted to Elle was true. Dez had been less than half a man. Broken and lost. Understandably so. And for whatever reason, Noah had suspended his rules that night, too. He'd shared some—though nowhere near all—of the pieces of his own past, and he'd told the other man how he'd found purpose.

"I didn't expect it to have any effect," he murmured.

"Didn't expect what to have any effect?" Elle replied.

Noah didn't open his eyes right away, even though he knew he should've. He just felt too off balance. Or maybe more like he was balancing on the edge of something. On one side of it was what he'd just acknowledged, just reaffirmed—that emotion equaled weakness. On the other side of it was the need to tell Elle everything.

"Noah?"

Her voice dragged him back to reality, and he forced himself to lift his lids. He met her gaze. Her bright blue irises seemed to absorb the darkness, turning their color from cloudless sky to deepest ocean. He stared into them, then gave his head a shake.

"C'mon," he said gruffly. "Let's get the hell out of here."

He didn't wait for her to answer, or even offer her his hand this time. He was afraid if he did, that balance would tip. He'd sink into her eyes. Dredge up the past. His past. Which would throw away any chance at all of maintaining the distance he'd just sworn to keep. So he inhaled, and just slid past. It was impossible not to notice, though, how quickly she followed. It wasn't just the narrow space, either. Yeah, he could physically feel her nearness as he navigated the hidden corridor by memory. Her soft, slightly floral scent filled his nose, too. Except if he was being honest, it felt like more than that. He had an awareness of her that was entirely unreasonable. So when the awareness broke off abruptly, Noah spun back, and he wasn't surprised at all to see that Elle had stopped just a few feet behind.

"Something wrong?" he asked.

"I think I'm stuck," she replied, her hands moving behind her.

He stepped toward her. "Here, let me—"

"No."

"I can—"

"I've got it."

Noah gave his chin a scratch and hung back as Elle wiggled and wriggled and tried to free herself. When it became apparent that she wasn't going to get loose easily, he tried again to offer her some assistance. She again waved him off.

"My shirt's just stuck on a nail or something," she said.

"I can probably get it off more easily than you can," Noah told her.

"No," she repeated. "I said I've got it."

He frowned. "Okay. But— No. Never mind. You go ahead."

He watched as she twisted and turned, and he wondered why the hell she wouldn't just let him help. As she pulled, yanked and fiddled, the seconds ticked by. But just when Noah was about to override her random determination to do it on her own, Elle abruptly stopped and lifted her eyes up to him.

"You think it was him, don't you?" she asked.

"What?"

"That guy out there… He was talking about the first hunter or whatever. Saying he was dead. And you think it's Dez."

Noah started to argue, then thought better of it and nodded instead. "Yeah, Elle. I do."

Her eyes dropped to her fingers, which she squeezed tight around the fabric of her T-shirt. Of his T-shirt.

"It's my fault," she said softly.

Realizing her stubbornness was a foil for her feelings, he forewent his need for space, and he stepped toward her. He closed one of his hands over hers, and he used the other to grip her chin and lift it so he could see her face again.

"It is not your fault," he told her.

"If I'd gone with him…"

"If you'd gone with him, you'd both be dead. Or he'd be dead, and you'd be bound and gagged, and on your way to wherever it is Trey Charger wants you."

"Maybe they would've let him go."

"Do you really believe that?" he asked her softly.

She drew in a shaky breath. "No. But I don't feel any less guilty."

"Elle, you don't need to feel responsible for his death. This job comes with risks. There are dangerous clients and dangerous operations, and God knows most people don't want to be forcibly retrieved."

"He didn't deserve to die."

"No, he didn't. And I'm not trying to make it sound lighter than it is. All I'm saying is that it wasn't even close to your fault. Dez was well aware of the risks, and he took them anyway. Hell. He liked to push the boundaries." He dropped her chin and let out a heavy sigh. "Let me help you with the shirt, and we'll mourn Dez when the time is right. I promise."

Noah felt like he'd made more promises to Elle in the last few hours than he'd made to anyone in a year. It was worth it, though, when she blinked away her tears and nodded. When Noah reached behind her, though, another surprising sentence popped out of her mouth.

"I'm not good at taking help," she said.

Fumbling for the offending nail—and not finding it as easily as he assumed he would—Noah frowned. "What do you mean?"

"I just—I can barely even admit that I need help, okay?" She sounded a little embarrassed and a little defensive at the same time, but she went on anyway, her voice tickling his neck when he had to lean in even more. "I'm used to being on my own. I take of everything for Katie and me. I hate owing anyone anything."

Noah felt a chuckle build, and it escaped before he could stop it. And he still hadn't found the damn spot where her shirt was stuck.

"What?" Elle said. "What's funny?"

One side of his mouth went up, and he seized the fabric and slowly worked his fingers along in search of the snag. "You chased me down and ordered me to help you."

"I…" She trailed off like she hadn't thought of that, and muttered, "Usually."

"Usually?" he echoed.

"I'm usually terrible at admitting it."

"Okay," he said doubtfully.

"Seriously," she replied. "Last month, I got a flat tire, and a tow truck literally stopped in front of me. Pure lucky coincidence. When the driver pulled over and offered me a spare, I told him to stuff it."

"Why would you do that?"

He finally found the thing that the cotton was stuck on—it was actually somehow wedged between two beams—and he yanked it free. He leaned back, a small smile playing over his mouth at her apparent stubbornness. His amusement faded, though, when he saw the look in her eyes. Haunted. The same way she'd looked when he'd first seen her in the park. Concern reared up. But then Elle blinked, and her expression changed.

"I guess I feel like if I can't control the big things around me, then I should at least be able to control the little ones," she explained.

Noah nodded. Just once. Tightly. Then faced the other direction again. He believed her explanation, at least on a superficial level. In fact, he completely understood it. The problem was, he didn't buy that there wasn't something more behind her words.

Do you really need something more than a single mom who not only has a missing kid, but who's also mixed up with a notoriously shady businessman?

Noah's mind slipped to Elle's reaction to the opening in the closet. Then to her comment about not wanting to disclose the whole truth because he might not want to help her anymore. He thought of her guilt over Dez. It all mingled together in his head and told him that yeah, there was something else behind that fleeting look. And that as soon as they were safely on their way, he was going to find a way to ask her what it was.

It was strange. Elle knew she should've felt relief that things had finally sped up. They made it through the rest of the hidden corridor without interruption. They slipped out another closet panel into a second motel room—this one empty and pristine—which Noah casually mentioned he rented, too. Just in case. He snagged a pair of keys from under an umbrella stand and an expensive-looking suitcase from under the bed.

Elle barely processed the oddity of all of that before he guided her to the door, explaining in a low voice that it was the very last unit in the building, and due to a construction flaw, the exit was located on the side. In spite of the relative cover and lack of visibility, they still moved through it with caution, taking care to look for any would-be assailants. But the care they took didn't slow them down much at all. In moments they were cutting through the residential streets of Low River at a clipped speed. Five minutes of quick turns brought them to a stop in front of a sealed garage at a seemingly random home. There, Elle watched as Noah punched in a code to the keypad on the side. The door chugged open to reveal a surprisingly elegant car—sleek maroon paint, two chrome-lined doors and a leather interior that screamed of money.

Noah offered no explanation for the vehicle, and Elle didn't ask for one as she climbed in and buckled up. The engine purred to life, the A/C kicked on, and they were off. Headed for the highway and into a nearby town where Noah said another underhanded, well-connected acquaintance hid out. One who would be able to help them out for the right price.

It was strange. Almost surreal. Yet all in all, it was the least eventful chunk of time in Elle's day. There were no more stuck shirts. No more murderous visitors employed by Trey. And no drawn-out conversations that brought her dangerously close to revealing the more disturbing parts of her past. They were finally physically moving—toward Katie, with any luck—and Elle knew she should've been feeling nothing but relief. Instead, she felt off-kilter.

The thick pit of worry was still in her gut, shortening her breath every time she thought about the little girl and her current fate. About Trey. About the way their lives intersected, and how hard she'd worked to keep the three of them apart. The devastation at having failed. And—in spite of Noah's reassurances that she wasn't to blame—there was Dez's death.

The collateral damage.

Elle would do almost anything to protect Katie. She'd sacrificed personal goals and dreams and any semblance of a normal life. And she didn't resent it. Not even a little bit. But when people started dying, her heart couldn't help but twist with regret. What kind of person would she be if that didn't bother her? And what if Dez wasn't the last one to die? What if someone else got caught in the crossfire?

What if it's Noah?

Elle's hands tried to knit together with worry, and she forced them to stay still, flattening them against her bare knees. She stole the smallest look at the big bounty hunter. His mouth was set in an even line, his hands gripped tightly on the steering wheel. He looked tense. Harried. But like he was trying not to let on.

Guilt washed over her, and she refocused her attention out the front windshield.

Anything for Katie, she thought. *But is it fair to expect a good man like Noah to give up his life for her?*

She inhaled a breath that she hoped wasn't too noticeable, and she watched the scenery—residential had given way to highway, and rural properties dotted the horizon now—go by for a few very long seconds, considering what her options were.

She needed Noah. At least until she had a proper lead on where Trey had taken her little girl. But once she had that lead…

I can promise to pay him what I owe him, and I can sneak off.

The thought no sooner formed than Noah's voice—deep and laced with warning—startled her.

"Whatever it is you're thinking about doing…" he said. "Don't."

She flicked her eyes his way and infused her reply with innocence. "I don't know what you're talking about."

"Bull," he responded immediately. "I have a sister. I

know exactly what that look on your face means. You're plotting something I won't like."

"I—" Elle cut herself off and went back to staring at the trees.

Because a denial would be a lie. Even if she hadn't yet thought through the sequence of events that would be involved in leaving, she had silently used the words *sneak off.* Which meant that some part of her subconscious knew that Noah wouldn't like it.

Maybe because you owe him over three thousand dollars in expenses? She winced a little as she realized it should have been a much bigger number. Specifically, thirteen thousand. Because Noah would've been paying Dez, too. And now he wasn't.

Elle balled up her hands. "As soon as we get a tip that's good enough, I'll pay you, and you can go."

The car jumped a little, then jerked to the side. A passing driver laid on the horn, but Noah didn't seem to notice as he brought the vehicle to a haphazard stop on the side of the road.

"You'll pay me…" he said woodenly. "Then you'll go."

"I wasn't thinking straight when I hired you," she replied, knowing full well just how lame the statement came across.

"You weren't thinking straight."

"Are you just repeating everything I say?"

"I'm just trying to make sure I get it right," he replied, his tone just as stiff, his words just shy of clipped. "What I'm hearing is that hiring me was an error in judgment, which you've just now realized, and that you're dismissing me before I can get the job done."

"I'm going to pay you," Elle said, trying to keep the desperate edge out of her voice.

Something unreadable passed across his face. "How?

Are you going to find the nearest bank? Use your debit card to withdraw thousands of dollars? Do you even have a debit card?"

Her face warmed. "I—"

"Save it," he said, now speaking with barely confined anger. "Even if you answered yes to any of those questions, do you really think I'd believe it?"

"If you don't believe that I can pay, then why are you here?" she countered.

He didn't answer. Not really. Instead he said, "You need me, Elle. If you didn't you would've got yourself a cab or hopped on a bus or stolen a car, and you would've made your way to Trey Charger on your own."

"He wouldn't have just taken her home!"

"You know him well enough to be sure of that?"

"Yes!"

Elle snapped her mouth shut as soon as the admission was out. She could tell by the look on Noah's face that she'd only further piqued his curiosity. She needed to backpedal. Find an excuse. But the words wouldn't come, and she had no idea why it was so hard to just lie to the shaggy-haired man. She'd done her fair share of telling untruths over the last six years. They were especially rampant in the first weeks after her escape from under Trey's thumb. And even this week, when she'd filled in the application at their new apartment, she'd laced it with false information. Phony jobs. A phony backstory. Aside from her love for Katie, a large chunk of Elle's life was—by necessity—a lie. So why couldn't she just spit out something convenient and fitting right then? Why did a pair of hazel eyes, a set of warm hands and a sincere stare like Noah's change everything?

"Tell me the truth." His tone rode an odd line between gentle and urgent. "Why are you cutting and running the second you can?"

Her eyes dropped to her lap, and she could barely hear her own whispered reply. "Because he'll kill you, Noah."

He didn't respond. But a second later, the hum of the engine kicked up, and the crunch of gravel and the roll of the tires told Elle they were pulling back onto the road. She lifted her attention to the window and waited for Noah to pull a wide turn. He didn't. He didn't take the next exit, either, and Elle's pulse did a nervous jump.

"Didn't you hear what I just said?" she asked.

"I did," he acknowledged. "And that's my risk to take."

"You're just going to sacrifice yourself?"

"I'm going to assume that my death isn't a foregone conclusion, and I'm going to do my damnedest to stay alive."

"But… Think about Dez."

"I am. I'm thinking about him a lot. And his death shouldn't be for nothing."

"Noah."

"Elle."

"What if I said I can't really pay you?" she asked, hearing the now-unstoppable desperation creeping into her voice.

He was silent for a moment before answering. "Then I'd have to admit I suspected as much."

"So why are you still helping me?"

His fingers tapped the wheel. "I don't know."

For some reason, the three-word admission made Elle's heart squeeze sadly in her chest.

What did you want? she asked herself. *For him to make some kind of big confession? Maybe for him to say that he was helping you because you have some weird, profound effect on him? You know...the way he seems to have on you?*

The long answer was that it was a ridiculous thing to even consider. Elle ought not to care about a stranger's reasons for doing something—even when that something was helping her. She shouldn't be biting her tongue to keep from confessing that it mattered to her. But the simple answer was…it contradicted all of that. Because it was yes. Yes, she wanted to hear that there was some weird, cosmic connection happening between them. She wanted him to tell her she wasn't alone in the crazy feeling.

As she admitted it to herself, a blush spread across her face, and she turned her head to the side in case Noah happened to glance her way and catch the pinkness. But after a few heavy seconds of silence, the heat faded away. Because she realized something. There was one simple sentence she could say that probably would send him running. All she had to do was to announce the truth—that Trey Charger was Katie's father.

Chapter 9

Noah was used to tension. Used to uncomfortable situations where his personal, physical well-being was on the line. This, though. It was something different.

Saying aloud that he was pretty damn sure that Elle couldn't meet his payment demands had been an accident. Now he couldn't take it back. Which in turn meant he had to admit to himself that it was officially true. In the last few hours, he'd broken all his cardinal rules. A kid and plenty of attention. And in spite of all the action, he couldn't deny that it was emotion overruling the whole thing. The woman sitting beside him made him feel things he wasn't sure he wanted to put a name to. Worse than that—or at least as bad—was the fact that he had a sinking sensation that she was about to say something that would upset him.

Upset you? For crying out loud. You don't know her well enough for her to upset you.

The inward snarl did nothing to ease the feeling. He

needed to fill the quiet, so he could stop Elle from speaking first. Maybe discuss where they were headed. Ask if she thought they'd need to fuel up. Hell. Any inane thing would do. But his mouth seemed determined to share his thoughts instead, and when he opened his lips, something entirely *un*-inane slipped out.

"Did you catch that bit that Dez said about me living by a code?" Using the other man's name gave him a pang, but he kept his gaze on the road and went on. "That night when I met Dez, he asked me how I got by. How I shielded my brain. I told him I had three simple rules to keep myself sane. You want to know what they are?"

"Sure," Elle replied, sounding anything but.

"On the surface, they all make good business sense," Noah told her. "Rule one is so basic that I barely even think about it, and that's that I don't work for free. Rule two is that I keep a low profile. And rule three is that I don't get involved in situations that concern kids. I probably don't need to point out that I'm batting zero for three right now, do I?"

"No." Her response wasn't much more than an apologetic whisper.

"You most definitely have a kid," he said, "and I sure as hell suspect that I'll be getting some unwanted attention from your friend, Mr. Charger. On top of that, you owe me thirteen thousand, one hundred and seventy-three dollars, not including what I should collect when I actually find your kid." He waved a hand as she frowned and opened her mouth in an obvious protest. "Yeah, that amount includes Dez's fee. Because I'm going to make damn sure his sister-in-law—his only living relative—gets every cent of it. And we might as well add in gas money and mileage while we're at it. Let's say we're at thirteen thousand, two hundred and fifty dollars for good measure."

"I'm sorry." Her response really was a whisper this time, and Noah had to squeeze the steering wheel to keep from reaching for her.

"I don't want you to be sorry." The statement came out in a low, emotion-fueled growl.

"I—what?"

"I said those rules made sense on the surface, Elle. The truth is, they go a hell of a lot deeper for me."

"What do you mean?"

"I want to help you."

"But if it makes you go against your code, and it might get you killed…"

He hazarded a glance her way, and the misery on her face made his heart ache in a way he'd never experienced before. It made every part of him want to pull over, drag her into his arms and hold her close until she knew everything was going to be fine.

Just hold her? asked a voice in his head, and it took a significant amount of willpower and small, self-directed chastisement to shrug it off. *She needs you to find her daughter, not sit around thinking about how good it would feel to kiss her.*

"They're my damn rules," he told her gruffly as he flicked on his signal and turned onto a long rural driveway. "I'll break them if I want to."

For a second, her only response was silence. Then she let out a small sigh.

"Call it selfish," she said. "But I don't want to be responsible for your death, Noah."

He could tell that she meant it, and if he'd thought his heart hurt a second earlier, it had nothing on the feeling now. She was a woman desperate to find her daughter, yet she was worried about his life, too.

"Maybe I do know why I'm still here," he said.

He felt her eyes lift to his face, even though he hadn't shifted a look her direction. "Why?"

"Because I'd rather die knowing I did the right thing than live knowing I walked away because of my stupid code."

Her inhale was sharp, but if she was going to say anything in response, she didn't get a chance to. They'd reached their destination—an old farmhouse one of his professional acquaintances occupied—and it didn't take any kind of special training to see that something was wrong. A tall potted plant lay on its side, battered and broken. A string of patio lanterns looked as though they'd been ripped down, then tossed everywhere. That wasn't the worst of it, though. The most alarming sight was the all but shattered front door. The top half was missing completely. The bottom half was split up the center, and it hung from the hinges, flapping eerily back and forth.

All of Noah's hackles came up, and he swung his gaze from side to side, searching for the culprit of the destruction. There was no sign of anyone. Not another vehicle, and nowhere to hide one. That still didn't mean it was worth the risk to stick around and find out for sure. Regretful that they wouldn't get to use his acquaintance's considerable resources, he dropped his hand down to shift into Reverse. He barely managed to take ahold of the gear stick before Elle's fingers closed over his, stopping him.

"We can't just leave," she said.

"You want to confront whoever the hell did this?" he replied.

"No," she admitted. "But you said this guy could help us."

"He's likely to be beyond being able to help at this point, Elle," he told her as gently as possible.

She shook her head. "But you don't know that for sure.

And what if it's the reverse? What if your friend needs our help?"

"He's hardly a friend."

She let his hand go and pointed out the front windshield. "There's no one around. And you can see the fresh tire tracks spin out and leave in the other direction."

He eyed the spot she'd indicated and saw that she was right. There were clear marks. Someone had left in a damn big hurry.

"Please, Noah," Elle added. "I feel like if we leave without checking, we might lose an opportunity to get closer to finding Katie."

Noah eyed the destruction at the front of the house, then brought his gaze back to her. He stood zero chance of saying no to the half-hopeful, half-plaintive look on her face. Gritting his teeth and cursing his own softness, he cut the engine but left the keys in the ignition.

"I'm taking my gun," he stated, "but I'm leaving you my phone." He yanked it from his pocket and set it down in the cup holder. "When I get out, I want you to climb over the console into the driver's seat, and I want you to wait and watch. If you see anything go wrong, lay on the horn. If you think I won't get back to you in time, then you just get the hell out of here. Once you're somewhere safe, use my phone to speed dial a guy listed under the name 'Spud,' and if he sounds dubious about our relationship, tell him I said 'Norah.'"

He knew she was going to argue about at least some of it—possibly all of it, actually—so he didn't give her a chance to say a word. He lifted a hand to her cheek, leaned forward and placed a soft, slow kiss on her lips. Her mouth was warm. Sweet. Everything it ought to have been. And regretfully, Noah had no time to enjoy it. He pulled back and grabbed the door handle, and as Elle stared at him with wide, startled eyes, he slid from the car. He tapped the automatic lock and closed the door quietly. Then he crouched low and slunk toward the house without looking back.

. Elle was too surprised to react. All she could do was stare in mute, worried silence as Noah made his way stealthily across the yard, slipped up the stairs, then disappeared into the house. Which, she suspected, was fully his intention. And when the surprise wore off, she was just plain annoyed. Except she couldn't quite pinpoint the source of her irritation. Or maybe it wasn't that she couldn't pinpoint it; maybe it was that she couldn't narrow it down because there were too many things to choose from.

For starters, she didn't like the orders Noah had issued, and she'd be damned if she would leave him there if that's what it came down to. It also irked her that he'd kissed her to keep her from protesting. And she disliked his sneaky maneuver in getting out of the car, too. But maybe what pricked at her most was that he'd stolen the moment. It was kind of petty to think about it. Elle knew that. But there had been all those perfect chances before. Heat simmering between them. Eyes on lips. Tension—the good kind—galore. And yet there went the first kiss. Grabbed as a trick.

See? said her conscience. *That's what you get for not seizing the opportunities when they arise.*

But as unexpected and slightly underhanded as it might've been, it still hadn't been unenjoyable. In fact, it was the opposite. And as Elle kept her eye on the front door, she could still feel his lips on hers. Firm but tender. Quick but somehow unhurried. Unconsciously, she brought the tips of her fingers up to her mouth. She felt along the edges of her lips, thinking about how the brush of his stubble had added a hint of roughness that she would never have guessed she'd like. But she did. She had. A lot.

"Dammit," she murmured, her eyes on the empty doorway, and the last of her annoyance slipping away. "You'd better come out of there in once piece. Because I—"

The abrupt buzz of Noah's cell phone cut her off, midsentence. She dropped her gaze to the screen. The name "Spud" was on display. Elle bit her lip, thinking it couldn't be a coincidence that Noah's fail-safe contact was texting him that very second.

With an uncomfortable prickle of nerves coming to life between her shoulders, she lifted the phone and swiped a finger across. She half expected a prompt for a password, but instead was rewarded with the most recent text alert— a set of numbers that took her a second to place. GPS coordinates. But she didn't get a chance to consider what the coordinates might signify before the phone buzzed an incoming call. And Spud's name was there, too. She let it go to voicemail, but the buzzing no sooner ended than it started up again.

Her finger hovered over the answer button. She bit her lip a little harder, glanced up at the house in search of Noah, then let voicemail take it again. And it started to buzz once more. This time, with another text from Spud.

Pick up the phone!!!

Elle's pulse jumped, and when the cell alerted a third call, she finally gave in and tapped the answer button. Then she held her breath, brought the phone to her ear and waited.

"What the hell, man," said a masculine voice on the other end. "Are you trying to mess with me?"

Elle blew out a breath. "I'm sorry. Noah's not here."

There was a drawn-out silence on the end before the man—presumably Spud—answered. "I'd ask who this is, but I'm not sure I really want to know. So I'll just ask this instead. Have you killed, maimed or otherwise harmed Noah Loblaw?"

"Uh. No?"

"Is that a question?"

"No," she said more firmly. "Noah is helping me. I haven't hurt him."

An audible exhale carried through the line. "I really want to believe you."

Elle's brain kicked up a reminder. "This is Spud, right?"

"Yeah."

"He told me to tell you 'Norah.'"

There was another pause, then a low whistle. "Well, damn."

Elle tamped down her curiosity. She wanted to know who Norah was, and what she meant to Noah, and why the name made the stranger on the other end sound so surprised. But now wasn't the time.

"Why did you want to know if he was messing with you?" she asked instead.

"He asked me to track a car," Spud replied. "You know about that?"

"Yes."

"All right. Well, I found it. Helped that the car has a permanent tracker on it, and I was able to—" He cut himself off with a throat clear. "Never mind. You don't need to know all that. My point is, I was able to get a clear visual of the car's route. I pinged that off Noah's location—he asks me to keep tabs, so don't freak out—and I noticed something weird. The location where you are now? The car was there about twenty minutes ago. And it just rerouted to head back in that direction."

Elle's breath stuck in her throat. "He's coming back?"

"So that answers my question about whether or not it's a planned meeting."

"Definitely not."

"Damn."

"How much time do we have?"

"Pulled the U-turn three minutes ago," Spud said. "So if he's going the speed limit…"

"Seventeen minutes," Elle filled in.

"And I'd be willing to bet that he's putting the pedal to the floor whenever he can."

"Thank you. I'll tell Noah right away." Her hand was already on the unlock button.

"Wait!" Spud almost yelled.

Elle paused. "What?"

"Tell that son-of-a-you-know-what to call me when you guys are safe and sound."

"I will," she promised.

Then she tapped the phone off, stuffed it into her shorts pocket and clambered out of the car. In the back of her mind, she knew she should be exercising caution. But her fear of the man chasing them overruled it. He'd already killed Dez. He'd kill Noah, too, if he caught up to them. And God only knew what his plans for Elle herself were. So she ran up the driveway, thumped over the front porch and rushed through the shattered door and into the house. Then froze.

The scene in front of her was macabre.

Crimson darkened the cream-colored area rug in the living room. A man's leg jutted out from behind a brown leather sofa. Blood spatter dotted the wall between the piece of furniture and the partially hidden body.

Oh, God.

Sickness swirled in Elle's stomach, and she turned away

in an attempt to stop it from rising up. Her spin brought her sight in line with something else. An enormous desk, a half dozen wall-mounted computer screens, and reams and reams of printed paper and magazines and cut-out articles. Pens covered every surface. And Noah was there, too. He stood between an oversized, well-worn office chair and the desk. In his fingers, he held a single, partially crumpled piece of computer paper. His eyes were on Elle. His expression was dark, and for no good reason that made her feel worse than the murdered man on the floor.

"What?" she breathed, her intention to break the news of the imminent arrival of an unwanted guest completely swept to the wayside. "What's wrong?"

"You told me this wasn't a custody issue," he said.

Elle's heart dropped impossibly low. "It's not." Her eyes flicked to the paper in his hand—she could just see an official-looking letterhead—and she swallowed nervously. "What's that?"

"A photocopy of a birth certificate. Do you want to see it?"

"I don't need to."

"Her name is Kaitlyn Marie Charger."

"I know that."

"A coincidental last name, Elle?" he asked, his tone suggesting he knew it was anything but.

"No," she admitted.

She could tell he was waiting for an explanation. A denial of Katie's parentage. But the words stuck in her throat. She wasn't sure why she couldn't defend herself. She wanted to think it was because she didn't owe Noah— or anyone—an explanation. But she knew that wasn't the truth. Maybe it was shame, for what she'd let herself endure for so many years. Maybe it was that he knew she'd broken laws and done bad things in the name of the greater good. Either way, she stood still, her mouth shut, her voice silent.

Speak, she ordered herself. *Tell him that it's not what he thinks.*

But as her tongue refused to cooperate, the vaguest, farthest-away rumble of an engine carried through the air. And the reason for her sudden burst into the room came back.

"Spud called," she gasped, finally finding something she was capable of saying aloud. "The car you had him track is on its way here."

Noah let out a curse, turned and dropped the partially crumpled birth certificate onto the crowded desk, then grabbed a file off the desk before he spun back.

"Let's go," he said, his tone urgent. "This is chock-full of info that should help us get another step closer to your kid, and the last thing we need is to lose what little ground we've gained."

Elle was a little surprised when he followed the statement with an offer of his hand. Hadn't she just given him every reason to retract any extra show of kindness or familiarity? But she wasn't going to question it too hard. She slid her fingers into his, and together, they bolted back out the way they'd come in.

Chapter 10

Trey Charger was Katie's father.

Noah knew he didn't have time to dwell on that particular reality. He didn't have time to think about the fact that Elle hadn't been honest about there being a custody issue. He sure as hell didn't have time to think about which thing bothered him most—the custody, the parentage or the fact that she'd out-and-out lied. Yet as they bounced down the steps, tore across the dirt driveway, then jumped back into the car, his thoughts refused to still. Instead, they ground along with the roar of the engine. They rumbled with the tires. The crunched like the gravel-marked path under the car.

Noah could understand the why of her end of it. Really. After all, he'd flat-out told her he didn't do custody-related cases. On top of that, Trey Charger wasn't exactly the kind of guy who'd earn a father-of-the-year medal. But why did it make his jaw clench hard enough to ache? Why couldn't

he shake the sensation that he'd been betrayed? It was beyond stupid. Elle was a stranger. A client.

A stranger and client who you kissed.

That was true. A spontaneous move, and maybe a bit
ill-advised. If he was being honest, though, it was also
a move he'd been craving since the second he spied her.
He'd immediately noticed her beauty. Been unable to ignore it, really, in spite of the situation. But did a kiss and
that magnetic attraction really justify the all-over disappointment he felt at the revelation? Did it explain why he
felt like that birth certificate was a personal affront? Noah
somehow doubted it.

He hit the gas pedal hard, willing the bumps and thumps
to drive away the churning of his mind, but it was Elle's
voice—hesitant and soft—that finally pulled him from the
anger-tinged musings.

"I didn't lie to you," she said.

"Doesn't matter," he muttered.

"It matters to me."

He swiveled a quick look her way. Her blue eyes were
on him, her expression sincere. It made him feel that much
worse, and he exhaled a sigh.

"Which part wasn't a lie?" he asked.

"You didn't ask me if Trey was her father," she replied.

"Kind of what I meant when I asked about custody."

"Look… I know it's a fine line, but there's a difference."

"Explain it."

She didn't say anything right away, and he glanced in
her direction again. She wasn't looking at him anymore.
Instead, her gaze was on her hands, and he could see that
tears had started to flow.

Dammit.

Even factoring in their time constraints, he couldn't
let her cry. He couldn't be the source of her sadness. So

he slammed—too roughly, probably—on the brakes. The car jerked to an immediate halt, and Elle bounced against her seatbelt, but she didn't lift her eyes. Guiltily, Noah reached a hand out to clasp hers. She let him take it. When he squeezed, though, she didn't tighten her fingers back around his in the way he would've liked.

"Don't tell me you're sorry," she said.

"It's fine, Elle."

"I know you might classify it as a lie of omission, but that's only because you don't understand."

"I want to understand," he said gently. "But only if you want to tell me."

Her breath hitched like she was holding in a sob. "Trey might be Katie's biological father, but he has no right to claim that he's any kind of parent. He's the kind of man who locks a little girl in the basement and tells her she can fight her way out because it will build character. Or who will stuff her into a closet, so she can listen while he works out the finer details of how to violently end a man's life. Who thinks his daughter is a bargaining chip, and who doesn't think twice about selling her. Literally. Selling her for some kind of payoff. He's the kind of man that will force a woman who's barely more than a girl herself to get married." Her eyes came up, and they were full of pain. "I don't know if you would call that a custody issue, but I sure as hell don't."

A wave a revulsion coursed through Noah, and his reply was roughened by it. "I call that a police issue."

Elle shook her head, and her reply was small and sad. "You say that because you don't know Trey. What he's capable of. Who he's connected to. The stuff I just mentioned… It's only the tip of one enormous iceberg for him. How do you think he managed to get away with murder and then thrive afterward? And on top of that—" She cut herself off and swallowed, then spoke again in a way that made Noah think she'd changed her mind about what she'd been planning on saying. "On top of that…some things are better not repeated aloud."

He waited another second to see if she'd add anything else. When she didn't, he nodded his acceptance of the partial explanation. He wanted to know more. Not because he liked to hear about her suffering. He hated it. He hated the man he'd never met, too, and it made him sick to think that a kid had been treated that way. But he wanted to know it all, so that he could offer comfort for every bit of it. Except he could tell that it hurt her to talk about the finer details, and he suspected more time and a different environment would be necessary for her to share everything.

Not to mention getting her kid back.

Realizing that was the thing he needed to do before any of the rest of it—and that he was wasting time on self-centered thoughts rather than propelling them forward in their search—he cleared his throat and answered her in an emotion-tinged voice. "Okay, sweetheart. Let's get Katie back, then let's find a way to keep her as far away from Trey Charger as humanly possible."

She shot him one of the most grateful looks he'd ever seen, and his heart tightened, then expanded so hard that he had to bring a hand to his chest to give his breastplate a rub. As he put the car back into Drive, he wondered how he'd ever considered not helping her. What would've happened to her if he hadn't? His mind strayed to Dez, and to the dead man—a guy known none too fondly as Spider— back at the house they'd just left. He'd barely processed the former, and the latter had been shoved to the back of his mind for later. Even with the compartmentalization, the loss of life saddened him. But the idea that the same could've happened to the woman sitting in the passenger seat…that filled him with an entirely unreasonable sorrow.

He stared out the window, his throat burning. He felt like he should say something more. Tell her a bit about what he'd seen on Spider's computer, and what was in the file that he'd tossed onto the back seat. Hell. He could just tell her where they were headed. Except he didn't trust himself to speak. Which was why he was almost glad when a flash in the distance caught his attention.

He held still, tipped his head and listened. And sure enough, the engine noise was far too close for comfort. It made him realize that if he kept going straight, they'd likely encounter the man who was hunting Elle. In fact, if they hadn't stopped for the last two minutes, the run-in would've been inevitable. At least now they had a chance to get away.

Noah cast a look back and forth. They couldn't go back. The couldn't go forward. So they had only one choice left.

"Hang on tight," he growled.

Then he spun the steering wheel and drove the car over the shoulder and straight into the head-high grass on the side of the road.

Elle clutched tightly to the seatbelt with her right hand, and with her left, she held on to the seat with a death grip. The car was sleek. Well crafted. And nowhere near de-signed for the off-road trek it was currently undertaking. The wheels bounced like crazy. Every bump made the un-dercarriage shudder.

She wanted to close her eyes to block out the unrea-sonable slap of tall grass against the windshield. But she forced herself to keep looking. She was afraid that if she didn't, she'd never know what foreign object they slammed into right before they died. But after a minute—that felt like ten—the wildly tall, crazily thick grass gave way to a few thinner patches. Then a few more. Then visibility improved, and Elle could see that they'd made their way across a large patch of farmland and were now headed back toward the road. More specifically, it looked like they were about to jump onto the highway.

Elle finally let herself breathe. "Do you think we avoided him?"

"For now."

There was more than a hint of grimness in Noah's two-word reply, and Elle wanted to shiver. She fought it, though, and turned her thoughts to Katie. She hated that the hours were starting to feel like days, and even more than that, she hated the sinking feeling that they were getting farther away instead of closer. Her eyes stung, and she willed herself not to cry. The tears had come more times today than they had for the last six years altogether. It made her wonder if she was truly as strong as she'd believed. How could she be, if the second Trey was back in her life, she fell apart?

Her hands tried to tighten into fists, and she forcibly made them stay relaxed. She'd bested the cruel man once before, and she'd do it again.

Then—as if he could sense her mounting need to act— Noah reached into the back seat. And without looking, he retrieved the folder that sat on the leather, then held it out.

"Here," he said. "Have a look through the first three pages."

Elle took the file from his hand and opened it. On top, there was a picture of Dez. A mugshot, to be more accurate. Her heart squeezed with sadness, and she made herself flip to the next page. It was the photocopied and enlarged driver's license of a different man.

"Klause, Henry James," read the words beside his picture.

He was gray haired, and craggy-looking—probably old enough to be her grandfather—but with a ring through one of his eyebrows, and a tattoo peeking out from under his T-shirt sleeve that lent him a little bit more of punk rock vibe than any senior citizen she'd ever met. Elle stared at the photo for a few seconds, then moved on. The third sheet was another mug shot, this one for a man named Beldon Shields. He appeared to have an affinity for breaking and entering.

"Aside from Dez," she said, "should these mean something to me?"

Noah shook his head. "Not to you. But to me they do. The second dude there goes by the name King Henry, and he's a two-bit crook who does some retrieval on the side."

"Another bounty hunter?"

"Sort of. I wouldn't put him in the same category as me, or even as Dez. King Henry is more of an enforcer. Collections. Watched too many gangster movies as a kid and likes to break fingers."

"And this other guy? Is he the same?"

"Yeah. He's not from around here, though. Somewhere back East. The only reason I know who he is at all is that he did an interview on some news piece a few years back. Ticked off a lot of people in the business."

Elle flipped through the sheets again. "You think these will help us find Katie somehow?"

"Not at all," he replied.

She wasn't she sure she'd heard right. "What?"

"Look at the fourth page."

Frowning, she did as he'd suggested. It was an outgoing email, the same message sent to two people. The language was nonsensical, though. Sentences joined together that seemed utterly unconnected. Almost gibberish. The replies were there, too. Each only a single word. Aborted. After another second of rereading, Elle gave up.

"I don't understand," she said, looking back up at Noah.

"It's coded," he told her. "Did I mention that the man who owned that house back there was named Spider?"

She tried not to picture the too-still leg and all the blood, and she made herself answer in as smooth a voice as she could manage. "No, I don't think so."

"Not even sure what his real name is. Was, I mean." He paused, strummed a thumb on the wheel like he was still processing the other man's death, then sighed and went on. "He earned the nickname because of his affinity for creating webs of connection between people and things. Based on that email there, I'd say the three men—Dez, the King and Beldon—were each other's competition. Spider must've figured out that it wasn't going to go well, and he warned them. The King and Beldon heeded the warning."

Elle glanced down at the four sheets of paper again. "I don't understand why you're showing me—"

She cut herself off as she clued in; Noah wanted her to know that no one else was going to die on her behalf. Not based on hunting her down, anyway. Her heart expanded with appreciation. But then sank again right away.

"Two people are still dead," she said.

Noah's hand came out to give her elbow a quick, reassuring squeeze. "You need to remember that it's not your fault."

"I'm trying." She closed her eyes for a second, doing her best not to let the pit in her stomach grow any bigger than it had already become. "Can I ask you something?"

"I dunno." He had a mildly teasing smile on his face. "My mom always told me to avoid that question."

Elle felt her own mouth curve up, just a little. "Probably not horrible advice."

"That's probably the most apt description of my mother I've ever heard."

"What? Not horrible?"

He let out a chuckle. "Exactly."

She was suddenly curious about Noah's family life. She tried to picture him, sitting at a table, surrounded by loved ones. She thought about the ruined picture in the motel room. Were those kids a part of his family? Was he an uncle, maybe? Or did he have kids of his own? The idea hadn't even occurred to Elle until right then, and it made her heart do a strange lurch. Bouncing a kid on his knee seemed like something that would be at odds with so many parts of him—his career choice, his looks. But then again, she could somehow see it anyway. A baby on his hip, a grin on his face. And as she thought about it, the picture morphed to include Katie, laughing at his side.

Elle's face heated. It was a ridiculous thing to imagine. Beyond ridiculous. She needed to rid herself of the fantasy fast. But when she opened her mouth, her intention to change the subject got derailed by her own question.

"Are you close with your family?" she asked.

Noah's jaw stiffened just the tiniest bit, and his smile disappeared, and Elle expected him to change the subject. Instead, he gave his head a small shake.

"I was," he told her. "A long time ago. But things happen, and you grow apart, right?"

Elle wished she could say she understood, but she truly had no idea. "I don't know. Katie is the only person I've ever had in my life that I'd call close enough to be real family. I loved my mom a lot. But she died when I was young, and I feel like I never really got enough time to appreciate or know her."

His head swung her way, and his eyes held hers for so

long that she thought it was amazing that they didn't crash. She saw curiosity in his gaze. But thankfully, no pity.

"Was that the question you wanted to ask?" he said, at last turning his attention back to the road.

She thought about saying yes. She really did want to know more. And she wanted to tell him more, too. But Katie was still gone, Trey was still winning, and that meant everything else could wait.

"No," she said after another moment. "I was actually just wondering if your job is like this a lot. With the violence and the death."

His thumb bounced again, and Elle was starting to take it as a sign of reflection. As though the light rhythm helped him carefully choose which words to say next.

"No," he admitted after a moment. "I've been doing this job for sixteen years, and most of the violence I've seen is in-the-moment anger. A fistfight here or there. The odd black eye. I once had a target break a beer bottle over his own head, then throw a billiard ball at *my* head. This whole time, though, I've never seen anyone get murdered. Closest I've come is dragging a near-dead woman from the ocean after her ex hit her with a fishing rod." Tap, tap went his thumb. "I guess that's probably not what you wanted to hear."

"No. Or maybe yes." She sighed. "I don't know. I want the truth, but I want to feel less responsible, too."

"I wish I had some better words to offer," he replied.

His statement was followed by a brooding silence, and Elle directed her attention outside. The highway looked never ending, and the sunlight was starting to wane. Time was passing too quickly and too slowly at the same time. Clouds had started to set in, and the sky was showing signs of darkening instead of the clear blue it had been just hours earlier.

Elle pressed her forehead to the window, wondering if Katie could see it, or if Trey had her closed in some dark room. She hoped for the former. So desperately that it hurt to breathe.

Please, please, she begged silently. *Please let her be okay.*

Her mind wandered to that dark promise Trey had made. He'd said he'd keep her alive. But what if it was a lie?

Swallowing against the sick feeling that threatened to overwhelm her, she tried to drag herself back to being solution oriented. Noah was quicker.

"Onward and upward, okay?" he said. "Have a look at the final page in that file."

Elle flipped to a creased-up paper, which showcased what appeared to be a map of some kind. There were no street names and no indication of what city it was, and the only marks aside from the intersections were three red dots in the upper right-hand corner.

"Whoever killed Spider did a pretty good job destroying everything else that looked important, I think," Noah stated. "But he wasn't quite thorough enough. The pictures of Dez, King James and Beldon were jammed inside the printer, which is how they got overlooked. And that map was sticking out of Spider's pocket."

Trying not to imagine Noah touching the dead man, Elle studied the map for another moment. "But what does it mean?"

"That's what I was trying to figure out when—"

He cut himself off, and Elle knew immediately what he'd been about to say. That's what he'd been trying to figure out when he found the copy of Katie's birth certificate. She waited for him to add it. Or at least try to cover it up with something else. But he just let out a little cough, then said something else completely.

"I'd bet my left arm that that's a map of Vancouver," he told her. "I know there aren't any street names, but a lot of my work is done in the city, and a few of the intersections are easily recognizable. I'd know the Georgia Viaduct anywhere."

"And what about the dots?"

"I don't want to jump the gun or anything…but three dots, three names…"

Three dots. Three names.

"You think they met there somehow?" Elle asked.

"I think they *emailed* there," he corrected. "I'm not very techy, and I usually outsource that kind of work, but I'm pretty sure that handwritten sequence of numbers on the back of that map is an IP address. Or something similar, anyway."

As she flipped the page over and glanced at the number in question, she couldn't quite fight off the immediate bubble of hope, and she couldn't keep the excitement out of her voice, either. "We have to go there. It could be where he's holding Katie."

"We will," he assured her.

His tone dampened her optimism. And sure enough, he tapped his thumb, then went on.

"I want to know what we're heading into first," he said. "Whether it's an apartment or a house or a hotel. Whether it's guarded, and if it is, by how many people. I want to know who owns the property, and to be a hundred percent sure it's the right location. Because if it's not, and we run in with guns blazing…we expose ourselves."

Elle's throat tried to tighten, and she forced out a breath. "How long of a delay?"

"We've got a couple hours' drive until we get into Van," he replied. "Then I want to run the details by Spud. He's the fastest in the business. I promise. But before that…"

He shifted awkwardly in his seat, dug a hand into his pocket, then yanked out an unfamiliar cell phone. "We get rid of this."

Elle frowned. "Whose it is?"

"Pretty sure it's the reason our friend in the sedan was coming back. I found it under Spider's desk, and I know for a fact it doesn't belong to him."

"And you took it? What if they can track it?"

"That's exactly what I'm counting on."

"What?"

He held it out. "Take it."

She recoiled involuntarily. "Why?"

"I want you to power it up, then toss it out the window."

"What good will that do if they already know we've come this far?"

"We've been driving in the wrong direction for about twenty minutes. By the time they track it and follow up on the tracking, we'll be long gone."

"Seriously?"

"Yep."

Elle palmed the slightly warm phone, started to reach for the power button, then hesitated. "What if there's valuable information in here? Phone numbers or actual locations or something. Can't we just take out the battery or whatever?"

"Nothing stored on the phone itself," Noah said. "I already checked. It wasn't even password protected. Incoming calls are anonymous, no names in there, and the recent texts are suitably generic. But I pulled the SIM card already, just in case, and I'll give that to Spud, too, to see if he can dredge up anything useful."

"Okay."

She pressed her thumb the rest of the way into the button and rolled down the window while she waited for the screen to light up. As the wind blasted in, she drew back her arm, then gave the phone a hardy toss. It was strangely satisfying to see it hit the ground and shatter. For a second, Elle felt pretty good. But once she'd put the window up again, and Noah had pulled a wide U-turn and turned them back in the other direction, her mind decided to run rampant with renewed worry.

What if it they got to the location on the map, and it turned out to be the wrong place? Then they'd have wasted an awful lot of time waiting for nothing. Or what if it was the right place, but Trey moved on before they got there? What if his personal thug—or worse, multiple personal thugs—caught up to them before they even got there?

Noah's voice cut into her thoughts. "Hey."

She inhaled deeply before answering him. "Hey."

"I know your brain doesn't want to shut off, and you're worried about everything that could go wrong," he said. "I can practically feel the doubts bouncing around in your head. But you'll feel better if you rest."

"I don't think I can."

"You can try."

She shook her head, but then closed her eyes anyway and leaned sideways so that her cheek rested on the cool window. No semblance of rest seemed near. The lump in her throat and the hard knot in her stomach were both far too thick to let her feel comfortable. But after a few seconds of sitting that way in silence, Noah's hand came out to rest on her shoulder. It slid gently back and forth, warm and soothing. And without even realizing it was happening, exhaustion took hold, and Elle drifted off.

Chapter 11

The blare of a horn ruthlessly yanked Elle from sleep. She jerked into wakefulness, startled to find herself leaned back in the passenger seat with a plaid jacket draped over her body. For a second, she was completely disoriented. Then it came rushing back.

Katie. Noah. Trey.

She tried to sit up quickly, but she failed to do anything but flop back as her muscles protested and refused to co-operate. She settled for letting out a groan, then turned her head in search of Noah. Instead, she found an empty seat. Her heart danced a nervous jig. Where was he?

Against the scream of her stiff body, she managed to sit up a little, performing a visual search for the missing man. She didn't immediately find her target, but her quick look around did bring her surroundings into focus.

The car was parked in an open lot, and on her left was a busy city street—presumably the source of the honking. In front of the vehicle was the building that belonged to the lot. It was a tall glass-fronted structure with an ornate archway and enormous, burnished wood doors and gilded vines climbing up the sides. Elle stared at it for a second—both impressed and intimidated at the same time—before she swiveled her head the rest of the way to the right. A row of thick eight-foot hedges blocked most of her view. But just in front of the greenery, she finally spied the big blond bounty hunter. He had his back to the car, but he was only a dozen feet away, and there was no mistaking his solid form.

Elle let her eyes close for another moment as a surprising amount of emotion rolled through her. There was relief, obviously. But there was more than that, too. A warmth deep in her chest that felt an awful lot like affection. And the slightest ease of all the tension that plagued her body, too. And under that, a sense of longing she wasn't a hundred percent sure she was ready to define. She lifted her lids and let herself stare at his wide shoulders for another second. And right away, her fingers tingled with a need to touch him, and she very nearly flung open the door before realizing that Noah wasn't alone. But her shifted position let him see that he was with another man.

Elle's initial reaction was worry. But Noah's body language suggested that he was there by choice, and the discussion didn't seem to be causing any agitation.

Elle leaned forward a little more, squinting and trying to get a better view of Noah's companion. Who was he?

Spud, maybe? she wondered, recalling that he'd said he wanted to meet up with the other man.

She decided to wait for him to finish rather than rushing out to demand answers, and she sighed and leaned back against the reclined seat. Through the top of the front windshield, her eyes found the sky. She could see that the weather had changed drastically while she slept. The deepening clouds suggested that it would only be a matter of time before they opened up for a summer storm. And even if the grayness hadn't already been creeping in, the sun had done a rapid descent into the west, too, further darkening the sky. A little belatedly, Elle realized that she hadn't just napped; she'd slept so soundly that they were likely at their destination.

Guilt stabbed at her. How could she possibly have slept for hours while Katie was still under Trey's control? She made herself sit up again, searching for confirmation that she was right. Instead, she saw Noah again. The man he'd been talking to was gone, and now the bounty hunter was striding toward the car. When he spotted the fact that she was awake, a smile tipped up his mouth, and Elle's heart tripped. How did he manage to make her feel like that? Hopeful and happy and safe, in spite of everything. The itch to touch him was back, and it took a significant amount of willpower not to jump out and throw herself into his arms. Forcing her hands to stay still, she waited until he reached the car before making her move. And even then, she just cracked the door enough to call out a question.

"Is everything okay?" she asked, pleased that her voice sounded far calmer than her pulse felt.

Noah's smile widened, and he swiped a hand over his face like he was trying to contain it. "Peachy on this end. Spud wants an hour or two to narrow it down, but he agrees that the numbers are something to do with an IP address. Made me feel smarter."

Deeper relief washed over Elle. "That's good news. About the IP address, I mean. You were already smart."

A blush immediately followed her statement, but Noah just chuckled and pulled the door open the rest of the way.

"C'mon," he said. "We need to check in."

Elle started to swing her legs out, but got only halfway before she clued in. Forgetting her embarrassment, she lifted her eyes to the opulent building.

"We're staying here?" she blurted.

"Figured we could both do with some momentary luxury."

"But…"

"What?"

"How much does it cost?"

Noah shrugged. "I dunno. Spud booked it on our behalf."

"It's got to be at least three hundred dollars for the most basic room," Elle said.

"So?"

"I already owe you more than thirteen thousand dollars."

"Thirteen thousand, two hundred and fifty dollars," he corrected easily, holding out his hand as he spoke. "And that doesn't include my usual fee."

She stared at his hand for a second, then brought her gaze up to meet his eyes. "I wasn't kidding when I asked you what would happen if I couldn't pay."

"You can work it off. I was thinking of taking on an apprentice anyway."

"Noah…"

Unexpectedly, he dropped down to one knee, putting him just below her eye level. He reached out and took both of her hands, which in turn pushed his body against her inner thigh. Elle's pulse thrummed in response to the contact.

"Listen to me," Noah said, his voice low and urgent. "I told you I'm not here for the money. I want to help you. I want to get Katie back as quickly as possible, and I don't expect anything in return."

Elle refused to let herself be swept away by his tone, his words, and the look in his eyes, too. "We're not talking about pocket change. I could maybe accept the cost of the pizza. And because it's Katie… I'd find a way to get the cash for Spud, and for your neighbor, Roget. But the rest…the money for Dez…" She trailed off, a little choked up, then cleared her throat and nodded toward the hotel. "Especially this. There's no reason why we can't find some crappy hole-in-the-wall to stay at for a few hours."

"It's not a problem."

"How is it not a problem?"

"Because I have money, Elle." He said it almost resentfully—so much so that Elle thought she must've heard him wrong.

She could hear the puzzlement in her own voice as she replied. "What?"

"I have money," he repeated. "Enough that I don't care about recouping the cost. Thirteen grand might not be pocket change, but they're my damn pockets. And if I want to dig around inside of them to pay for stuff, you're going to have to physically fight me to stop me."

Elle stared at his face. His grim expression was utterly at odds with his generous words, as was his tone. She didn't know if she was supposed to laugh or cry. So instead, she did something else. She freed one of her hands. She brought it up to grip Noah's shirt. Then she yanked him forward and pressed her lips to his. Hard.

For a moment, he didn't react. His mouth was still. Completely unmoving. And in the back of Elle's head, she pictured them as a tableau. Two people, locked together in a frozen moment.

Then Noah came to life. His hands slid up her thighs to her hips, where they landed and stayed with a familiarity that belied the newness of their meeting. He pushed forward, bringing his body flush against Elle's in a way that made her light up from the inside out. And for several seconds, his mouth roved over hers, alternating between demanding and yielding, giving and receiving. But just as Elle really started to lose herself in the kiss, Noah pulled back, his eyes slightly glassy, his breathing more than a little ragged.

"Just tell me one thing…" he said. "This isn't because you suddenly realized I'm sugar daddy material, is it?"

His teasing tone was undercut by the rawness of his voice, and Elle vehemently shook her head.

"I don't care about money," she told him. "I had access to plenty of wealth for the worst period of time in my life."

He let out a little groan. "You know that's a statement that begs for follow-up questions."

In response, Elle grabbed him again and brushed her mouth over his, then gave his lower lip a tiny tug between her teeth. "You want to waste time talking?"

"Hell, no." He said it with so much force that Elle laughed.

"Questions and conversation aside…" she replied, "I'd just like to point out that this is what our first kiss should've been like."

One of his eyebrows went up, and his mouth quirked a little, too. "Is that where this came from? You're punishing me for kissing you at the wrong moment?"

Her face heated, but she couldn't quite deny it. "Possibly."

His fingers left her hip, and they came up to trace the line of her blush. "You're not very good at punishment."

She knew he was teasing her, but the moment the words were out of his mouth, Elle's heart immediately dropped. Her mind went to Katie, recalling a recent time the little girl had come home and asked what "grounded" meant.

Elle had laughed about it, saying that Katie would probably rather not know. But in her usual, adamant six-year-old way, the little girl had insisted on having it explained. When Elle had gone over the finer details, Katie had first wondered why she had never been grounded, then came to the same conclusion made by Noah right then. Elle wasn't very good at doling out punishment. The memory didn't seem quite so endearing now. Instead, it brought back the ache in her chest with a vengeance. It seared away the pleasant heat brought on by kissing Noah, and she didn't even realize that she'd dropped her gaze until his hand—still on her cheek—slid down a little and tipped her face back up.

"We *will* find her," he said. "I promise you, Elle."

She let herself sink into his hazel eyes, and—even though she knew it could be perceived as weakness—she let herself believe him, too. Spud would be successful in his tracking of the IP address. She and Noah would confront Trey, and they'd win. And maybe somewhere at the end of that would be some kind of happily-ever-after.

"Kiss me again," she whispered. "Please."

And he did more than that.

He unbuckled her seatbelt and swept her into his arms.

He hip-checked the door shut, and he carried her across the parking lot and into the hotel foyer.

He waved a dismissive hand at the concierge—who acted like she knew Noah but called him by some other name.

He muttered something at a bellboy—who jumped to attention and practically ran toward the elevator—then he carried Elle through the brass door and pushed her to the wall with no regard for their company or the public space.

And finally, he laid her down gently on the oversized bed and helped her temporarily forget that it was actually the worst day of her life.

* * *

Noah knew he should be worried about the time. He should be leaning over to check his phone to see how much longer Spud was going to be with the promised street address. Or maybe he should be asking Elle if she thought they should get dressed so they could be ready to go at a moment's notice. Instead, he was busy living in the moment. Running his hand up and down her back. Relishing in the silky softness of her skin. Loving the way her head rested on his chest and feeling overly pleased that their bodies fit so well together.

The space around them was chaotic. The blankets were askew, the pillows tossed to the floor. The nightstand was a mess, too. The shade over the lamp had been knocked into a laughably crooked state, the phone was off the hook and the hastily procured, rapidly torn-into condom package sat in pieces. But Noah couldn't recall the last time he felt so settled.

He trailed his fingers over Elle's back once more, then smoothed back her hair. "Can I ask you something?"

She let out a little sigh—content sounding rather than annoyed—and spoke into his chest. "Weren't you the one who warned me to be wary of that question?"

He chuckled and kissed her forehead again. "Technically, it's my mother's warning. But yeah. You're right. Forget it."

She wiggled a little, shifting so that she could look at him. "No way. Now you have to ask."

"Mmm-mmm. I don't want to disappoint my mother."

"That's not fair."

He kissed her again—this time along the bridge of her nose. "I never said I played fair."

She pushed all the way up and sent a mocking glare down at him. But if she thought that was going to work, she was dead wrong. Her sudden motion made the sheet drop down, and the newly tantalizing view sent coherent thought from Noah's head. He kissed her a third time. Then a fourth. Then a fifth and sixth, too. Nose. Mouth. Throat. Mouth again. Then neck.

"That's *really* not fair," Elle said, but her voice had a catch in it that gave away her true feelings on the matter.

"I could stop," Noah offered.

"Not. Fair." She leaned down a little more as she said it, and he took advantage of the renewed contact and closed his mouth over hers in yet another kiss, this one lingering.

"You really aren't going to ask me whatever it was, are you?" she breathed as he pulled back.

He chuckled again. "I honestly can't remember what it was."

She wrinkled her nose, then settled against his chest and tightened her arms around him, too. "You're such a liar."

"If you're going to resort to name calling…"

"Maybe I'll just ask *you* a question."

"Go for it. Ask anything you like."

She went silent for a good minute after he said it, and Noah could tell that the light mood was about to change. He considered using the break in conversation to shift to something else. Either another quick, distracting joke, or back to the search for Elle's daughter. Instead, he let her query come, even though he was sure he wouldn't feel comfortable answering.

"You said you had money." Elle's voice was soft.

"Yes."

"But you live well below your means."

"I do."

"And you'd rather walk around in ripped jeans and an old T-shirt than anything else."

"Yes," he said again.

She paused for another second, her fingers twirling a maddeningly sexy circle along his ribcage. "I think you don't want anyone to know that you have money."

"I haven't heard a question in any of that, sweetheart."

Elle snorted. "Don't be impatient, *sweetheart*."

Noah fought another laugh. "Not a fan of endearments in general, or just that one in particular?"

"Oh no you don't. You gave up your chance to ask questions."

"Sorry. My bad. Ask away."

Her tone immediately turned serious again. "The concierge knew you."

"She did," he replied.

"But she didn't call you Mr. Loblaw."

"She didn't."

"You come to this hotel…regularly? Sometimes?"

"Somewhere in between the two," he told her.

"But not for work."

"No. Definitely not for work."

"How many cases do you take on every year?"

Noah didn't bother asking where she was leading, or why she hadn't queried about a shorter timeframe. He could tell that she was working through it all aloud, and for some reason, it mattered to him that she get there on her own rather than him just handfeeding her the truth about his life.

"Not many cases," he said. "I average about three."

"And you charge ten-thousand dollars per case," she mused. "Which is nowhere near enough to afford a car like the one you have out there, and nowhere near enough to afford a place like this. Not even for one night."

"Probably not," he agreed.

"I'd say that means you have family money, except…"

"Except what?"

"Who's Norah?"

"She's my sister. Twin, actually. Forgive my parents for the indulgent names. Noah Liam Loblaw and Norah Lisa Loblaw." He smiled, absently twirling a strand of Elle's hair through his fingers. "She's three minutes older, which makes her the smart, responsible, level-headed one, of course."

"Of course." Elle paused, then added, "It sounds like you and your sister get along?"

"Mostly. She's not crazy about my chosen profession. But then again, hers isn't my favorite, either." After he made the statement, he expected her to press for more information about the subject, but surprisingly, she didn't.

"So I don't think it's quite a family money issue," she said instead. "But I do think you don't want anyone to know about it."

Noah's heart tapped an unwelcome nervous beat. "Thinking about becoming a detective?"

"Does that mean I'm getting close?"

"Guess you'll have to keep up the interrogation to find out."

She tipped up her head. "If you feel like you're being interrogated, I can stop."

He stared down at her, his mouth trying to turn up in a smile. He had a feeling that she would stop, if he asked her to, and he liked that.

"Nah," he said. "I need you to keep going so I can hear your conspiracy theory conclusion."

She wrinkled her nose. "Funny."

"I'm waiting."

"It's more of a bigger question than a conclusion. But here it is… Why keep doing the work if you don't have to? And if you do it just because you want to, then why not use the money you have? Why hide it?"

"That's a little more than 'a' question," he teased.

She gave his chest a gentle tap. "You're avoiding giving me an answer. What happened that made you think you need to pretend to be something you're not?"

Internally, he tensed. He waited for the wall to come up, slam in place, then lock itself shut and prevent him from saying anything else. There was already a denial on his lips. A deflection. A hastily crafted plan to deliver each, then make her forget about it all with a kiss. When he took a breath, though, it was easy. No anxious pain in his chest, no stab of worry or regret. And the words flowed like they hadn't in years. Like an uncorked bottle.

Chapter 12

"Norah and I were almost twelve, when our baby sister, Greta, was born," said Noah, and he was genuinely surprised that saying his little sister's name aloud didn't send a searing pain through his chest. So he said it again. "Greta. She was tiny and perfect. But I mostly kept my opinion about that to myself."

He went on, explaining how he let Norah take the lead in the older sibling role. How his twin sister's natural affinity for bottle feeding and getting the baby to sleep—and even diaper changing—earned her the nickname of Little Mama. He told Elle about his parents, who were both dedicated to their high-powered, time-consuming careers, and who'd been totally surprised by the late pregnancy. How, once their mother finished her maternity leave, the whole family began to rely on Norah to help out. They hired a nanny, but when Norah was home, Greta was in her arms or at her feet. Even as they got a little older, the two were inseparable. Matching blond curls, matching love of purple, and quick giggles. They liked to dance and sing, and Norah had endless patience for Greta.

"I used to say that *they* were more like twins," Noah said, hearing the roughness in his voice, and he cleared his throat before adding, "At least twice a week, I teased Norah that somehow, Greta and I had managed to switch places right before I was born. Like a freak science fiction–style accident. It made her mad every single time."

"It sounds like you were pretty good at playing the little brother role," Ellie replied.

"Oh, I was. For sure. Probably still would be, if Norah would tolerate it." He smiled, but the happy memory was quickly superseded by what came next. "When Greta was three, my parents took a mini vacation, just the two of them. On the fourth day after they were gone, the nanny came down with a stomach bug. So Norah volunteered to take our sister to the park. And she roped me into it, too."

Noah closed his eyes as he recalled the day. Sunny and bright, but crisp. Just before autumn got into full swing, and just a week before he and Norah would turn fourteen. He pictured Greta's little face. Her hazel eyes, the very same shade as his own. The pert nose and the rosy cheeks and her tiny, perfect teeth. In his head, he could still see the fluffy, lilac-colored coat she'd been wearing. She'd had on stretchy dark purple pants, too, and brown boots that were a touch too big. It'd been gorgeous out, and Noah would rather have been anywhere but surrounded by snot-nosed kids and their parents.

He opened his eyes and swallowed, cleared his throat yet again, then said, "I let Greta go up to the top of this big curvy slide. Norah thought it was too high, but I told her there were even littler kids going up and down just fine. We argued about it. Norah said I was making a scene and embarrassing her. I reminded her loudly that she wasn't Greta's mother. The fight lasted maybe a minute. And then Greta didn't come down."

His eyes sank shut again, and he shivered in spite of the heat between his and Elle's bodies. It'd been such an awful, heart-sinking moment. The worst, though, was yet to come.

"She never came down," he stated. "Or maybe she never actually made it up. I don't know. Either way, she was gone."

"Oh, Noah." Elle's voice was infused with understanding, and he latched onto that and made himself continue.

"Norah was hysterical. I was so furious with myself that I could barely move. She had to punch me to get me going. And we searched that playground from end to end. We asked every parent in sight if they'd seen her. Norah kept screaming Greta's name." Noah drew in a breath, then blew it out. "Someone must've called the cops, because suddenly they were all over the place. Asking us questions. Sweeping the place with dogs. A lot of the rest is a blur."

"I'm so sorry," Elle said, and this time, her tone told him she knew already what the outcome had been.

He made himself say it aloud anyway. "They didn't find her. Not alive. The ransom demand came to my parents at home, but they were on their way back from Cabo. The kidnapper..." He trailed off, choking on his words.

Elle's hand slid down to clasp his. "You don't have to tell me."

"I do." He squeezed her fingers. "I want to."

It was strange to realize that it was true—he did want to tell. For the first time since he sat down with a counselor a decade and a half earlier, where he resentfully spewed out his anger and sadness and guilt all at once, he wanted to talk about Greta and the aftermath of losing her. So he did. Glossing over the truly horrific details a little, he told

Elle about the police suggestion not to pay the ransom. He explained how that, plus the delay, meant it was too late to save Greta. He described the wedge it drove between his parents, the way it made him and Norah closer—at least for a time—then how the divorce divided their loyalties. There were the countless days that became months that became years. Noah dedicated far too much of his time to researching kidnappings and the abysmal statistics that bogged him down. There was a short while that he thought of getting into law enforcement. There was the bitterness that stopped him from following through. Moments of weakness that paralyzed him. His father's suicide, and the subsequent lawsuit his mother initiated against a well-known news outlet for the horrific deluge of slander and disgusting and false allegations of abuse. The settlement. The investment. The wealth that followed—a richness that could never aid in the healing. Noah laid it all out, holding back none of the emotional devastation that it wreaked on his life and on the lives of the people he loved.

"I had to do something productive," he said after what felt like the longest speech of his life. "I needed to use my brain but not get bogged down by all the feelings."

"And that's why you made your rules," Elle filled in.

"Yes. Exactly."

Silence filled the room, then, but it wasn't awkward. It was strange, though. After revealing so much, Noah thought he should feel vulnerable. Exposed. Instead, calmness reined. The hurt was still there. It always would be. But for the first time since that horrible moment when he first noticed that Greta hadn't come down the slide, Noah glimpsed a future with hope. And with that came a sense of wonder.

Marveling over it all—and hesitantly embracing it, too—he trailed a finger up Elle's spine. He paused at the back of her neck to gently knead the skin there. When she let out a small murmur of pleasure, warmth surged up and made Noah's chest expand. He dragged his hand to Elle's jawline and tipped her face up. For a long moment, he just stared into her blue eyes, drinking in the matching heat there, and hoping to God she was experiencing the same rush of emotion.

"You make me feel…" He trailed off and gave his head a shake.

When he didn't finish, the tiniest frown creased her perfect forehead. "Feel what?"

"Just…feel," he replied. "Everything."

"Is that a good thing?"

"Pretty much the best damn thing in so long that I can't even describe it."

A smile tipped up her full lips, and it danced in her eyes, too. The warmth running through Noah intensified even more. It consumed him. Had he really just met Elle this morning? Were they together because something bad happened, and had he started his day, not knowing she existed? The idea was baffling.

It was all too much, too soon. Noah knew that in every logical part of his being. Yet there it was anyway. He couldn't fight it. He didn't want to. So he didn't. He let it carry him away instead. He shifted just enough that he could reach her lips with his own. Hungrily, he pressed his mouth to hers. It was more than a physical want. He poured emotion into the kiss. Gave her as much as he could give her, doing his best to share his feelings with his touch. She reciprocated with an equal fervor. Her hands roved over his face, then combed through his hair, then slid across his shoulders and pulled him close. She fit him so perfectly that he wondered how he'd been passing his days without her. When his cell phone buzzed with an incoming call, the intrusion was a most unwelcome one. But as he pulled his mouth away from hers, he realized that while the phone might've broken the moment, there was no way it broke the spell she'd cast on him.

It took Elle several, long moments to catch her breath. Far longer than it took Noah to growl an irritation-tinged greeting to Spud. Longer than it took the big blond man to retrieve his boxers from the edge of bed and slide them on. And longer than it took for him to dive into conversation, too.

She watched him move through the room, picking up his various pieces of discarded clothing as he talked. She liked the sureness of his step and the ease he clearly felt with his body. She more than liked the way his attention kept flicking her way every few seconds—unconsciously, she was sure—and how he smiled as though he couldn't help it. She smiled back, too. Only half of her brain was listening to his murmurs of "uh-huh" and "good." The other half was focused on realizing that she wasn't sure she even wanted to catch her breath. Because she was enjoying the burgeoning sense of rightness building inside her. A lot.

Elle pulled the sheet up to her and studied Noah a little more. He'd finished buttoning his jeans, and he'd moved to the kitchenette, where he was pulling open a drawer. As he dragged out a pen and paper, he cast yet another smile in Elle's direction. What was it about the curve of his lips that made her warm so thoroughly? She knew it wasn't just the residual effects of the best kiss of her life, or even the afterglow of sleeping with him. It also wasn't the perfection of his body, though the ripple of his forearm as he scratched something onto the paper was captivating all on its own. And it wasn't even his eagerness to help or the promise that he would help her get Katie back. No. The breathlessness—and the fact that it was so pleasant—had a different source. An emotional one. For whatever reason, this almost stranger had captured a small piece of Elle's heart. And that piece pulsed for him. Ached for him. It made her see a fast, hard trajectory that led right into deep, meaningful territory. Because if she felt this thread between them now, what would it be like in a day? Or in a week?

The thought should scare you, a voice in her head cautioned.

Except it didn't. It just made her tingle with anticipation of what was to come. She was almost giddy with it. Or maybe more than almost.

What about Katie? the voice added.

But just to add to the strangeness of it all, the question didn't bring any unease to Elle's mind. She still desperately wanted to retrieve her—more than she wanted anything, of course. Now, though, there was something extra to go along with that need. She wanted to introduce her to Noah. That on its own should've been startling. It should've made her stop and take a step back to assess just how quickly things were moving. It was one thing to let herself become lost in a moment. Even the sex—the incredible, toe-curling, heart-pounding, passion-filled sex—could be excused. It was a whole other thing to be thinking about her favorite little person sharing an ice cream sundae with a man like Noah. But she couldn't shake the feeling.

She stared at him as he clicked the pen, then he said something else to Spud, and she wondered if she was going crazy. And when he lifted his gaze and gave her a nod, her heart definitely jumped in a way that wasn't quite sane. Did he feel the same? She thought he did. She hoped he did. He'd literally said he felt everything, hadn't he? In a good way. But as his conversation finally seemed to be winding down, Elle's mood dampened. Because she realized that as much as he'd shared with her, she hadn't quite reciprocated. And if Noah didn't know everything, then it didn't matter much how he felt now. It only mattered how he felt after. The thought made Elle's hands sweat and her heart drop. And then a worse idea occurred to her.

Maybe this is common for him. Maybe sex is just sex to him.

She drew in a small breath. He didn't seem like the one-night stand type, and Elle didn't really believe that he just went around spilling his family history with people, either. But then again, he also hadn't seemed like the kind of man who had so much money that he didn't know what to do with it. There was a reason people said looks could be deceiving. And this right here was it. She exhaled and tried to erect a bit of a wall between herself and her emotions. She needed to be prepared for something other than a happily-ever-after with a man she barely knew. But the moment he tapped the phone off and stepped toward her with the notepad in his hand, she felt the wall waver. And it was clear that Noah could read the change on her face, too. His own expression went from pleased to concerned.

"What is it?" he asked right away.

"It's—" She cut herself off and shook her head. If she told him now, it wouldn't make a difference to what had already happened. But it might change their current course. And it wasn't exactly a five-minute conversation, either. She met his eyes. "I'm just worried about Katie. What did Spud say?"

Noah's eyebrows pressed sharply together, and his mouth opened, then closed, then opened again. Elle braced for an argument or an insistent question. He didn't formulate either one. He just ran his free hand over his head, then held out the notepad again.

"Good news," was all he said, his tone neutral. "This is the address attached to those numbers we gave to Spud. He did a little research for us, too. Even drove by to check it out."

Hope rushed in, and Elle's mind immediately shifted gears. "What did he find out?"

"It's an apartment building. The units in the building were all rentals up until last year, when the landlord served them a mass eviction notice. The place has been completely vacant for a month now, and it's slotted for demolition next week. Take a guess at which company bought the property and kicked everyone out."

She didn't even have to think about it. "Iris International."

"Bang on," he replied.

"We're going, right? I mean…we have to." Elle stood quickly, her hope morphing into determination and eagerness to get moving. "Were there a lot of guards? Could he tell if Trey himself was there? And did he see a way we could get in stealthily, or…" She trailed off as she realized Noah was watching her with a strained look of amusement. "What?"

"I'm not sure how you define stealth," he said, his eyes moving up and down her body. "But in my opinion, it usually requires clothes."

Elle's gaze dropped down, and she couldn't stop a blush. She was still utterly naked. Which might not have been so bad, considering that Noah had just spent at least an hour thoroughly exploring that nakedness. But the fact that she'd taken a few steps toward the door without even thinking about it was downright embarrassing.

"Don't get me wrong," Noah added teasingly. "It's not that I mind."

She did her best to shoot him a dirty look, failed miserably, then sighed and yanked the sheet off the bed in a belated attempt to maintain some dignity. "Could you just shut up and help me find my bra?"

His mouth widened into a grin, and instead of immediately assisting in the search for her strewn-about clothes, he stepped forward and swept her in for a firm but quick kiss. And when he pulled back, his expression was serious once more.

"You know that if there's something you want to talk to me about…something you're worried about…you can say whatever you want to me," he told her.

She stared up at him, wishing she believed it as sincerely as he'd said it. Questions formed in her head. *What does this mean to you? What do I mean to you?* But as quick as they came, Elle pushed them away. No matter what he said, they weren't things one ought to be wondering after knowing someone for this short a time. And if he answered in a way that she didn't like…she wasn't sure she'd handle it well.

She nodded, but she didn't offer anything up. Instead, she freed herself from his arms and moved through the room, grabbing her clothes from the spots where they'd been dropped or tossed. But after just a moment or two of silence, Noah spoke up again.

"Elle?" he prodded. "Did you hear what I just said?"

"I did. And I'll find a way to pay you back," she promised as she wriggled into her underwear.

"What?"

"All thirteen thousand, two hundred and fifty dollars."

He smiled like he thought she was kidding. "It's actually thirteen thousand, five hundred and seventy-eight dollars now. Factoring in this overpriced room and all."

"That much, then." She spoke over her shoulder as she

quickly fastened her bra. "It might take years to get the amount together, but I'll do it."

His forehead creased as he seemed to clue in that she was being serious. "That's not exactly what I meant when I said you could talk to me."

"I don't want there to be anything hanging between us."

"There isn't," he said.

She slid into her shorts, then popped her borrowed T-shirt over her head and met his eyes. "For now."

"What are you saying, Elle?"

"Just that money like that creates a string."

"A string?" Noah repeated, his frown deepening so much that it looked almost painful.

She fought to keep her voice even. "Nothing. I owe you. A lot more than money, really. And if something were to happen... I don't want you to feel any obligation."

"I'm not following your logic. If I were expecting you to pay me back, wouldn't that make *you* obligated rather than me?"

"No. Well, yes. Technically. But I don't mean my financial obligation. I mean if you felt like I owed you something, you wouldn't be able to walk away."

He stood still, his hazel eyes sharp and fixed on her face. "I'm not going to ask why you think I'd walk away. But I am going to ask if you're trying to deflect me from whatever's really bothering you."

A denial formed automatically. But it didn't quite make it out.

"Are we ready to go?" she asked instead, reaching for her shoes.

Noah's arm shot out, stopping her just as her fingertips brushed the straps. "Elle."

She swallowed and forced herself to look right at him. "Yes?"

"I have no intention of taking off the second we get your kid back."

"Things can change really quickly, Noah."

"You think I don't know that?"

Her mind went to his sister's abduction, and her heart squeezed. "I know that you know."

He let go of her elbow. "I'm also well aware of how crazy it would sound if I offered some kind of commitment speech after less than a day together, so I won't do it. All I'm asking is that you don't write me off so easily. Please."

Elle started to nod. But before she could bob her head more than once, or even get a word out, a bang on the door—too hard to belong to hotel staff—stilled both her movements and her voice.

Chapter 13

Automatically, Noah's brain shifted into action mode. He didn't waste time wondering how Trey's men had discovered their location. He knew better than most what skilled tracking could lead to. So he simply stowed the emotions he'd been struggling to express, readied his weapon and positioned himself between Elle and the potential intruder, then listened. The ominous smash against the reinforced metal door didn't ring out a second time. Noah counted to ten. Then fifteen. After thirty seconds of continued silence, he hazarded the smallest movement—just turning his head to whisper over his shoulder.

"I'm going to check the door," he said.

"What for?" Elle whispered back. "You know already it's not room service. We need to find a way out."

He wished he didn't have to tell her the truth, but he took a breath and did it anyway, his voice still low. "There is no other way out. Not unless we want to try to break through the industrial-strength window and jump down ten stories. And since that's probably not a very viable option, we need to see what we're up against."

"And then what?" she replied. "We try to fight off a half-dozen skilled gunmen who have no qualms killing for money?"

He didn't answer her question directly. If he had, he would've had to remind her that Trey didn't want her dead; he wanted her brought in. Because the reminder would've prodded her to point out that the morally bankrupt businessman wouldn't have any issue ending Noah's own life. He settled for a noncommittal response instead.

"If we get separated in the scuffle, I want you to book it out of here as fast as you can," he told her.

Her eyes widened. "You think I'm just going to leave you?"

He ignored the protest. "Make your way to the back of the hotel, then use the alleys to head east for two blocks. Hang a left at the lights there, go one more block, then turn left again. On the right side of the road, three doors up, you'll find a little shop called Rosie's Relics. There'll probably be a closed sign on the door. Ignore it. Knock twice, tell Rosie I sent you, and she'll help you get to the apartment building." He pressed the notepad into her hand. "This is the address."

"Noah, I can't—"

"If it's a choice between staying safe and being captured, then you'll have to."

He bent his head, dusted her lips with a kiss, then moved smoothly to the door before she could argue anymore. From his new position, he leaned forward and peered through the peephole. He had a surprisingly clear view. But what he saw made him frown. Instead of the expected armed thug, Noah spied a slick-looking businessman. He stood with his back against the wall on the opposite side of the hall, and his whole appearance was just upper-class enough that he fit in with the hotel's usual standard of clientele. From the carefully shorn hair to the expensive suit and shoes to the manicured hands flicking over the sleek cell phone in his hands, he gave off a wealth-imbued vibe. He also seemed completely disinterested in anything but the phone under his tapping thumbs.

Mistaken identity? Noah wondered. Wrong room?

His nerves wouldn't settle, though, and his instincts told him to keep watching. A heartbeat later, he was glad he listened to his gut. A tiny woman—not over five feet tall, and definitely under a hundred pounds—came backward through the door next to the spot where the man stood. She pulled a tray of cleaning supplies along after her, and she jumped back, visibly startled by the businessman's presence. Even though Noah couldn't hear their conversation, he got the gist of it.

Mr. Suit-and-Tie was laying on the charm. Full, veneered teeth on display. A hand on the small woman's elbow. At first, the housekeeper smiled back. She even looked like she was laughing. Then the well-dressed man gestured to the door that Noah stood behind, and the woman's smile faltered. She shook her head. The charmer tried again. His teeth flashed even wider, turning more predatory than friendly. The petite woman took a small, seemingly unconscious step back. She shook her head a second time, and then her eyes dipped to the spot where the man's hand still held her arm. She gave a little tug. When it didn't dislodge Mr. Suit-and-Tie's grip, her face came up, and it was easy to see the genuine fear there.

Noah couldn't stop his protective instincts from jumping to life. Cursing under his breath but still keeping his eye on the peephole, he reached for the door. He wasn't quite quick enough. Before his fingers could actually close on the metal knob, the man in the hall executed a swift blow to the woman's head. Her body immediately slumped, and her attacker fixed his gaze on the door.

For an eerie moment, Noah felt like the other man was looking right at him. Mr. Suit-and-Tie dropped his attention to the fallen woman. He bent to one knee and began what looked like a pat-down.

What the hell is he doing?

Almost too late, Noah realized what the other man must be in search of—the master key cards.

He pulled back and spun to face Elle, and even though she couldn't have any idea what Noah had just witnessed, her face was ashen and consumed with worry.

"What?" she whispered. "What is it?"

He shook his head, then stepped toward her. "No time to explain. I just need you to trust me. Closet or bathroom?"

Her eyes flicked to the still-closed door. "Closet, I guess?"

Moving fast, he grabbed her hand and tugged her to the space in question. He opened the door as quickly as he dared, put his finger to his lips, then pushed her gently inside. The moment the latch clicked—closing Elle in for at least a few moments of added safety—Noah sprinted back to the main door. He flattened his body on the wall beside the hinges, settled his gaze on the door handle, and readied his weapon once more. There was no way to know what the intruder was thinking—whether the man believed the room was empty and was simply there to gather intel, or if he was coming in hot. It didn't matter. Noah had no intention of asking. A plan had already formed in his mind. It was quick, and lacked any kind of style, but he thought it would work anyway. It also took a page out of the other man's book, and he liked the karma.

Just three more seconds ticked by before the telltale beep of the electronic lock announced that Mr. Suit-and-Tie had met with success.

Noah tensed in preparation as the hinges let out a low rattle of protest. He sucked in a deep breath, then held it as the door inched open. He kept utterly still, watching as the other man made his way in with painful slowness. First came the tip of one of his designer shoes. Then the flash of his crisp dress pants. Next were his fingers, gripping the edge of the door. Finally, Mr. Suit-and-Tie stepped completely into view. For another second, he continued to hold the door open, his eyes scanning the open room, obviously unaware that danger lurked behind him rather than in front of him.

Noah's lungs burned from the effort of not making a sound. He continued to hold the oxygen in anyway, waiting for the perfect moment. At last the other man released the door, and it whooshed shut. The intruder was fully exposed. And Noah was ready.

Almost dizzy from the pent-up air, he pushed away from the wall, gun over his head. With a hard swipe, he smashed the weapon into the other man's skull and expelled the long-overdue breath at the same time. As the impact reverberated up his arm, Noah saw stars. For a second, he thought the plan had somehow backfired. That he'd been the one to take the blow rather than the one to give it. But just a few heartbeats later, the stars and accompanying dizziness retreated, and he saw the other man lying at his feet, jaw slack, blood seeping from a wound on the top of his head and his chest moving in slow, unconscious breaths.

"You get what you give," he muttered.

He spun away from the violence, strode to the closet and flung open the doors. Immediately, Elle collapsed into his arms. She was shaking and crying a little, too. When she pulled back to look up at him, though, Noah knew it wasn't because she was scared for herself. She was worried about *him*. Her next words confirmed it.

"Are you okay?" she asked.

He almost wanted to laugh. "Not a scratch."

Her body sagged against his again, and this time, her arms slid up to his shoulders. She stood on her tiptoes to kiss him, then shook her head.

"Can you please try a little harder not to risk your life at every turn?" she said.

Now he *did* let out a small laugh. "All right. I'll try. So long as I'm able to keep you safe at the same time." He reached up and touched her cheek with the back of his hand. "We should go. Before any of that guy's friends decide to show up."

Elle's eyes sought the fallen man, and as she sank back down on her heels, her face went a little paler. Was it just the bloody display, or was it something more? Noah studied her for a second, trying to place the sudden sense of off-ness that rolled over him.

"You okay?" he asked after a moment.

Her gaze jerked back to him, and she exhaled. "Yes," she said quickly. "Let's hurry."

Trying to brush off the need to ask another overly unspecific question about the change in Elle's expression, Noah moved to the door and stole another look through the peephole. The hallway was clear. Even the housekeeper's body was nowhere that he could see. Maybe that wasn't necessarily a good thing, but he didn't have time to stop and dwell on it, so he grabbed the door handle and gave it a tug. But as he stepped through the frame, then held it open for Elle, he caught her staring at the fallen man again. Her visage was even paler—almost sickly. Under that, Noah caught a hint of something he could identify. Recognition. Not the good kind, either.

"I take it you know him," he stated.

"Yes," Elle replied, her voice tight.

Noah frowned at the lack of explanation. "That's it?"

"Yes," she repeated, stepping out into the hall.

"You sure?" Noah prodded. "You don't want to at least give me a name?"

Her lips pressed together for a second, then dropped open. Before she could speak again, a male voice cut through the air, answering on her behalf.

"His name is Detective Lance Townsend," said the unseen man. "And his superiors are going to be none too pleased that you've assaulted him."

A half dozen questions swirled up—not the least of which was why a detective would need to break into a hotel room, and why he would need to knock a woman unconscious—but Noah stowed them all as the speaker revealed himself by stepping out into the hall, arms raised in a surrendering gesture that Noah didn't buy for a second. Instinctively, he started to step in between Elle and the suited, fiftyish man. Except he didn't get a chance to finish the protective maneuver. Elle moved faster. She stuck an arm out to stop him from going by. And if that didn't surprise him enough, her words sure as hell did the trick.

"Your partner is alive, Detective Stanley," she said. "He's just going to wake up with a bad headache."

Noah's head swiveled in her direction, and he saw nothing but guilt and sadness written across her beautiful face.

Elle let herself look at Noah for only a solitary moment before sliding her attention back to the man standing in front of them. It'd been more than half a decade since she'd seen him, but he hadn't changed at all. Same prematurely silver-gray hair, same crinkle around his eyes. He was an undeniably handsome man who would probably continue to age well for most—if not all—of his life. Yet Elle knew better than most that the adjective that suited him most was "ruthless." There was nothing he wouldn't do to follow a case. Even if that case was motivated by something other than true justice. And his smile made her want to shiver. His eyes had always contained a trace of something sinister and out of control. Something that made Elle believe he was just this side of coming unhinged.

"Ms.….what is it now? O'Malley?" he asked.

She didn't dare look at Noah. She could feel the tension and curiosity rolling off him already. And if she was being honest, it made her want to cry. Then again, honesty hadn't been her strong suit since meeting Noah.

She steeled her nerves and addressed the detective instead. "It's always been O'Malley. You know that."

"I suppose I do," the older man replied, his smile becoming a Cheshire cat grin. "Though in professional circles, we might call that a technicality."

"You can call it whatever you want. That doesn't change what it is, Detective Stanley."

"Agreed. And speaking of the inevitable…" His slightly wild, gray eyes flicked to Noah, then back to Elle. "I guess it's up to the two of you to decide how this plays out. I'm going to go out on a limb and say that you haven't told him the truth, the whole truth and nothing but the truth, so help you God?"

Once again, Elle refused to turn and look at Noah. "He doesn't know anything except that Trey is Katie's father."

Noah spoke up then, his voice edged with concern and confusion. "What the hell's going on, Elle?"

She gave the barest head shake, willing him to keep

quiet as she ignored him in favor of speaking to Detective Stanley again.

"I want to talk to him," she said softly.

Uncharacteristic surprise registered on Detective Stanley's face. "You want to talk to Trey?"

Elle nodded. "That's my condition for coming with you without a fight."

The older man cast a speculative look her way. "I can try. But I don't know if he'll—"

"He will."

"All right. Give me a sec."

Seemingly unconcerned about leaving himself exposed, Detective Stanley slid a hand into his pocket to retrieve his phone, then turned away as he placed the call. Elle knew Noah would try to take advantage of the perceived opportunity, so she adjusted herself so that her body shielded the detective from an attack.

"What are you doing?" Noah asked under his breath.

"If he had any doubt about his own safety, he wouldn't be looking in the other direction," she told him. "There's nothing Detective Stanley values more than his own life. He's got a fail-safe plan of some kind. Trust me." She winced as the last two words escaped her lips. Right then, he had little reason to take her word for anything. A fact which Noah was clearly aware of as well.

"I want to trust you," he said. "I want to keep trusting you. But you need to give me something here, Elle. A little bit of a hint as to what all of this means."

She made herself meet his eyes. "The less you know, the safer you are."

"That's a copout."

"I know."

"I don't even give a damn about my safety at the moment," he said.

"Which is exactly why I have to do this."

"You can sacrifice yourself, but you're demanding that I don't do the same?"

"If I'm alive…there's still a chance that I can save Katie. And that's all that matters."

"I've been doing nothing but trying to save her," he pointed out.

"And if you keep trying…" She inhaled to steady herself to say what she thought would keep him from launching an attack.

"If I keep trying, then what?"

"I won't forgive you for it. Ever."

He blinked at her, and the undisguised hurt on his face cut her like a knife. Automatically, she started to reach for him. She managed to stop herself just as the detective turned back their way, and she was glad she'd found the tiniest bit of self-restraint in time. The last thing she needed was for the older man to find yet another way to exploit her.

"Here," said Stanley, holding out the phone. "Guess you're getting your wish."

With sweatier palms than she would've liked to admit to, Elle reached out and took the device from his hands. Both her fingers and her lips trembled as she brought the phone to her ear. She willed herself to sound stronger than she felt.

"Hello?" she greeted.

"Hello yourself," said Trey.

Elle couldn't stop her eyes from sinking shut. Nausea swept in, too. So did a hundred bad memories. She fought through it all.

"I'm not going to bother asking how you are," she replied.

His chuckle wrapped around her like a medieval hair shirt. "I don't suppose you would. But I'll tell you all the same. Business is good. Thriving, even. Only dampened by the fact that I've been bleeding money to find you and Kaitlyn."

"Katie," she corrected without thinking.

"Katie?" echoed Trey.

Elle wished she could rewind and unsay it, but she made herself answer anyway. "It's what she prefers."

There was the briefest pause. "Funny. She didn't mention that to me."

His words were a slap. Katie hadn't just been taken by Trey's men; she was with Trey himself. The reality of that hit her hard enough to make her sway on her feet.

God help me.

She refused to let a hint of her fear seep into her voice. "I could make a sarcastic observation about being so very surprised that she didn't share her nickname with the stranger who kidnapped her, but it'd be a waste of time for both of us. So I'll just tell you that I'll come with Detective Stanley. But first… I want two things."

"You want things…" The statement was speculative rather than amused.

"That's right."

"I'm listening."

She opened her eyes, but she kept them fixed on a spot on the wall because she didn't trust herself to stay in control if she so much as glanced at Noah. "I want to talk to Katie. So I can hear her voice, and so she can hear mine."

Trey barely missed a beat. "And the second want?"

Elle straightened her shoulders. "You need to let the man who's been helping me go."

"Pretty tall order."

"Maybe."

She waited. She knew there was a strong possibility he'd simply say no. The man was unpredictable, and he had every reason to want to punish her. But instead of a flat-out denial, he posed a question.

"Do you care about him, Elle?" he asked. "On a personal level?"

"He thinks so, and that matters more," she replied.

"Hmm."

Her eyes closed again, and she adopted a tired tone—one that wasn't too far off from the exhaustion she actually felt. "What, Trey?"

"He *thinks* you care." The words were a strange blend of flat and curious.

"That's right."

"Does he 'think' it so much that he told you who he really is?"

"He does." Elle said it easily because it was true.

"Prove it," Trey ordered.

"I know why he can afford this hotel." She dropped her voice low and prayed that Noah wouldn't hear. "And I know about his sister."

"Does that mean he knows who you really are?"

"No." Now her voice was small. "Like I told Detective Stanley, all he knows is that you're Katie's father. I want your word that he won't be hurt. And not the kind of so-called word you give your usual clientele. I want the kind of word you'd give if your life depended on it."

"That sounds a little like a threat, Elle," Trey replied.

"Not a threat. A plea."

This time, the pause had a different feel. Weighted. As though Elle could feel Trey's mental deliberation through the line. And when he spoke, his voice held the first hint of sincerity it had since the start of the conversation. It also lent her the first hint of real hope that he'd comply with her requests.

"Mr. Loblaw would have to agree not to come after you, and I'd have to believe he meant it," he said.

Elle's throat tried to close. "I know."

"There are things I'd have to tell him. Probably not in a nice way."

"I know," she repeated.

"Put Stanley back on. I'll tell him what's what, and the second you're in the back of his car, I'll put the kid on the phone."

She just barely bit back a heartfelt declaration of gratitude, pressed her lips together, then turned to the detective and held out the phone. And the next sequence of events happened almost too quickly to be real.

Detective Stanley had a quick, monosyllabic conversation with Trey, then tapped the phone off and yanked a pair of cuffs from his belt. He slapped them onto Elle's wrists. And before she could even wince over the tightness, he looked her in the eye and called out a single word.

"Clear!"

His holler prompted two more men to appear in the hallway. One stepped out from around the corner at the end of the corridor, while the other seemed to unfold himself from a doorway just five rooms up. Both were armed. Both were in armored vests. And both were aiming their weapons right at Noah. And he looked from them to her, every shade of disappointment playing over his features. But that wasn't what made Elle have to fight to hold back her tears. What prompted the increased sting in her eyes, throat and chest was the third man. The one who appeared behind Noah. The one who quickly—with the efficiency of a seasoned pro—jabbed a needle into his neck and depressed the plunger faster than a blink.

Chapter 14

Elle did her best to throw a mental brick wall into place. One that would block out Noah's expression as the needle hit. And the way he fell down without even a chance to fight, too. But it was almost impossible to keep it in place. The guilt was too strong. And even when Detective Stanley grabbed her shoulder, ordered her to move "quick and quiet," then gave her a shove to help her along the way— not because he had to, but probably because he wanted to—the ache in her heart didn't ease in the slightest.

Behind her, she could hear the other two men grabbing Noah. She also heard them complain about it. How heavy he was, and how inconvenient the task was, and how one had hurt his back already, raking the leaves from his lawn and how this was going to make it that much worse. She desperately wanted to rip herself away from the detective so she could run back, shove the men out of the way, and tell Noah she was sorry.

What good would that do? asked a snide voice in her head. *You already sold him out. And it's not like he could even hear you if you did apologize. You made sure of that.*

It was true. And telling herself that she'd only done it to save Noah's life did nothing to help. The farther away they got from him, the more Elle's breath burned in her lungs. But slowly. Like molten lava, making its way through her mouth when they hit the stairs. Down her throat when they pushed through a side exit on the first-floor landing. Then into her chest where it settled in a searing pool as they made their way through a pitch-black alley toward an unmarked police car.

She couldn't stop herself from second-guessing her choice, either. What guarantee did she have that Trey would keep up his end of the bargain? Yes, he wanted her. He was undoubtedly preparing to make her suffer in the worst way. Hadn't he promised that he would? She was plagued by the thought that maybe she'd done nothing but hand Trey everything he wanted.

When Detective Stanley placed his hand on her head and started to guide her into the back of his vehicle, Elle remembered the other half of her requests was still forthcoming. And it helped her strengthen her wall just a little. She pushed back against the detective's hand and straightened up.

"Katie," she said firmly.

"I'll make the call after you're in," the older man replied. "Just like Trey said."

"No."

"You really want to pick a fight with me?"

"It's not a fight unless you refuse to honor Trey's end of the bargain. The bottom line is, I'm not getting in until I've spoken to her," Elle told him. "And we both know that if I cause a scene out here or if you hurt me without your boss's permission—"

"He's not my damn boss."

She met the protest with a wordless stare. She knew his and Trey's history well enough to be sure that their bond wasn't one of friendship, or even one of mutual respect. The two men had been childhood friends. United in their destructive behavior. Somewhere along the line, though, Detective Stanley—back when he'd still been just plain, old Jimmy—had started to take a turn for the better, if it could be called that. At the same time, Trey had gone the other way. But years later, Jimmy had come back. Needing something. Begging. That's what Trey had called it. Elle didn't know the specifics, and she didn't want to. But she was certain it was nothing legal. And she was even more certain that whatever it was that Detective James Stanley owed to Trey, calling it a boss/employee relationship was probably the nicest way to put it.

After a few more moments, the detective let out a string of muttered curses, then violently yanked his cell phone from his pocket once again.

Elle didn't let herself heave out a relieved breath. The fact that she was about to hear Katie's voice again was the only sliver of light in the current situation. She could barely believe it'd been only hours since she'd last seen her. It felt like a million years. And when Detective Stanley pressed the phone to Elle's ear, and the familiar voice carried through the line, it took all she was worth to hold back her tears.

"Momma? Is it you?"

Elle closed her eyes. "Hi, baby. It's me. Are you doing okay?"

"I'm scared," Katie admitted, sounding unashamed of the announcement. "But I'm okay. I had some popcorn for dinner, and I want to come home." She paused. "Momma?"

"Yes, my little love?"

"Can I say something that's not very nice?"

"Sure, baby. Go ahead."

Katie dropped her voice to a whisper. "There are some men here…and I think they might be bad guys."

Elle bit back a ragged breath. Her mothering instincts told her to deny it. But her brain told her that it would be a mistake to let Katie think that the men in question could be trusted.

"Are you being brave?" she asked instead.

"Yes," Katie replied proudly.

"I need you to keep doing that, okay?"

"Okay."

"I'm going to be there soon." The unwanted tears couldn't be held in anymore and her next three words came out sounding choked. "I love you."

"I love you, too, Momma," Katie said. "But can you hurry up? Please?"

Before Elle could clear her throat and reply, Detective Stanley ripped the phone away again. He tapped it off without a word, and it was almost enough to send her heart over the edge.

Katie's alive, she told herself. *That's all that matters right this second.*

Not that she'd let herself truly consider a situation where anything else might be true. But that didn't stop the relief from making her limp. And when the detective put his hand on her head this time, Elle didn't protest. She let him push her none-too-gently into the back seat, where she leaned her head on the window's cool glass and counted the minutes in silence.

The first thing Noah became aware of was the throbbing in his head. His pulse pounded hard against his skull, and his brain felt…swollen. Too big for the meager size of the bone that surrounded it. It made him want to keep his eyes closed. To sink back into whatever oblivion he'd just been dragged out of. But the next bit of awareness was a man's voice. He couldn't understand the words, but the tone was insistent, impatient, and undoubtedly trying to pull him from his stupor. And if nothing else, that stopped Noah from giving in to the urge to let his mind drown all over again. Not because he cared that some stranger probably wanted him awake, but because the words brought in a rush of recent memories.

Elle.

One moment, Noah had been standing in the hall, trying like hell to make sense of what was happening. Was Elle a criminal? Was she a cop? Why, in God's name, was she negotiating with the man who'd kidnapped her daughter? For all his experience, he couldn't come up with an answer. Before he could even really try, the sharp prick on his neck had drawn his attention away from the scene in front of him. Too late, he'd realized what the pain meant. He'd only had time to lift his hand to cover the sting of the needle before the world swam.

And now…

The world was swimming again. Or maybe he was swimming. Pulling himself up from under the groggy current, pushing past the pressure in his head and straining to understand what was being said. He tried his hardest to open his eyes, but all he saw was a blur of darkness. So he dropped his lids again, trying to focus on his next best sense—his hearing. And at last he caught something.

"Don't know what the hell's taking so long," said the same voice that Noah hadn't been able to understand before. "The shot wasn't that potent."

Another man replied, issuing a curt expecting-obedience order. "Give him a shot of the other stuff."

Footsteps shuffled across the room, then back, pausing somewhere near Noah. Fingers closed on his forearm, and an instinct to fight off the intrusion reared up. Except his limbs were leaden.

Why the hell can't I move?

His pulse smacked hard against his veins, and he willed himself to fight. And he must've succeeded at least a little, because the hand on his arm tightened, and the first voice grumbled for him to hold still.

"You can relax, Mr. Loblaw," added the second voice. "If I wanted you dead, you'd be dead. This is just a shot of ADHD medication to counteract the propofol."

Propofol.

Noah was acquainted with the quick-acting anesthetic and its knockout effects. Two years earlier, he'd sustained a major break in his arm while chasing down a mark. A bit of reconstructive surgery had required that the doctors put him under, and propofol was their drug choice. There hadn't been any adverse reactions then, and with the exception of the loss of an unknown amount of time, there likely wouldn't be any now. That didn't mean he liked it. Or accepted that these men could just do whatever they felt like. He tried again to move and got the same result. He was immobile.

"Stop shaking your damn arms," snapped the first voice.

Noah was momentarily triumphant, and thankful that however sluggish his brain might be, his body was still doing its damnedest to avoid getting dosed with an unfamiliar substance. Except the battle didn't last long. Another set of hands abruptly clamped down on his arm, and the grip was far rougher than the first.

"Do it now, Lee," commanded the other voice.

With that came the jab of a needle. Then several seconds of silence before the second man spoke again.

"How long until he's lucid?" he asked.

"Not long," replied the first man. "He was already coming to anyway. Give him ten minutes."

"Ten minutes I'd far rather spend doing something else."

"Just the messenger, boss."

There was a barely audible sigh, presumably from the second man. "You can wait outside, Jack. I'll make sure you know if I need you."

Feet obediently hit the floor, and a door closed.

Noah gritted his teeth and peeled his eyes open once more. The dimness made him want to panic, but after a few forceful pounds of his heart, he clued in. He wasn't going blind. The world wasn't a blur. The issue was simply that something covered his eyes. The realization was enough to ground him again.

Ten minutes, he said to himself. *That's how long you have to figure out anything that might help you.*

Careful to keep his breathing even and slow, he began a physical inventory. The first thing he noted was the fact that he'd been strapped to a chair. His wrists were bound to the chair's arm, and his ankles were bound to its legs. Which at least explained the earlier perception that he couldn't move. He didn't let himself feel any relief; he just moved on, trying to catalog the rest of what he could figure out.

The air was a little stale, and it was also warm, confirming the fact that he was inside, possibly in a smallish space. Aside from that, it was also impossible to discern anything about his surroundings. There was the odd shuffle of someone else in the room. A small click that might've been fingers hitting a phone screen. A little cough. And a bit of concentration brought in the vague sound of something that may or may not have been traffic in the distance.

Great, Noah said to himself. *For all I know, I'm trapped in a giant fish tank.* Except as sarcastic and unhelpful as the thought was, it was immediately followed by another, more hopeful one. *Even if it really is a fish tank…it's a fish tank with a door. And that means potential for escape.*

He adjusted his focus to his own body, stealthily searching for a weakness in his bonds. There was the tiniest bit of wiggle room between his wrists and the rope that held them. Had it been caused by his attempt to fight off the needle? Or was it what had let him fight in the first place? He wanted to find out, but he didn't dare try to loosen them. Without knowing where his captor was, he couldn't take the chance. What he needed was a distraction. Except he had no clue how to create an effective one while sightless, sore and tied down. Frustration set in, and the slight fuzziness that hung on to his brain didn't help at all. But then an idea popped to mind. One that could possibly turn all of the disadvantages into the perfect ruse. Or maybe not perfect—but workable.

It'll have to do.

First, Noah let his fingers go extra limp. Then he counted to five and spread them out, assessing the width of the arm of the chair. He had plenty of room to get a good grasp on the wood. Satisfied with that fact, he moved on, trying to get a better feel for the chair itself. It was hard to truly measure its stability without moving around, but if he had to guess, Noah would say it was right in between rickety and stable. He hoped it leaned toward the latter, but whatever the case, he was sure it could be tipped. He exhaled a light breath and started to count again, this time down from thirty. Finally, as he reached the number five in his head—and with his nerves on high alert—he prepared to send himself and the chair to the ground.

Four... Three... Two... One.

But a heartbeat before Noah was set to fling the chair over, the unseen man's voice cut in and stopped him.

"You can stop playing dead, Mr. Loblaw," he said, his tone dry. "And whatever you're planning...stow it. I'm going to give you the chance to earn your way out of here."

Noah didn't bother to keep up the pretense that he was only semiconscious. "Like hell you are."

His angry words didn't appear to faze the other man, who replied in an even tone. "I don't usually allow people to swear at me, but we've barely gotten acquainted yet, so I'll let it slide this once."

Noah wished his eyeroll was visible, but he settled for a snide response instead. "Your idea of meeting someone is clearly different than mine. But I guess I'll let that slide, too."

"The blindfold isn't to keep you from seeing me, Mr. Loblaw. It's about power. Control. I'm sure you already know who I am, even under the haze of the propofol."

Noah started to argue that he had no idea who his captor was but stopped before he spoke a word. If he could've kicked himself, he would've. The other man's identity was beyond obvious.

Trey Charger.

Noah didn't realize he'd spoken the name aloud until the man himself answered.

"That's right," said Charger. "I'm sure our dearest Elle gave you an earful about me."

"If you're fishing for her opinion of you, there's no need," Noah said evenly, ignoring the burn in his chest at hearing the other man say Elle's name. "All she told me was that you're the kind of man who locks kids in closets.

Which is more than enough for me to come to my own conclusions about you."

Charger chuckled. "Her memory is slightly faulty. I only put naughty kids in closets. Then again, she always did prefer to pick and choose how to interpret our life together. She happen to share any other glorious tidbits with you?"

"None," Noah replied through gritted teeth. "Thank God."

There was a pause. "Lucky for you, I believe that's true. And before you say my ruling on the validity of your ignorance doesn't matter…it's the only thing that's keeping you alive right now. She was smart not to tell you anything else."

"Should we celebrate by having you untie me?"

"Not quite yet."

"What are we waiting for? The clowns and the balloon animals to arrive and make it a real party?"

"Control, Mr. Loblaw. I need you to understand that I have it." The words were arrogant, but Charger's voice contained nothing that suggested his statements were overblown.

It sent an uncomfortable chill straight through Noah, and he didn't like it one bit. "Just tell me what the hell you want and get it over with."

"It's very simple. I want to be utterly certain that you're not going to come after Elle." Charger paused as if to let the demand sink in, then added, "I know that's going to be no small feat for you, so I'm going to give you some incentive to go along with it."

"You don't have anything I want."

"But I do. I have the truth about Elle."

Noah's chest burned even hotter. He couldn't quite muster a believable lie about not caring. Charger seemed to realize it.

"You'll feel differently about it when I show you what I'm about to show you," stated the other man.

Noah tensed as he heard Charger approach, and he barely managed to fight what would've been a futile and embarrassing urge to try to kick him, too. But the only thing the corrupt man did was yank away the blindfold.

Noah blinked at the sudden onslaught of yellowish light, and while he waited for the bleariness to fade, he took a look at his surroundings. As he'd surmised a few minutes earlier, they were in a musty, gray-walled space, and though it might've been labeled as a living room at some point, it wasn't much bigger than a box. Aside from the chair where he sat, it was devoid of furniture. In fact, as far as could tell, there were only four things in the room at all. Himself and the chair. And the other man and the laptop that he held open in his hands.

Noah gave Charger a quick onceover. He had a fake tan, an expensive suit and artificially enhanced gray temples. His eyes were the same as Noah remembered from the news broadcast all those years earlier—cold and lacking in humanity. More important than the man's looks, though, was the gun on his hip. The weapon Noah was going to need to procure if he stood a chance of getting out of the room alive.

Yeah, he said to himself. *But how can you get it without getting shot yourself?*

"Don't like what you see?" Charger asked.

Realizing his forehead had folded in a frown, Noah lifted an eyebrow at the man and ran his gaze over him once more, this time slowly. "Yeah. A bit disappointing. I was expecting you to be bigger."

Charger smirked, but his voice was still cool. "You're clever. I can see why Elle doesn't want you dead."

Noah did his best to shrug from his tied-up position. "I can't help the effect I have on women."

"Speaking of which…" The other man reached over the laptop's screen and gave the spacebar a quick tap. "Make sure you watch right until the end. Just so there's no mistake about what you're seeing."

As much as Noah didn't want to obey the order, his eyes were already glued to the video playing across the screen. It was obvious from the angle that the feed had been pulled from a security camera of some kind—higher up and pointed down, which offered an unobstructed view of a blond ponytail, bobbing along as the person attached to the locks scurried through a courtyard.

And Noah didn't have to see her face to know it was Elle. He'd spent enough time looking at her—running his fingers through that same silken hair—to be sure. Unease crept in. For no pinpointable reason, he wanted to stop the playback. He forced himself to keep watching anyway.

As Elle and her ponytail disappeared from view, the screen switched from the courtyard to a concrete path that led to a set of stairs on the side of a house. There, she paused to toss a glance over her shoulder before running up them and disappearing through a door.

"There's a thirty-second delay here," said Charger. "If you're wondering why she wasn't smart enough to know she was being recorded, let me assure you that she did her best to disable the cameras the previous morning. She tore out one of the wires that powered the whole system. Clever, really. She knew just which one would disable the operation without setting off an alarm. Too bad she didn't also know that my security team had a previously scheduled service tech there later that same day. He noted and fixed the problem. He thought it was rats that had done the damage, actually." He smiled. "And I can't say he was wrong."

Noah opened his mouth to tell the other man where he could shove his opinion, but the words stuck in his throat. Elle was back on the screen, this time running back down the stairs. She had a large bag slung over one shoulder, and a small bundle tucked against her chest. She had her hood up now, but there was still no mistaking her. Especially since she paused at the bottom of the stairs to stare at the camera for a moment. The video quality was surprisingly good, and in those two seconds, Noah could easily read the surprise—then fear—in her gaze.

"That was the moment she realized her plan had encountered a huge problem," Charger stated. "And in case there's any doubt about what she was stealing…"

He swung the laptop toward himself, banged on the keyboard, then turned it back again.

Noah knew what he was about to see, but he drew in a sharp breath anyway. The image had been zoomed in on the bundle. And the bundle was a baby.

Chapter 15

Noah thought Charger would stop there. That it was the only trick—the only big reveal—he had up his sleeve. The fact that it was Elle in the video meant it didn't require much thinking to realize that baby had to be Katie. Before Noah could comment on that—or on his belief that the kid was clearly better off with Elle than with the man standing in front of him—Charger spoke up once more.

"Considering your past," said the crooked businessman, "I'd think that the kidnapping might be enough."

Noah met his eyes in a level stare. For the first time in as long as he could remember—maybe for the first time since his sister went missing—hearing a reference to her kidnapping didn't dredge up every imaginable emotion. He didn't feel the furious futility or the mind-bending grief. The sorrow was still there. Maybe knowing Elle, and feeling something positive and new and so very real for her, tempered all that rage and sadness. Or maybe Noah's disgust at Trey Charger's manipulation simply overrode it. Either way, he didn't need to jump into defensive mode.

"Having Greta taken didn't affect my ability to see what kind of father you are," he said instead, repugnance standing out clearly in his voice.

"Well. That's a real shame." Charger's upturned mouth belied his true feelings on the matter. "I was really hoping to appeal to our common ground."

"We have nothing in common."

"We have Elle."

Now the rage did bubble up, at least a little. Before any of it could escape, though, Charger had already brought something new on the laptop. And despite wanting to look away, the slightest glimpse of the photograph on the screen was enough to grab and hold Noah's attention. It was a macabre scene. Like something out of a crime show. A woman's body lay crumpled in a heap on the floor directly in front of a crib. Her outstretched arm brushed the edge of a discarded teddy bear, and her ankle was twisted at an awkward angle. All around her body were numbered yellow markers.

"What the hell is this?" Noah asked roughly.

Charger's reply was a shrug. "My nanny. And the aftermath."

Noah stared for another moment before truly clueing in to what the man meant. "Elle didn't do this."

"No?"

"No."

"Let me give you a little more evidence."

Quickly, Charger tapped through a series of photos, identifying each one as they came onto the screen.

Picture one was a dead woman lying under a sheet, eyes closed, shoulders exposed, face scrubbed but bruised and marred.

"See that mark on the nanny's forehead?" Charger asked. "That's the blunt force trauma that killed her."

The second photo showed three matching cylindrical metallic vases. A mess of dried flowers sat at their base, and a measuring tape indicated that each one was two inches across.

"There were four of these," Charger explained. "All heavy. All at the top of the stairs just outside Kaitlyn's room. They line up perfectly with the wounds on the nanny's face."

Next came a picture of a broken window with shards of glass strewn along the sill below.

"That's in the nursery," Charger told Noah. "The police believe Elle was trying to make it look like someone broke in, kidnapped the baby and killed the nanny in the process. And before you ask, yes, I admit that I pulled some strings to have my friend on the force run the case and keep it all very, very quiet. But this is the report."

An official-looking form, covered in messy handwriting, popped onto the screen. It was easy to pick out key words. *Victim. Blunt-force trauma.*

"You can read it in detail if you like," added Charger. "But I know your bias will tell you not to buy it anyway. So to settle your completely founded worries, let me present the last exhibit in my little case."

Finally came the same freeze-frame shot of Elle, staring up at the camera. Only this time, it was zoomed in, and digital circles had been drawn over the picture. The first was on Elle's face. The second was around a metallic object hanging out of the bag hanging at her side.

"In case you had any doubts…" said Charger. "The answer is yes. That *is* the missing vase. That *is* a smudge of something that looks a hell of a lot like blood on her pretty cheeks."

Noah stared. There was a denial in his head. Utter disbelief. It wasn't possible.

Isn't it, though?

He tried to stuff the question back into the mental box it'd popped out of, but he couldn't quite do it. What did he really know about Elle? The answer was simple. Nothing. For all their intimacy, she hadn't told him much. What she had told him could all be a lie. No matter how badly he wanted it to be otherwise. And as much as he didn't want to, Noah couldn't help but recall Elle's response when Dez had suggested she'd killed the last man to try to bring her in. *No one has ever tried to bring me in*, she'd said. Or something pretty damn close. It'd felt deliberately vague then. Now it felt even more so.

"I didn't want to believe it either," Charger said, his voice laced with false sympathy.

Noah brought his eyes to the other man's face. "What I really don't believe is that you care, one way or the other."

"Maybe, maybe not." Charger snapped the laptop shut, then set it on the floor. "Either way, you need to look at the facts, Mr. Loblaw, and you need to mull them over. You need to listen to me, too. Carefully, because this is your one shot at living. I'm not telling you I'm an angel. God knows I'm not. Hell. That baby's mother was barely more than an overpriced hooker. So all I'm saying is that Elle isn't exactly a peach, either. She's sneaky and manipulative. She's a kidnapper and a murderer." Charger shook his head and let out a dramatic sigh. "But I made her a promise that I'd let you go so long as you stayed gone, and I'm a man of my word, so…" He trailed off, pushed back his suit jacket and freed his weapon—a handgun equipped with a small silencer—and aimed it at Noah. "This'll hurt a bit. I'd say I'm sorry about that, but it'd be a lie."

Noah's eyes flicked from Charger to the gun and back

again. "You're kidding, right? You're going to shoot me? How the hell does that help you keep your promise?"

"It helps because it stops you—at least temporarily—from chasing Elle down and asking for some kind of excuse. In turn, the slowdown will give you a chance to think about the dead nanny's face. About whether or not there's any excuse that could cover that."

As soon as the other man had finished speaking, he raised the gun again. And this time, he didn't pause. In fact, he moved so quickly that Noah barely dragged in a breath before a muffled bang sent him into a spiral of pain that radiated from his foot up the rest of his body.

A moment later, he felt Charger's hands on him, freeing him from his bonds. Not that it mattered. The burn of the bullet was so fierce that Noah simply slid from the chair. He knew he should get up and do something. Anything, probably. There was even a small, tiny part of his brain that urged him to get up and take a swing at the other man. Except all he could do was breathe. Even when Charger's fingers came at him again, this time to tuck something into Noah's partially clenched fist, he wasn't yet ready to move. And through the blur of the pain, he heard the other man's voice.

"That card'll get you one freebie with a doctor who won't feel obligated to report that GSW to the cops. And in two minutes, there'll be a courtesy cab downstairs, ready to take you there. The tab's on me, of course. All you have to do is get there. He won't wait long."

Then the other man's feet thumped lightly away, leaving Noah to fight to get to his feet before the taxi left without him.

As tense and emotionally overwrought as she was, Elle found it easier to let herself drift in and out of consciousness. It was simpler than talking to Detective Stanley. Better, too, than thinking about where Noah was, and whether or not he was actually okay. Being half-asleep had the added bonus of not giving her too much time to wrestle with the giddiness at the upcoming reunion with Katie. Because she couldn't be giddy. She didn't have that luxury. She had no idea what Trey had in store for the two of them, and she wasn't sure she even wanted to speculate on it. So she let herself drift. But there was a downside to not letting herself dwell on the details. And that was that her subconscious took hold, and it wasn't pretty.

Images and memories and the accompanying emotions flitted along the periphery of Elle's partially awake mind. Some were vague, wispy demons. Others were far more specific. Like the first time she'd had to take Katie in for a medical appointment. It'd been terrifying. And not just because her sweet, six-month-old baby had been crying for hours, gasping for breath, and choking on her own tears. Not even because Katie's fever had been so high that Elle could feel the burn of her skin from inches away. What had paralyzed her was the fear of being caught. Of being asked for proof that the still-tiny infant was her own. Of being forced to hand over documents that would allow Trey to track them. She'd rushed out of the hospital the moment the doctors said she could. But then there'd been the terrifying moment in the parking lot. A dark-haired man had stepped out of a sleek sedan, and Elle had been sure—so sure—that it was him. And instead of running, she'd frozen. When the man had finally turned, revealing that he was a complete stranger, Elle had nearly collapsed from relief. And for three weeks following the incident, she'd questioned her ability to keep Katie safe. Finally, she'd enrolled in a Momma-and-Me running group, determined to teach her own body that staying still wasn't an option. But she'd never quite shaken that "what-if-he-really-finds-us" feeling.

And now you've let it come true.

The thought—the accusation—jolted Elle awake. Almost blinded by the stab of guilt that hit her gut, she blinked a look out the window, watching the raindrops hit it in a rhythmic way.

She peered through the wetness, trying to discern their location, but the light was too scarce to allow her to even hazard a guess, and after a few, fruitless moments, the tap-splash, tap-splash against the glass almost lulled her. But the retreat back into the restless, semi-conscious state brought along another, specific recollection. One that was even older, and even darker. That day had shared a lot with the current one. It was also rainy, fraught with fear, and with Katie's life—and Elle's own—on the line.

Elle had just turned twenty, and it'd been two long years since she'd set foot in the place where she grew up. The place she refused to refer to as home. That she'd sworn never to set foot in again, no matter what. But circumstances had changed, and she'd needed to make the trip, just one more time. So she had. Except it wasn't exactly a smooth, painless return. It took two weeks in a hotel to work up the nerve to even go and look. It'd taken two more to come up with a plan. Another two days to set it in motion. But finally, the moment had come.

Elle remembered very little about the hours leading up to that night. She did know that she'd barely slept for two days, and that the weather had suited her mood. Wind bashed against the windows. Rain pelted down. And she'd hoped the chaos would work to her advantage.

But it didn't really, did it? said the lucid part of her brain.

She acknowledged the question with a nod. But in actuality, things had started out okay. Aside from the unpredicted rain, the initial plan went off without a hitch. The camera feed had been cut. The nanny had taken the bribe. The guard had consumed the dosed coffee and been forced to take a break at the right moment. And Elle had gotten in. Which was about the same time all hell broke loose.

Even in her dozing state, her heart rate started to accelerate. Her chest tightened, too, and sweat beaded across her brow and lip.

In the dreamlike memory, she was just reaching the top of the stairs. Just hearing the unexpected sounds from behind the nursery door and just reaching for the vase atop the little table in the hall. Elle could practically feel the cool metal in her palm. But before she could get to the next part—the part where she came face-to-face with the woman whose life she was responsible for ending—the car jerked to a stop, yanking Elle firmly back into the world of the living.

Heart thumping with a renewed combination of nerves and hope, her eyes found the car window. She squinted through the dark and the rain, and right away she spied the yellow porch lights ahead. And she realized that she now knew exactly where they were. From the log cabin exterior—a front for the distinctly *un*rustic interior—to the wraparound porch to the swing hanging from the evergreens in the back, Elle was familiar with it all. They were at Trey's summer home on Wavers Lake, just a couple of hours away from Vancouver. In fact, the very last time she'd seen the man in question, it had been almost in the very spot where she and the detective were stopped right now. And the memory of it came back, hitting her as hard as any of the ones that had surfaced on the long drive.

That day, at six o'clock in the evening, she'd stepped onto the porch and stared at the back of the abusive man's dark head. He'd been watching the sunset, and she'd taken a few steps toward him without even realizing it. Elle had been going to ask him something, but it'd gone out of her head. Because her movement had sparked something. An epiphany of sorts. Because he hadn't noticed her movement. And he'd left his gun unattended on the arm of one of the Adirondack chairs there on the porch. It meant Trey Charger was human. Fallible. For all the evil he'd planned for her future, he could be stopped.

Elle's brain—and her fighting spirit—switched on. She seriously considered grabbing the gun and simply firing. Emptying every one of the chambers. But then she thought of Trey's police connections, and the fact that no one would buy her story of self-defense, no matter how true it might be. Then she'd done a remarkable thing. She'd left. Turned back into the house. Grabbed a bag and stuffed it with a few necessities. Stolen whatever cash she could find. And just walked away.

She'd known he would come after her. Relentlessly, probably. But the world was big, and even without a passport, it was easy enough to put space between them. Cash jobs hadn't been hard to find for a fresh-faced eighteen-year-old woman. And yeah, maybe she'd been on edge sometimes. But overall, Elle had felt far safer away from Trey than she could ever had felt under his roof. But that was two entire years before Katie.

Katie.

Thinking of her seemed to conjure the sound of her voice. A wordless whimper that Elle had comforted away after the onset of a nightmare, or after Katie had skinned her knee or had her feelings hurt. And for a second, Elle thought she was imagining the noise. But then Detective Stanley's voice carried in—along with the sudden whip of wind and a barrage of raindrops—and she realized it was real. Katie was out there in the storm.

Ignoring everything but the cries, Elle whipped off her seatbelt, launched herself past the detective, then tossed her gaze back and forth, searching. It took only a moment to find her. She was lying limp in the arms of a strange man, and their silhouetted forms sent every protective-parent hackle up. Why was he holding her? Who was he? How dare he put hands on her? And then, as if brought about by the force of her anger, a zap rang out, and the porch lights went black.

And Elle bolted. She couldn't help it. Detective Stanley was yelling at her, but she didn't care. Her feet smacked against the soaked ground, and mud sprayed up while her immediately-sopping ponytail smacked against her face. None of that meant anything either. She dashed all the way up the driveway, her tears mingling with the rain as she finally reached the stoop and gasped out an order at the short, squat man who held Katie in an awkward, cradle-like position. As though he'd never had a child in his arms ever before. And it made Elle's stomach roll.

"Give her to me," she said, stretching out her still-cuffed arms. "Now."

Katie stirred immediately, and her blue eyes opened—sleepily at first, then widening as she caught sight of Elle. "Momma?"

"Come here, baby," Elle replied, holding out her cuffed hands.

The unknown man stepped back, his overly full mouth twisting into a grimace. His movements made Katie wriggle to get free, and when he didn't let go, Elle had to fight an urge to stomp on his foot. She forced herself to take as calming a breath as she could manage. But she couldn't stop her words from coming out in a bitten-off form.

"Give. Her. To. Me. Now."

The squish of boots in mud told her that Detective Stanley had come up behind her, and Elle swung toward him, her anger and frustration ready to be unleashed. But he spoke first, directing his words toward the other man.

"Let her have the kid," the detective said, his voice utterly dismissive as he reached out and undid Elle's handcuffs. "Trey won't be back for an hour or more anyway. Might as well give them what little time they have."

Elle wasn't sure if she was more grateful for the gesture, or more scared of what the second part of his statement implied. But she decided there wasn't much point in dwelling on the latter. Not while she was at last taking Katie back into her arms, the little girl's arms clinging to her own like she was never going to let go. So Elle chose to embrace the gratitude, and she pressed her chin to the top of Katie's head, then let the two men guide her into the house.

Chapter 16

If Noah had been thinking about it at all, he wouldn't have accepted the cab ride. He sure as hell wouldn't have gone to some off-the-record doctor who'd been recommended by Trey Charger. Of course, it was pretty damn hard to be rational for the first ten minutes after being shot. So by the time he was clear-headed enough to really consider not accepting the assistance, Noah had already stumbled his way out of the apartment. He'd already pulled himself in the back seat of the taxi and laid himself across the bench as the tires rolled underneath his body. He'd even already let himself be yanked into an oversized house by a small myopic man—who'd opened the door, taken a nervous look around, then grabbed hold of Noah's elbow, pulled hard and slammed the door behind him.

Noah was thankful, at least, that the room where he was currently undergoing treatment appeared to be clean and professional. Soft green walls. The smell of ammonia and various medical accoutrements arranged in tidy place. No visible sign of dirt or corruption. It was more like a home-based hospital room than anything else.

The man working on him appeared no less business-like, either. He'd donned a lab coat then both washed his hands and covered them in rubber gloves before getting near Noah's foot. With a calm, perfectly cultivated bed-side manner, he'd explained that he was going to need to cut through the laces of Noah's boot before being able to see what was going on, and he'd also asked permission be-fore jabbing him with a shot of lidocaine. His subsequent motions were quick and sure. And from all of that, Noah deduced that the man must be a real medical professional rather than some de-licensed hack, like he would've ex-pected.

Not exactly complete peace of mind, Noah said to him-self, *but I'll take it.*

The only problem—aside from all the obvious wrong-ness—was that being able to breathe also meant being able to think. Which meant that his mind automatically went to Elle. In fact, his brain didn't even bother trying to skip around her. It simply dived right in, sifting through the divulgences Trey Charger had offered up.

Divulgences? They weren't just divulgences. It was cold, hard proof in video form, he reminded himself. *Elle lied to you.*

He tried to focus on that. To use it as a shield against the ache he felt when he thought of her. It was hard. Not just because he didn't want to face the truth about her, but be-cause trying not to think of her somehow only intensified his short-term memory. His senses were full of Elle. Her scent. Her voice. Her touch. He was well aware that it was over-the-top. She had no right to be laying so much claim to him. After all, he really didn't know her. How could he, after so short a time? Even if the video hadn't proved as much, there were other things to consider. Like the fact that the intimacy between them could've been as fake as her story. Something nagged at him anyway. Maybe it was just that Charger wanted him to be aware of Elle's past. His whole song-and-dance routine was intended to keep Noah away. To make him feel angry and betrayed. Why? Noah supposed it could just be because of the promise the other man had made to Elle. It was a simple enough explanation. So how come he felt like it didn't quite fit?

Wishful thinking, Loblaw. It's as straightforward as that. You were all set to start falling in love with her, and then you found out she was a murderer.

The thought was so startling that Noah jerked to a sitting position without even realizing it. The bald head at his feet bobbed up, and the glasses-clad man cleared his throat.

"Sorry, sir," he said. "I'm just going to need you to relax for a couple more minutes, here."

Noah muttered his own apology, then lay back again, trying to divert his mind once more. Because people didn't start falling in love in hours. They didn't even consider it in the offhanded way that Noah's conscience had just done. That was pure insanity. And even if it weren't, it didn't matter anymore anyway. His role in Elle's life was over.

He cleared his throat and tried a new distraction tactic—addressing the man who was taking care of his wound.

"Gotta admit, Doc," he said. "You don't seem like the pay-for-play type."

"And you don't seem like the usual type that Mr. Charger sends my way," the other man replied mildly. "Aside from the GSW and the blood, of course."

"What? Am I too clean-cut for maximum thug-ness?"

"No. You're plenty scruffy enough. But you're also capable of forming a complete sentence without dropping an f-bomb, you're not calling me names, and you're not demanding stronger drugs. So…"

Noah let himself chuckle. "Yeah, well. Maybe 'Mr. Charger' isn't usually responsible for the bullet in question."

The doctor paused in his work and lifted his eyes. "I would guess not. No offense to Mr. Charger, but I suspect that the people he takes down are usually intended to stay that way." He lowered his gaze again. "And actually, you're quite lucky, sir."

"Noah."

The doctor's attention came up once more, surprise and caution mingling on his face. "Names aren't necessary."

Noah shrugged. "I've got nothing to hide. My last name's Loblaw, while I'm at it."

"In that case…" The man stood, snapped the glove off his right hand, then extended his palm. "I'm Ford McMillan. And yes, I'm a real doctor. I do most of my work out of Van General."

Noah clasped the other man's fingers and shook firmly. "That's incredibly reassuring."

"It's equally nice to have someone in here who isn't going to steal my narcotics." He took off the other glove and tossed it into a nearby trash bin. "You want the good news now?"

"Please."

"Your boot took the brunt of the bullet."

"Felt like it hurt a hell of a lot more than a graze."

Dr. McMillan nodded. "That'd be because of the burn."

"The burn?" Noah echoed.

"The bullet went through the topside of your boot just past your pinky toe. Then it got lodged in the sole. Here. Let me show you."

He turned around for a second, then spun back with the

boot in his hands. Noah winced at the footgear's state. As the doctor had said, he'd cut open the lace in order to remove it. The side where the bullet had entered was charred and shredded, and the inside—which had once been off-white—was darkened with dried blood. Nothing about it looked "lucky."

As if Dr. McMillan could read Noah's mind, he spoke up right then. "Just think. That could've been your foot."

Noah sighed. "Yeah, man. You're right."

The doctor offered a smile and set down the boot. "As it stands, you're just going to be mighty sore. It was partially cauterized already, but I made sure it was cleaned up, slathered it with some strong topical stuff and bandaged it as well."

"Thanks, doctor. What do I owe you for all that?"

"Nothing. You came in as a referral."

"There's no chance that I'm letting Trey Charger pick up my tab for a coffee, let alone for a visit to a doctor."

The other man's lips curved. "No sweeter words have ever been spoken. So I'll tell you what, Noah Loblaw. This one's on me, rather than on him. I'll even toss in a bottle of good old-fashioned penicillin tabs and a couple of pain pills. The ones from my secret stash upstairs, strictly no placebos. Maybe a pair of size twelve work boots? Never worn."

Noah nodded. He was grateful, and he wanted to be relieved. Except he honestly wasn't sure what came next. Hell. He didn't even know where to go next. He couldn't head back to the hotel where he and Elle had been staying. It was assumable that Charger's thugs would do a cleanup mission, but Noah didn't want to risk any staff recognizing him and asking questions. Even going home seemed like a bad idea. It had lost its anonymity.

And Elle?

Noah raked a hand over his hair. Was he supposed to go to her? Demand an explanation, then get one that he might not even want to hear? Or simply walk away? Neither seemed like a solution. The former could get her and her kid killed. The latter left her stuck with the man who'd pushed her into murder. Neither seemed like an ideal cure for the sharp throb that pulsed unpleasantly through his veins. The doctor's light touch alerted Noah to the fact that he'd been sitting and staring at nothing for a little too long.

"Look," said the other man. "I'm normally in a hurry to get guys out of here, and they're not usually interested in staying. But if you want to stick around…"

Noah shook his head. "If you don't mind, I'll just…" He trailed off as something caught his eye—a framed photograph, sitting on the tiny desk in the corner. It was of a beautiful woman with a swaddled bundle in her arms, and he couldn't look away.

Dr. McMillan followed the direction of his stare, then cleared his throat. "My wife and son. The day we brought him home from the hospital. Connor's eighteen now—almost nineteen, really."

Noah's eyes stayed fixed on the photograph, trying to figure out what it was that had made him want to fixate on it. He was only half listening as the doctor explained that his family had moved down south years earlier. He wife was American, and they both felt it was safer for them to be as far away from Trey Charger as possible. Especially knowing that Charger had been banned from crossing the Canada–US border.

"I'll get down there one day," the other man said, his voice full of undisguised wistfulness. "Hopefully before my son has a baby of his own."

Then it finally struck Noah. *A baby.* Elle had taken Katie as an infant. The video evidence had shown it. And he was sure that she'd said something about the kid being six, and that she'd been taking care of her on her own for that same number of years. But she'd also said Charger was the kind of man who locked a little girl in a closet. Who taught her a lesson. There was no way she'd been talking about a baby. If that had been the case, she would've stated it outright, further illustrating the darkness of Charger's character.

What did that mean?

"Has Trey Charger ever mentioned a wife?" Noah blurted, cutting the other man off, midsentence.

Dr. McMillan's puzzlement was evident in his frown. "A wife?"

Noah couldn't have explained the question if he tried. Maybe it was the fuzziness of the recently administered drugs and the leftover shock of being shot, or maybe it was just that his brain hadn't managed to catch up to his mouth yet. Either way, he gave his head a little shake. Something was just out of mental reach—something he damn well needed to figure out.

"A wife," he repeated a little more firmly. "Or a long-term girlfriend? Maybe the mother of his child?"

The doctor frowned. "I don't think I've ever heard a word about a wife, but one thing I am certain of is that Mr. Charger lost his daughter years ago."

"Yes," Noah replied softly, his mind churning in what seemed like a useless, hamster wheel of a way.

"Aside from the obvious…is something wrong?"

"No, I— You know what? Can I take you up on the boots and stuff? I'd like to make a call."

"You need to borrow a phone?"

Noah patted his pocket, relieved to find that his cell hadn't been taken. "I'm good."

Dr. McMillan nodded. "All right. I'll give you a few minutes."

Noah waited until the other man had slipped out a door across the room, then dragged his phone free and dialed without looking. Halfway through the second ring, his sister's familiar voice answered.

"This is Norah," she said.

"Don't pretend you didn't know it was me," he replied.

"You know I don't believe in that twin sense garbage."

"So you didn't know?"

Her sigh carried through clearly. "Fine. I did. But I don't have to like it. And for the record, I also don't like knowing that you're about to ask me for help."

Noah couldn't help but smile. "It's a good kind of help, though."

"That's a thing?"

"It is when I'm giving you a chance to prove that you're smarter than I am."

His sister sighed again. "Your attempt at flattery will get you nowhere. And are you seriously calling me from Vancouver?"

"Are you seriously pinging the location of my phone?" he countered.

"Not you, personally."

"Oh, I see. You stalk every caller."

"Job hazard," Norah said easily. "But really, little bro? You come into Van the one weekend I'm away?"

"Sorry," he replied. "Are you at least somewhere hot and tropical?"

She snorted. "Hardly. I'm staying at this place called Wavers Hollow. Gingerbread cabin. I kid you not. That's what it's called. And the town has a population of about fourteen, I swear."

Noah's smile widened to a grin. "Sorry. Again."

"Yeah, I'm not sure I buy either of those apologies," said his sister. "You take peculiar pleasure in harassing me. So. Go ahead. Get it over with and hit me with whatever favor you need."

His amusement at the familiar banter faded quickly as he launched into a summary of the last twelve or so hours. He went into as much detail as he could in as few words as possible. The only things he left out were the more intimate details and his own, overblown feelings about Elle. His sister picked up on the omitted facts anyway.

"You *like* this woman," she said as soon as he was done.

"I barely know her," he responded.

"Yet you suspended all your dumb rules. You have a perfectly acceptable reason for walking away. Or for contacting some real police. And instead, you're calling me and asking what you should do."

Noah didn't bother to argue with her; he was never very good at lying to his sister.

"I'm not asking you what to do," he grumbled instead. "I'm asking you what I'm missing."

"Amounts to the same thing," Norah told. "But since it means you'll have to concede that I am, in fact, the smarter sibling, I'll tell you. What's the first thing you normally do when a client tries to hire you?"

"Asking me a question and telling me the answer are two very different things, sweet sister."

"I'm serious."

He started to close his eyes to think about what she'd asked, then realized he didn't really need to think about it at all. Mentally kicking himself, he nearly jumped off the hospital bed. He didn't need to tell Norah that he'd figured it out, either.

"See?" she said. "I'm totally brilliant."

"Love you, Norah."

"I'll take that as agreement. Let me know when to expect the engagement announcement."

Unsurprisingly, she didn't give him a chance to respond. The line went dead in Noah's hands. That was fine with him, though. He was already sliding down the mattress, hobbling toward the door where the doctor had disappeared and calling up to ask if the other man had a computer he could borrow.

Elle was wasting time. A fairly loud voice in her head kept telling her so. And she knew she should listen. Figure out just what she needed to do in order to escape the current situation. Or to be more accurate, she should figure out what she needed to do in order to save Katie. But every time she turned a look toward the girl's face—now restful in sleep once more—a different voice piped up in Elle's head. One that whispered to spend as much time with Katie as possible, because who knew how long they had. She actually hated that second voice. But that didn't mean she could completely block it out. Because what if it was right? So she'd heeded it for a while. Stolen long moments of cuddling. Of hair smoothing. Of whispering endearments. And admittedly crying a little.

But now Elle was pacing the length of the room, over and over, trying not to think about the war going on in her psyche. Trying to redirect her brain back to a workable solution. Except the space where she moved was, all on its own, an unpleasant reminder of the way her and Trey's pasts were linked together. Because it had been her room. And not much had changed in the last almost-decade. Her feet hit the same hardwood floors. The same board squeaked beside the same ornate dresser. Even the same midnight blue curtains hung over the panes of glass. Elle knew every inch of it. But it wasn't a good kind of fa-

miliarity. This was the same place where she'd lain awake at night, stared up at the ceiling and hoped that Trey would forget she was there. The bed where Katie was sprawled out, starfish style, was the exact spot where Elle had been sitting when he busted in—reeking of rum, and too pleased with himself to be anything but full of bad news—and informed her of his plans for her future.

Elle shivered, thinking about it now. The only good thing about being in the room was that Detective Stanley had left Katie and her alone. The smallest of mercies. And before she knew it, she'd stopped again, her eyes hanging on Katie's dark locks, her mind silently counting the rhythmic rises and falls of her little chest. Her life was wrapped up in that small body, her heart tethered to it, too. Elle loved her so much that she'd give up anything to keep her safe. If she needed any proof of that, all she had to do was take a look at the last few hours. Let her mind brush over Noah Loblaw.

God, how she hoped he was okay. She'd done everything she could to protect him, too. Right that second, though, in the quiet and the dark, she wished she hadn't made so sure that he wouldn't come after her. But she had. She'd made Trey promise to let him go, and out of necessity she'd demanded that he do it in a way that would keep Noah out of her life for good. She wasn't certain what Trey would choose; she just knew he wouldn't hold back. A threat. A piece of blackmail. An irreparable rift. It was what Elle needed. What she'd asked for. Yet she still would've given almost anything to be able to ask for Noah's help. To throw herself into his arms and immerse herself in his scent and the safety of his presence and the feeling of finally coming home when she'd been homeless for so long.

And there it was. What she'd given up. Something—

someone—she'd barely had a chance to really get to experience, yet which—who—she was so very sure was meant to end.

She closed her eyes, trying to brush off the very recent memory. But it backfired. Noah's stubble-dotted face and too-long hair leaped right to the front of her mind. For a second, the image was so powerful that she could almost smell him for real. Then the windowpane rattled with a sudden gust of wind, and Noah was swept away once more. The only problem was that Elle wasn't relieved. She was just sad.

She forced her eyes open, then chastised herself when she realized she'd completely stopped moving again. Not just physically, but mentally. It was one thing to waste time on Katie; it was a whole other to pine away over Noah.

Stealing another glance at the sleeping girl before averting her eyes once more, Elle moved to the window and stared out, trying to gauge the hour. The sky had cleared a little, and she was almost positive that there was a hint of dawn in the air. But it wasn't comforting to know that she wasn't going to be stuck in the dark anymore. It just meant that it was getting closer to the time when Trey would arrive.

Elle clutched her hands together. Because now it was *his* face filling her mind rather than Noah's, and her gut churned. She couldn't recall the last time she felt this powerless. She needed to act. Desperately. But she was weighed down by fear and tied up by the fact that the chances of the two of them successfully sneaking off were slim. And there was no way their escape could be simple.

When Katie had first fallen asleep, and Elle had managed to pry herself away, she'd taken a few moments to make a quick trip to the bathroom. The brief foray out of the bedroom had let her know that there was an armed

guard sitting in the hall. Back in the room, she'd stolen a look through the window. And that had told her that a man waited there, too. He was chain-smoking in a Jeep with a phone in his hand. The light of the former flickered fore-bodingly, while the glow of the latter illuminated the out-line of the rifle that sat on the dashboard.

Trey clearly wasn't leaving anything to chance, and even with the power still out, there was little hope of get-ting free undetected. Walking away from the property wasn't going to be as easy as it had been eight years ear-lier. And if Elle did manage to find a way to get out of the house—either by magically overpowering every guard surrounding it, or by some kind of uber-clever trickery—there was still the matter of how to get off the property. And getting back to the city, too. The property was close to three hours outside of Vancouver, so it wasn't as though they could just walk. Could she steal a car? Pry the keys from the hands of the man in the Jeep and take that vehicle?

Would I even be able to put him in a state that would require prying?

She honestly didn't know. It was one thing to fight in self-defense. It was another to strike in cold blood. Even when the cold blood in question might be the difference between life and death. And of course, there was Katie. Elle's eyes drifted to her sleeping form once more. She couldn't help but wonder how much damage had already been done. What would it do to Katie if she saw her com-mit some atrocious act? That kind of thing would undoubt-edly leave a scar.

But then Elle let out a sigh, because she suspected that it'd take some kind of miracle to even leave the top floor of the house, anyway.

She turned her attention out the window again, and she

stared a little longer. The sky was definitely less murky now, and it made her heart thump.

Think, Elle. There has to be something else you can—

The door creaked open, cutting off her thoughts. She tensed. But she knew she had to turn around and face Trey, so she took a breath and spun. And it wasn't him. Instead, it was Detective Stanley. His bulky form took up most of the doorway, and his presence was only slightly less unnerving than Trey's would have been.

Elle let out the breath. "Can I help you?"

He took a half step, then stopped, and his eyes lifted past her to glance at Katie. "I think we have something to discuss. In private."

Most of Elle wanted to say no. She didn't care what he had to say. She wasn't the least bit curious. And the slightly lascivious undertone in his words made her skin crawl. But she had just enough common sense not to argue. She issued a quick, wordless nod, then followed him out. And the moment her feet hit the floor in the hallway, she realized that this was it. The miracle moment. Because not only had the guard disappeared from his post, but Elle noticed something she'd somehow managed to overlook before. Just outside her door was a familiar object. A heavy cylindrical vase. It'd clearly been set there on purpose. Probably intended to incite guilt and fear and horror. But at that moment, all it did was inspire. And before the detective could even speak, Elle had grabbed the decoration in question. And with all her might, she swung it right at his head.

She watched him fall.

Made sure he was truly unconscious.

Checked that he was still breathing.

Grabbed his keys.

And tossed her weapon-of-the-moment aside.

For a second after it was done, Elle stared down at the dropped item, letting the regret wash over her. She studied its metallic glint. She saw how it was both beautiful and deadly at the same time. And truthfully, she'd never forgotten what that particular vase was capable of, and she'd never forgotten the nanny's dead-eyed stare, either. But just as she had done back then, she knew she had to move on.

"I'm sorry," she whispered into the air.

Then she turned her back on the unconscious man and hurried back to the bedroom to scoop Katie from the bed.

Chapter 17

In a moment that felt eerily similar to the one six years ago, Elle stared down at Katie's sweet face. She noted the way the shape of it looked so much like her own. She saw how the cap of dark hair matched her father's now-dyed locks. And she loved her. So hard. So desperately that she wondered how she had ever lived without her and hoped to God she would never have to do it again.

I have to save her.

The compulsion was as strong now as it had been then. Of course, when she slid her arms under Katie this time, the little girl didn't smack her toothless gums together and coo. Instead, she woke up and offered first a yawn, then a sleepy blink, then spoke up in a dream-tinged voice.

"Momma?"

"Hi, sweet pea. I'm sorry I woke you up. But we need to hurry."

Katie's blue eyes immediately became more wakeful. "Are we getting away?"

Elle nodded, and replied firmly, "Yes."

"I knew those guys were bad." She paused, and a slightly saucy smile turned up her lips. "Am I allowed to say, 'I told you so,' Momma?"

Elle couldn't hold in a laugh. "Just this once. But we're not going to let them keep us here, okay?"

"Okay." Katie paused again. "Momma?"

"Yes?"

"I told you so."

Laughing again, Elle held out her hand, and Katie grabbed it without hesitation. Together, they made their silent way across the floor—pausing only long enough for Katie to slide her feet into her shoes—then stepped out into the hallway. Too late, Elle realized she should've shielded the girl from seeing the unconscious man, or at least have warned her what to expect. But thankfully, Katie took his slightly disturbing presence in stride.

"Is he dead, Momma?" she asked.

Elle shook her head. "No, baby. Just asleep."

"Did you make him asleep?"

"Only because I had to protect us. Which is why we need to go before he wakes up again."

She started to guide them around the detective. Katie, though, stopped once again.

"Momma?" she said.

Elle channeled every ounce of patience she had and said, "What is it, honey?"

"Do you think he came here in a car?"

"I know he did. He brought me here in it. Why are you—" She cut herself off as her seemingly slow brain caught up with her six-year-old's quick one, and she dropped down to kiss the top of her mussed-up hair. "You really are a genius, aren't you?"

"You said we don't use that word because it sounds pretend-shush."

"Pretentious," Elle corrected automatically, stepping away, then bending down again, this time beside the fallen detective. "Remind me. What did we settle on, instead of genius?"

"Smart cookie," Katie replied, sounding suitably unimpressed.

"Smart cookie. *My* smart cookie. And I love cookies." Elle finished the distasteful task of digging through Detective Stanley's pocket to retrieve his keys, and she stood up. "All right. Let's get the heck out of here, okay?"

Katie still didn't move, and she spoke again, her voice quavering. "His gun, Momma."

Elle glanced down. In her hurry to grab the keys, she'd accidentally left the detective's coat open, and his weapon was on display. Its cold silver shine made Elle's heart trip, but as she strengthened herself and started to say that there was nothing to be worried about, she realized something. It wasn't concern driving her daughter's statement; it was another suggestion.

One you should've come up with on your own.

But she shoved away the admonishment as quickly as it came. Yes, she should've thought of the car and the weapon on her own. In retrospect, she couldn't believe she hadn't. But the six years that she'd spent protecting Katie had all been evasive. They'd been hiding. Elle's brain was accustomed to running and hiding. That was second nature to her. But going on the offensive wasn't even third or fourth nature to Elle, and her focus had been lasered on getting Katie to a safe space. All of her instincts urged her to bolt rather than to prepare for a confrontation. She was all flight, not fight. And acknowledging that made Elle realize something. It was exactly what Trey would be expecting. So she needed to find a way to do the opposite.

"Momma?" Katie's hesitant prod alerted Elle to the fact that she'd momentarily frozen.

Forcing a measured breath, she bent down a third time so that she could look straight into those blue eyes that were so like her own. "We need to change the plan a little bit. And it might not make much sense, and it might seem a little scary, but I'm going to ask you to keep being brave for a while longer."

Katie sucked her lower lip in, but she nodded her agreement anyway. "I can do it."

"That's my girl. It's not even a big thing that I need you to do," Elle said, trying to make herself believe the statement, too. "Come back into the room, and let me show you a hiding place."

"We're not leaving?"

"We are," Elle said firmly. "But first there's something I need to do to make sure we're safe."

"Okay," Katie replied, the trust in her eyes clearly outweighing her fear.

Elle fought a wave of choking guilt, but she stuffed it back, straightened up and took Katie's hand. She led her into the bedroom, then guided her to the closet and opened the door.

"You want me to get in there, Momma?" The question was heartbreaking.

Elle did her best to pretend that it wasn't. "Think of it like hide-and-seek, but Momma is the only one who's allowed to find you."

"But you already know where I am."

"Exactly."

"Oh." Katie tilted her head thoughtfully. "So…am I hiding from the bad guys?"

The breath left Elle's lungs with a violent whoosh, and she was surprised that her reply managed to come out sounding reasonably normal. "I don't want you to worry about them. Just concentrate on being as quiet as you can be, baby. You can even curl up with a blanket if you want, and go back to sleep. But can you do me another little favor?"

"What?"

"Give me one of your shoes and the hair tie from your wrist."

"That's weird, Momma."

"I know. But do you think you can do it anyway?"

Katie nodded solemnly, and as she set out to comply with the request, Elle did her best to set up the closet as a refuge rather than as a prison. She grabbed a pillow from the bed, and a fleecy blanket from the chest near the footboard. She tucked both into the small space, mentally crossing her fingers that whoever inspected the room wouldn't note the oddity of the missing items. Once that was done, she pulled Katie in for a hug so hard that the little girl let out a squeak. And finally, she helped Katie settle into the newly cozy-fied closet. But for a second, the sight of her little body—all tucked in and deceptively comfortable in appearance—made Elle sick to her stomach. The last thing she wanted was to subject Katie to being stuck alone in the dark, trapped in the teeny tiny, claustrophobia-inducing space. But she forced herself to do it. She had little other choice.

Blowing a kiss toward her favorite, little round face Elle whispered, "I love you," and closed the door. She let herself have a moment. She ran her fingers over the wood, and she stared at the panels, willing Katie to be strong and praying that her plan wouldn't fail. Then she straightened her shoulders, steadied her resolve and marched out of the room. She paused only long enough to snag the detective's gun.

And it felt wrong. Really wrong. But just the same, Elle knew it was right. Because for the first time in all her years, she was going to confront Trey Charger head-on. She just needed to use a trail of metaphorical breadcrumbs to lead him as far away as possible from Katie first.

Noah stared at the computer, frustrated by the lack of digital information available. He'd rephrased the same simple question in multiple ways with the same results—almost nothing.

Who is Elle O'Malley?

There was no solid answer. In fact, there wasn't anything he could even call a hint. Yeah, it was true that when he'd typed it up and pressed enter the first time, he hadn't been expecting much. But he'd hoped for something. Even just a sliver that would lead him down a path to understanding. Instead, his search had yielded watered-down, internet soup. There were a few social media profiles. None of which belonged to his Elle O'Malley. There was a popular chain of ladies' clothing shops in Alberta, owned by a woman of the same name. Clearly not related.

But there has to be some kind of footprint, he told himself. *No one is that invisible.*

Idly, Noah scrolled down the current list of results, wondering if he should give up. Or at least close out the search to try something else. Except as his finger hovered over the delete key, something at the bottom of the digital page finally caught his eye—a link to some kind of online forum.

He stared for a moment, then read the headline aloud, trying to figure out how it might fit. "Missed Encounters."

The post was years old, and it struck Noah as odd. With his forehead creasing in curiosity-infused puzzlement, he gave the seemingly out-of-place link a click, and was immediately routed to a specific ad. His brows split out of their frown, then shot up as he scanned through it.

You call yourself Elle O'Malley. You are a natural blonde. You have blue eyes, and the saddest smile. I believe you may have accidentally left with something that belongs to me. It would give me the greatest pleasure if I could find you and get it back.

Under any other circumstances, the brief paragraph might've seemed innocent. A man looking for a woman he'd met only briefly. Just long enough to catch her name. Maybe she'd picked up his cell phone by mistake. Or grabbed his scarf as she'd hurried off to work. Noah could think of a dozen scenarios where something like that might happen. Yet he was sure that none of them was true.

Wanting to find evidence to back up what his instincts told him, he read the words again. Slowly this time. Dissecting their flaws.

First was the phrase "call yourself." It seemed strangely put. Deliberately so. The more natural phrasing would've been—at the very least—in the past tense. With that in mind, Noah tapped his thumbs on the lower edge of the keyboard and considered the next oddity. It was the use of the word *something*. Wouldn't someone in desperate search of a missing item go out of his way to be specific? Especially considering the use of a specific name. The omission was clearly unrelated to a need for secrecy. Finally came the closing sentence. The words "greatest pleasure" were dripping with intimacy and violence—they were a dark promise. One that made Noah grit his teeth to keep from slamming a fist into some unsuspecting, inanimate object.

Exhaling, he leaned back from the computer and thought about what his next move should be.

"'You call yourself Elle O'Malley,'" he murmured.

Then an idea struck him, and he pressed his fingers to the keyboard again, wondering why he hadn't thought of it before. Women who escaped from abusive relationships didn't keep their husbands' last names. Why would they want to?

"Who is Elle Charger?" he wrote.

A tenth of a second later, a new selection of links appeared on the screen. For a moment, he felt let down. There wasn't much change from the offerings. More social media, some suggested spelling corrections, and four ads for phone chargers. The last bit made his mouth twist into a wry smile, but the rest of it just made him shake his head.

Frustrated, he tried a third search.

Elle Charger and Trey Charger.

The computer stalled, and Noah swore, then pulled back from the desk a little. He felt like he was trying to solve a riddle—except it was a riddle where he hadn't been given any of the clues, and he was just hoping to stumble upon the answer. His foot was starting to throb again, too, and that didn't help at all. He eyed the pain pills that the doctor had given him. He knew he was going to have to take one eventually. Right then, though, he wanted to be clearheaded enough to keep searching. So instead of the meds, he grabbed the mug of coffee—also provided by the doctor—and he took a hearty slurp, then closed his eyes.

Who is Elle? he thought.

Noah's sister had been right. The first thing he did when he got a new client was to take a look into what made them who they were. Although his strict rules didn't really include a not-working-for-criminals clause, he did take it into consideration. Even putting morality aside, he had no desire to be inadvertently caught up in some crime, labeled as an accessory, then tossed into jail. But he hadn't had a moment to stop and explore Elle's past. He hadn't even felt like he needed to. Not until Norah pointed out the oversight. Now it seemed a little crazy to have so thoroughly jumped in without a single bit of verified background. And that wasn't even factoring in the video and the dead nanny.

"So who is she?" Noah wondered again, this time aloud.

He opened his eyes and took another sip of coffee before turning his attention to the computer again. He was relieved to see that the stall had stopped, and a slew of articles were now on display. Unsurprisingly, nearly every one of them had to do with Trey and his business. More than a few related to the man's old criminal charges, too. Nothing mentioned Elle.

Noah scrolled down the list, searching. No headlines jumped out, but when he clicked over to the third page of articles, something other than words snapped up his attention. It was a photograph. Trey stood in the foreground, one hand at his temple while he seemed to squint into the distance. In the background was a line of people. Their black ensembles gave away the location—a graveside. None of that was what drew Noah in. The thing that made him look closer was the man who stood just to Trey's left. Not quite behind him, not quite right at his side. He wore a familiar blue uniform, and a small child in a puffy dress held his hand, and Noah knew the guy's face. It was Detective Stanley.

Curious and slightly uneasy, Noah clicked on the picture. The image filled the screen, and with it came a caption.

Funeral for famed adult film star Tawney O'Malley (stage name, Sassy Sammi) draws eclectic crowd. Shown here: Vancouver-based business mogul Trey Charger and Officer James Stanley.

Noah drew a breath. He read it again. O'Malley. No way was that a coincidence. His eyes dropped to the little girl in the picture. Blond hair. Downturned mouth. And he knew—unequivocally—it was her; the child was Elle. The photo was twenty years old, making her about six years old in the shot. The same age as her daughter was now.

"But what the hell does it mean?" he murmured.

How had she gone from holding hands with the cop to being dragged off in cuffs by him? How had her childhood led her into a relationship with a man who was at least twenty-five years her senior? The answers that floated just under the surface were chilling.

His gaze hung on the photo for several more seconds, as though he might be able to will it into giving him a proper explanation. Of course, nothing changed. No magical article appeared below, and the caption remained the only bit of insight into the truth behind the picture.

"Okay then," Noah said with a sigh. "Let's see what else I can find out. Like maybe an idea about where he'd take them."

Shaking his head in frustration, he typed a new phrase into the search bar. "Properties owned by Trey Charger and subsidiary companies." His slammed his finger to the enter key, then let out a groan. The search was clearly too broad, the results were far too numerous, and even if he could be sure which listings were current, there was no way to figure out where the man might've gone with Elle and Katie.

"Think, Loblaw," he grumbled to himself. "What're the options to narrow this down?"

He drummed his fingers on the edge of the keyboard and thought about calling Norah again. Maybe she'd have insight into where a man like Trey Charger would take his two kidnap victims. After all, finding kids was her area of expertise. But before he could even pick up his phone again, the call was rendered unnecessary by Dr. McMillan, who knocked lightly on the door, then called out to Noah.

"Permission to enter?" he asked.

"What kind of person would I be if I kept the man who saved me out of his own office?" Noah swiveled the chair to face him, and he found the doctor's expression a mix of grim and apologetic. "What's wrong?"

"Just got an urgent page from our not-so-friendly mutual friend," the other man said. "He's up at his place near Wavers Lake, and he's requesting that I make a house call."

Wavers Lake. The spot where Trey was hiding out. *Wavers Hollow.* The town where Noah's sister was vacationing.

What were the chances that these two pieces of his life would intersect this way?

Noah met the doctor's eyes. If he'd been the sort of guy who believed that things were meant to be, then this moment would've proved it.

Chapter 18

Elle wasn't breathing hard. She hadn't had to exert her-self at all to get where she was now. But her lungs burned anyway, and she wanted to cry. She held it in. More than enough tears had been shed because of Trey over the twelve years she was forced to live with him after her mother had died. She didn't owe him a single drop more. She just clutched Katie's shoe a little tighter, loathing the fact that she was going to have to let it go soon and laugh-ing without humor at the misplaced sentimentality, and pressed on.

So far, her slightly haphazard plan was working. She'd left the bedroom door open. Abandoned Detective Stan-ley in the hall. Sneaked past the small group of men play-ing cards in the living room. Made her way to the kitchen and its adjacent sunroom. There, she'd pushed open the door, and stepped into the musky early-morning air. She'd paused long enough to very carefully deposit Katie's hair tie—bright red and strung with three heart-shaped beads—in the center of the concrete pad at the bottom of the steps, then carefully evaded the man smoking in the Jeep and worked her way toward the detective's car.

Except now that she stood there—exactly where she'd intended to get—she was having the hardest time making herself take the next step. The edges of Katie's shoe dug into her palm. Her feet dug into the ground. And her heart had already dug itself into the house behind her, simply because that's where Katie waited. Elle had to fight to keep from getting buried altogether.

Slowly, she uncurled her fingers. Even more slowly, she moved her feet and faced the car. With shaking hands, she drew the stolen keys from her pocket, jammed them into the lock and manually opened it. She set the gun in the console and dropped Katie's shoe just outside the door. Then, with no regard for the attention she might draw, she turned over the ignition. That they would follow her was inevitable. In fact, it was what she wanted. She just had to make sure they did it exactly the way she wanted them to.

Calculating that it would take about a minute or less for someone to come out when they heard the noise, she stepped on the gas, making the tires spin hard in the mud. Then, figuring it would take more than a minute for someone to connect the dots, she slowed to just above coasting speed, and made her way down the driveway. Maybe the guy in the Jeep would pursue right away. Maybe he would get out of his vehicle and see what the commotion was first. Either way, Elle wanted to make sure they knew which direction she was headed. So at the fork at the end of the driveway, she paused. She counted in a painfully slow way up to fifteen—she didn't dare go any longer than that—and then she hit the gas pedal with near-to-maximum force while winding the steering wheel to the right at the same time. The tires kicked up a second splash of mucky dirt, and the car skidded out into the road.

Elle exhaled. She glanced in the rearview mirror once, then focused on the winding road in front of her. The twists and turns were enough to require most of her attention. But she also kept one ear cocked, waiting for a sign that Trey's men were doing as she wanted.

"Come on, 'bad guys,'" she murmured. "Do your thing."

And just a minute or two later, she finally heard the rev of an engine. It was in the distance behind her, but the calmness of the post-storm, early-dawn air let it carry clearly to her ears. They were coming. And Elle didn't know if she was relieved or just even more petrified. Doubt pricked at her.

What if this doesn't work? her subconscious nagged. *What if you can't get back to Katie in time? What if Trey figures out that it's all a ploy?*

Her hands tightened on the wheel. She couldn't afford to give in now. She concentrated on the drive, and after just another few seconds, she spied the first landmark through the front windshield. It was an old-fashioned mailbox painted to look like a cow that belonged to the next cabin along the road, and it eased the pressure in Elle's chest just enough. She'd made it a third of the way to her planned turnoff. Her foot pressed down harder, and her eyes dropped to the speedometer. She accelerated until the numbers hovered right above the speed limit, where she wanted it. Not fast enough to draw attention from any possible onlookers, not slow enough that Trey's men would immediately catch up. Yes, there was a great possibility that her pursuers would come in at a higher speed. But they wouldn't let themselves come under suspicion, either. Incautious men didn't last long around Trey.

Reassuring herself with that dark-edged thought, Elle

concentrated on the windshield once again. She was surprised—and relieved—to see that the sun had come up enough that the next anticipated feature was already in view. This one was a beat-up, rusted-out truck that had been hoisted onto stilts. There was a sign beneath the display, too. And even though it was illegible now, Elle knew that at some point it had announced the location of Bill's Brake and Muffler, a homebased garage business set back on the property. And the pressure in her chest eased further as she drove past it. She had to force her foot not to drop all the way to the floor in anticipation.

One more driveway. Just one more.

But as she approached another bend in the road, she was forced to speed up. Because the sound of a surging engine climbed through the air yet again. And this time it was far too close.

Instinctively, Elle slammed her shoe to the pedal and held on tightly as she spun the wheel and took the corner far too fast. But as firm as her grip was, it wasn't quite enough. The car fishtailed. Then it shuddered, and she could feel the passenger side wheels lift under her body. Her shoulder smashed into the door. Her head cracked against the window. And her heart didn't just jump into her throat; it lodged itself between her uvula and tongue, and it cut off her ability to draw breath. But the car didn't care how scared she was, or how many stars appeared behind her eyes. It just continued its wild, shuddering, two-tired bounce. And still she couldn't breathe.

The world went from star-speckled unpleasantness to near darkness. The road disappeared in a murky blur, and Elle braced for impact. For a flip. For the dark to become utter blackness instead. She closed her eyes in anticipation, letting a vision of Katie fill her mind, praying that somehow, someway, the little girl would be saved. A miracle. That's what she needed. And she was so busy waiting for it, that she almost didn't notice when it happened.

One second, centrifugal force pressed her to the door. The next she felt like she was in freefall. Then she clued in. The freefall was just a release. The pressure was gone. The block in her throat was gone, and the car was still. Too still.

Her eyes opened. Sight and air rushed in together. The car had finished its careening, her foot was on the brake and the sky was a blaze of red, yellow and orange. Momentarily stunned, Elle blinked. And the rapid flutter cleared her vision. Just ahead was the marker she was looking for—a white picket fence with a yellow gate. But she didn't have time to stop and feel relief. The pursuing engine was even closer now, the audible RPMs approaching with the ferocity of a fire-breathing dragon.

Shaking off the last of her daze and the encroaching, full-body stiffness that came alongside her adrenaline, Elle took hold of the wheel once more. And again, she pushed her sole down to the gas pedal. But the car stuttered. Once. Twice. And it cut out.

Elle's fear hollered a warning in her head, and it was even louder than her pursuer's vehicle.

"Please," she said under her breath. "Not now."

She flicked the ignition off. She said a three-second prayer. The she turned the key again and gave the gas another tap. And after another brief protest, the vehicle lurched forward.

"Thank God," she murmured.

Not daring to gun it again, Elle kept her approach steady. It was an achingly slow approach. But after an hour-long forty-five seconds, she finally reached the fence. The gate was open, as it usually was, and Elle guided the car through it, then down the slight slope of the driveway. Now at a crawl, she eased her way past the tiny farmhouse, then around behind the dilapidated barn. She barely had time to turn the car off before the noise of the fast-moving engine shook the air.

Elle held her breath.

She waited.

She wondered what she would do if it turned her way and followed.

She begged the universe not to let that happen.

The sound spiraled higher, then came to a crescendo.

And it passed.

Elle's entire body sagged with relief, and she closed her eyes for just a moment, letting the relief reign. But under that, more than a hint of doubt slipped in. What if the owner of this place had sold? Or passed? What if whoever lived there now simply called the police, and what if that call brought in Detective Stanley's very unimpressed cohorts?

And why didn't I consider any of that before?

But when Elle opened her eyes again, it was a familiar figure who filled her vision. He looked to be about a hundred years old as he hobbled toward her. But then again, he'd looked that way all those years ago, too. A straggly gray ponytail hung down to his shoulders, and his wizened frame seemed dependent on the cane in his hand. But his gaze was sharp. Just as it had been when Elle last stumbled onto his property, needing a place to hide while Trey went on a quiet rampage trying to find her. As she swung the door open and climbed out, tears of remembered gratitude pricked at her eyes. And if she hadn't had to grip the door to keep from stumbling, and her legs hadn't burned like she'd just run a marathon rather than taken a ten-minute drive, she might've launched herself at the man in spite of his frailness.

Instead, she had to settle for an emotion-laden greeting. "Hi, Mr. Quincy. It's good to see you again."

He eyed her up and down. "Mirabella. I could never decide if that son-of-a-you-know-what had actually killed you, or if you'd just gotten away with faking your own death."

A quavering laugh cut through Elle's tears. "Well. As you can see…"

"Indeed. You're not dead at all." The old man paused. "He had a funeral for you, you know."

Her heart squeezed unpleasantly. "I know."

"I went."

"Thank you."

"Don't mention it."

Elle wanted to laugh again—how bizarre was it to thank someone for attending your phony funeral? But the amusement was overridden by the way Mr. Quincy's attention was roaming over her appearance again.

"Take it that he's caught up to that fact that you're alive?" he asked, his voice roughened with more than age.

"He never believed I wasn't," she admitted.

"He really is a son-of-you-know-what, isn't he?"

"Yes."

"So, then. You here to get your room back? Gonna give me another speech about how helping you is gonna endanger my life, or are you gonna get straight to telling me what you need?"

Elle swallowed as her fear rose to the surface again, and she forced a lighter tone. "I guess that depends. Do you *remember* my speech from a decade ago?"

Clearly not buying the pretended breeziness of her tone, the old man lifted a craggy eyebrow. "A decade ago, Mirabella? According to my calendar, it was only eight years, one month, and two days ago."

Guessing she had her answer about his ability to recall details, Elle nodded. "I don't need anywhere to hide today, Mr. Quincy. I was just wondering if you still have the dirt bike that belonged to your granddaughter. The one with the special muffler you put on so as not to annoy the neighbors."

If the question surprised the well-wrinkled man, he didn't show it. "Yup. Keep it maintained, just in case, too. But as I remember it, you only spent time on it that one summer. When you fell off and banged up your knee, you were too afraid of what would happen if Trey found out."

Elle nodded. "That's right. But it was exhilarating. I felt freer on that bike than I had in years. So one of the first things I did when I escaped was to learn to ride properly."

"You gonna bring it back?"

"I hope so."

Without asking any other questions, he shifted his cane a little, then held out his hand. "All right. Give me the keys to your car. I can find a place to ditch it, or I can hold on to it until you want it back. And you can help yourself to the bike. It's in the barn, like always."

Wincing, Elle didn't drop the keys into his outstretched palm right away. "I should probably tell you that this car belongs to a police detective."

Mr. Quincy didn't flinch. "Dump it in the lake, then?"

She exhaled. "I might need it later."

"Or I could give you a ride wherever you need to be. Got a well-covered truck bed, and a whole lot of time on my hands."

"I don't know what to say."

He shrugged. "Say, 'Sure, Mr. Quincy. That's a lovely idea.'"

Now Elle did laugh, even if it was a little tremulous. "Sure, Mr. Quincy. That's a lovely idea."

He gave her a wink, and she handed over the keys. Or she started to, anyway. Because the old man closed his fingers on her with surprising strength, then held on for a moment as he spoke again.

"I've thought about you a lot over the last eight years," he said. "Wondered if there was more I could've done. Felt guilty in the moments where I believed he'd killed you. Woke me in the night more than a few times, and I'm unreasonably glad to know that you made it out. So do me a dang favor, and try to stay safe."

Elle's throat scratched, and she had to clear it before she could answer. "I will. I promise."

He smiled, opened his fist and—with no hint of being patronizing—replied, "Good girl. Now go. Don't want me to keel over before I get rid of this dang thing, do you?"

She shook her head, offered him a final look of gratitude, then turned to make her way toward the barn. Once inside, she didn't waste time with nostalgia. As the flood of emotional memories from that one summer rushed in, Elle shook them off in favor of the more concrete ones. Through those, she located the ring where the key hung, and the shelf that housed a protective jacket. She stuffed the former into the dusty pocket of the latter, then shook the debris off the leather as best she could, and slid her arms into the fabric. Unfortunately, the spot where the extra jeans were kept was empty, and so was the cubby that used to house the boots. But the most important piece of equipment—the helmet—was hanging from the bike itself, as always. It was also polished clean. Like it'd been waiting for her. Elle directed another, thankful thought toward the old man as she slid the cool plastic over her head and buckled up the strap at her chin.

Satisfied that she was as ready as she could be, she rolled the bike out to the gravel patch beside the barn. Both the stolen car and Mr. Quincy were gone, and Elle had to forcefully push aside a renewed stab of guilt-tinged worry. The old man was a war vet, a retired reform school teacher, and he had some high-level martial arts training, too. He'd told her all of that the first time she'd tried to refuse his help. And while he was well past his prime, Elle knew that if anyone was capable of knowing his own limits, it was him. She swung a leg over the bike, eyed the empty space where he'd been a final time, then refocused her attention.

As she turned the key in the ignition, she fully expected some kind of protest from the machine. But she was pleasantly wrong. The engine came to life with a purr, the custom-made muffler keeping the decibels to a very tolerable level. The seat rumbled a little under her body, and she recalled the sheer terror she'd felt the first time she'd climbed on all those years ago. Would she fall off? Break her neck? Embarrass herself? But surprisingly, none of that had happened. And the way that had bolstered her confidence had been nothing short of remarkable. What she'd told Mr. Quincy was true; it had been her first taste of freedom since the moment she'd been forced to move in with Trey. Now that came rushing back, too. The speed. The power. It was soothing. And when Elle pushed to a slightly wobbly start, her hope buoyed once more.

Chapter 19

As the taillights of Dr. McMillan's high-priced sedan winked out of sight, Noah wondered if he was doing the right thing. He could've chosen to go with the doctor. The other man had offered to take him along, even at risk to himself. On top of that, Noah was ninety-nine point nine percent sure that the house call would lead him straight to Trey Charger. Possibly directly to Elle and her daughter as well. And there was a large part of Noah that simply wanted to take the chance. In fact, over the course of the three-hour-long drive from Vancouver to Wavers Hollow, a fantasy about it had managed to take hold. He'd envisioned himself simply storming the metaphorical castle. Rushing in with sword brandished—or a pistol, as the case would have it—and with furious commands pouring from his mouth. In the white-knight version of himself, Noah reigned supreme. Trey Charger dropped to his knees. He handed over both Elle and Katie. And together, the three of them rode off into the sunset. On a randomly found horse. Obviously.

In reality, though, Noah knew that wasn't how things worked. The retrievals that worked best were the ones that were thought out. Carefully measured steps. Fail-safes. Option B, option C, and option D, too, just in case everything else went awry.

Action over emotion.

He hadn't used the mantra very much over the last day, but he knew he needed it now. As much as he itched to be back in contact with Elle—and yeah, to become her triumphant savior—he couldn't just go in with a reckless, unlikely-to-succeed move. He wanted confirmation of Elle's presence, but he sure as hell didn't trust himself to be able to hold back if she was on Trey's property. Which was why he'd solicited a promise from Dr. McMillan instead. The very second the other man knew for certain if Elle and Katie—or even either one of them—was present at Trey's summer house, he'd send a text. Then Noah could decide what to do. In the meantime, he would wait. He'd take a slightly slower, safer approach. One that would come closer to guaranteeing results. Except now that he was on the cusp, standing on the front walkway of a minuscule house on the edge of Wavers Hollow, he was second-guessing the choice.

He shifted from foot to foot and studied the cutesy blue shutters and the kitschy flower boxes under the windows. He examined the latticework that hung from the eaves and listened to the light melody of the chimes that were strung over the railing. There was no pretending that he'd come to the wrong place. Even if the cashier at the gas station hadn't given perfect, precise directions, there was no mistaking it.

The Gingerbread Cabin.

That was what Norah had said it was called, and the name was apt.

Noah sighed and scrubbed a hand over the back of his neck. He knew he needed to go up and knock. Enlisting some help from the best in the business made sense. The fact that the best just happened to be his sister was nothing but an added bonus. So why did it feel a little like the imaginary horse and the white knight scenario would've been a safer choice?

It wasn't that Norah wouldn't take him in or offer to help him. She would. In all likelihood, she'd be more than happy to do it. For bragging rights. But also because she loved him as much as he loved her. The problem was more complex than that. Despite their lighthearted banter on the phone, the years had been hard on their relationship. What he'd told Elle about it was true. The closeness he and Norah experienced as teens had suffered a deep break with the loss of their baby sister. The slowly rebuilt bond had been tenuous, and their parents' divorce had knocked it right over. Since then, most of what they shared was excuses. Reasons not to come to Easter dinner. Apologies and jokes about missing the birthday they shared. That wasn't to say they didn't keep in touch. They did. By phone. Text. Emails of funny cat videos. The lightness was comfortable. It was easy. Once he looked her in the eyes—a darker hazel than his own—it would be impossible to maintain that distance.

And you have so much time to think about this?

His conscience was right. He had to hurry. Lives depended on it.

He swiped his hand over his chin, then dragged his phone from his pocket and prepared to dial his sister's number again, this time to issue a far too belated warning. Before he could even get his passcode typed in, though, Norah's familiar voice carried to him from the tiny porch.

"Don't bother," she called. "I already tried calling the police, and they told me that my brother needing a haircut is not an emergency."

For a long moment, he just stared at her. Her hair was a shade deeper than his, just like her eyes were that little bit darker. She was shorter, or course, than his six-foot-four-inch self. Her head still topped close to five-eleven, though—a reasonably impressive height for a woman. Looking at her wasn't like looking in a mirror. It was something else entirely. Something that stripped away the years of separation and falsely casual conversation and left Noah raw. Maybe because over the last day, Elle had reminded him that there were more emotions than fierce anger and heart-searing sadness. Maybe because he felt like for the first time in forever, he could have another chance at life. He couldn't say with certainty what the reason was, but without thinking about it any more, he stepped forward and slammed Norah into the biggest, best brother-style hug he had to offer. And though she exhaled a squeak, she didn't fight him off like she always had when they were kids. Instead, her arms tightened, too, and she spoke into his shoulder.

"I never blamed you," she said, her voice breaking.

Noah gave her one more squeeze before he let her go.

"I know," he replied, and he meant it.

It was strange. The way the all-over pressure on his body eased up. He'd told himself the same thing over the years. It wasn't his fault. His sister didn't hold him accountable. No one did. He'd been a kid. They'd both been kids. Yet the underlying doubt had always been there.

But now...

It seemed to have dissolved completely.

Norah smiled, and she swept her hand toward the house.

"Come on in, little brother. I've got some stuff you're going to want to see."

He didn't bother to ask what it was, or to wonder how she knew he'd turn up on her doorstep. He didn't even notice the oddity of it. It was just the way things were with them. Which was why it didn't surprise him, either, when his sister led him inside, then straight to the couch and coffee table, where her laptop sat waiting.

"Sorry," she said as she sat down and indicated for him to do the same. "No room for a home office in this place."

"Roughing it, huh?" teased Noah.

"A girl's gotta do what she's gotta do to get some peace," his sister told him.

Concern flooded in. "Is everything okay with you?"

"Working too hard. Not sleeping too well. You know how it—" She cut herself off with a headshake. "You're not here to listen to me whine."

"I don't mind, Norah. You know that."

She sighed. "I do. I *do* know that. But I want to help you right now, Noah. We'll worry about me once you and your dream girl have settled down and made some babies, okay?"

He should've brushed off the idea as ridiculous. Even if he did believe that the hours he and Elle had shared were the beginnings of something that could last a lifetime, it was unreasonable to be thinking about whether or not their children would have her eyes. Yet the vision was there all the same. Maybe twins, like him and his sister. A boy and a girl. Noah couldn't deny that he liked the thought. And Norah was right about the other part, too. He had come for her help—urgently—so he'd take what was offered, and if she was burnt out and didn't want to talk about it then, he could respect that at the same time.

"All right," he said. "Show me what you've got."

She nodded, then swiped a finger over the laptop's mouse. The screen lit up, and Noah saw that she had multiple windows open, each one shrunk down so that the contents could be viewed side by side. He saw, also, that she'd started her search the same way he had—by typing in the question, "Who is Elle Charger?" Her results were similar to his, too. The digital breadcrumbs had led her to Sassy Sammi—aka Tawney O'Malley—and that particular wormhole had yielded his sister a flashing "safe search" warning. It might've made him chuckle if a photo under the warning hadn't distracted him from his own amusement. It looked so much like Elle that his heart stuttered.

"What's this?" he asked, tapping the window.

Norah swiftly enlarged it. "What do you think it is?"

"It looks like Elle. But it's not her." His eyes flicked over the image.

The woman had the same full lips. The same lush blond hair. Her demeanor, though, was nothing like Elle's at all. Her smile was coy—like she knew a secret—and her pose was deliberately provocative.

His sister's reply was gentle. "It looks like her because she's your dream girl's mother."

Startled, Noah jerked his attention up from the picture. "What?"

"Don't freak out. Just read the article."

With an abruptly dry mouth, Noah did as he was told.

"A Brief Biography of Sassy Sammi."

Below the self-explanatory heading was an easy-to-follow outline of Tawney's life. Her birthdate and place. Her three marriages and three divorces. Her sudden death at age twenty-four. And her only child. Mirabella O'Malley. The moment he saw the entry, Noah knew his sister was right. *Elle.* How could it be anyone but her? And if he had any doubt at all—if he thought for even a moment that the resemblance was an insane coincidence—the second photograph at the bottom of the page washed it away. It was the woman who looked like Elle again. Only in this shot, she held hands with a little blond girl. The same little blond girl from the digital newspaper clipping that Noah had found about Tawney O'Malley's funeral. It was troubling, even if he didn't fully grasp the implication of the puzzle piece.

He brought his gaze to his sister once more. "What else?"

She reached across to tap on the keyboard, then swung it in Noah's direction. "This."

A new window was on display, this one showcasing a website called VanCity Secondary High School: Online Reunions.

"Scroll through the list of names," Norah suggested.

With a graduating class of only thirty-six in the year in question, it was easy to immediately spot what it was that his sister wanted him to see. Tawney O'Malley, James Stanley and Trey Charger had been classmates. As Noah clicked through some of the candid shots, it was easy to see that the trio had been close. It answered the question of connection, but it also raised even more questions.

Seeming to read his mind, Norah spoke up again. "I went a step farther, and I pulled some digital strings to see if there was any old dirt on the three of them. There was the usual stuff that troubled teens get into. A drunk-and-disorderly and intoxication-of-a-minor charges for Tawney. A vandalism thing for James. And Trey stole a few hundred bucks from the student council."

"The records weren't expunged because they were minors?" Noah asked.

His sister shook her head. "Not automatically. And I don't think Trey or Tawney cared. They did a few dumb things later on, too. James tried to have his record erased, but when he applied to become a cop, it became public again. I didn't look into how. But either way, the small stuff isn't what matters. What counts is this…"

She clicked again, and a police report popped up. Noah raised an eyebrow, and the corner of his sister's mouth tipped up.

"Don't ask," she said. "Just look."

With a little headshake, he turned his attention to the report, which he read over quickly. The officer who'd taken the notes described an incident that happened on the side of a mountain. A camping trip gone wrong. Trey, Tawney and James had headed out right after their grad party on a Friday night, then been found the following Monday. A single photo accompanied the write-up, and it spoke volumes. The three teenagers stood a few feet from each other, with a red-clad rescue crew all around them. Tawney's face was pointed down, her shoulders hunched up under an emergency blanket. James had his arms crossed over his chest. His expression was just shy of furious. Trey, on the other hand, was smug. He was the only one looking at the camera, and a ghost of a smile covered his face in a way that made Noah's fist ball up.

What had happened up there, over those three days? he wondered.

"I think it was the turning point for all three of them," Norah said, answering his unasked question. "And whatever it was…they went their separate ways after it was over. Go back to the grad page and have a look at the 'Then and Now' tab."

Noah clicked from one window to the other, and he saw that his sister was right. It was impossible to say for

sure that the nights in question had been their last ones together, but the three friends had clearly gone in different
directions. James Stanley shifted to the right side of the
law, joining the police academy when he was twenty. Trey
attended business school straight after graduation, and he
finished a four-year program almost eighteen months early.
Tawney slipped off the radar for about a year, then reap-
peared under her pseudonym, gaining a little bit of notori-
ety from a small scandal involving a local politician. Their
careers and lives were completely distinct, and Noah suspected that further research wouldn't bring in any more
overlap. Not until Tawney's death and the photograph at
her funeral, anyway.

Feeling unsettled, Noah started to close the tab. Before
he could click, though, yet another picture snapped up his
attention—mostly because it was such a sharp contrast to
the one attached to the police report. This one was a year-
book candid, and it took only a moment for the truth to
hit him. To smack him in the face, really. He stared down
at the shot of the three of them, realization rolling over
him like a boulder. In the picture, James stood to the side,
middle finger raised, but blurred out. Trey was looking
straight ahead, that same, cocky smile on his face, and
somehow—even though he was just a kid and even though
his lips were turned up—his calculating nature was written all over him. It was Tawney, though, who gave it all
away. Her eyes weren't on the camera; they were on Trey.

To say her expression was one of adoration would've
been an understatement. Tawney O'Malley had clearly
been desperately in love with Charger. Whether or not it
was reciprocated was practically irrelevant, because there
was also one more, little factor that changed everything.
That answered everything. The way Tawney's hand rested
on her abdomen. The way her fingers splayed out protec-

tively. The tiny bump that no one would've thought to look for unless they had baby on the brain. For Noah, though, the conclusion popped up right way.

Tawney was pregnant with Trey's baby twenty-five years ago. And that baby became Mirabella. It—she—became Elle.

For a long second, all he could do was gawk at the picture, absorbing the reality it offered. Trey Charger wasn't Elle's abusive ex. He was her abusive father. *She* was the little girl who'd been locked in the closet in that illustrative story. That fact meant something else, too. A hugely important detail. Katie wasn't Elle's daughter. She was her sister. And Elle had been trying to save her from whatever horror she'd had to endure herself.

"Damn," Noah whispered. "Damn, damn, *damn*."

He needed to get to her. To them. He looked up at Norah, mentally cursing himself for not letting the white knight fantasy take over. He had to rush in. He had to save her. Save them both. Waiting for the doctor's word be damned. Except as he started to push to his feet, his phone chimed with an incoming message. When he yanked the device from his pocket, his blood turned to ice. The message from Dr. McMillan was the one they'd prearranged.

The tests came back positive.

It meant that the other man had evidence that Elle and Katie—both, because of the plural—were at Trey's house near Wavers Lake. That wasn't the issue. The problem was the words that followed.

Unfortunately, it looks like the specialist wants to do a full removal.

It wasn't a part of the code, but it didn't take any kind of genius to figure out what it meant.

Noah slammed his body back from the table hard enough to knock over the laptop and shot a desperate look in his sister's direction as he stood.

"Tell me you have a car here," he said, not disguising his desperation at all.

But his plea was unnecessary. Norah already had the keys in her hand.

Chapter 20

Elle's movement through the woods wasn't quick, and at first, it wasn't very steady, either. If anything, it was slow and rocky. Her riding skills were rusty, and aside from the initial burst of freedom, all she felt was sure that she was about to go flying off. The path that ran from Mr. Quincy's house, all the way along the edge of his property, then into the woods was overgrown to the point of barely being distinguishable from the low-lying foliage and loose dirt. Every bump jarred Elle, every kicked-up rock made her cringe. One particular divot made her bite her tongue hard enough to taste blood. But the farther she went, the surer she got.

After a few minutes, she started to believe there was a chance that she wouldn't fall. After a few more, she stopped looking down to check her speed on the aftermarket speedometer. Another few minutes after that, her palms were drier, and her breathing came easier. And by the time the path ended, she was at last traveling at more than a crawl. She wasn't quite able to ignore the thickening trees, but she was able to guide the dirt bike through the woods and down to Wavers Creek, where she paused to reorient herself.

Through the helmet's shield, she eyed the rain-heavy water. It flowed thicker than she'd ever seen it, its ripples heading eastward toward the lake. It looked dangerous and foreboding. Unlike the summer that she'd snuck off to meet with Mr. Quincy's granddaughter, when it had been nothing more than a trickle. She and the other girl had climbed down the embankment to dip their feet in. Lying on the pebbled edge, they'd talked about building a raft, climbing on and sailing down to Wavers Lake without ever opening their eyes. For Elle, it had been a real wish. And at the time, she'd wondered if the other girl really understood that.

No time for nostalgia, she reminded herself. *You don't want Katie to be wishing she could float away on a raft, too.*

With a final glance at the creek, Elle revved the bike up again, and she kept going. For the next few miles, the bike sailed smoothly over the dirt. She traveled east—the opposite direction of flow of the water—and kept going all the way to the footbridge that led over a particularly narrow part of the stream. There, she had to dismount and pull the machine across to the other side manually, but that was fine with her, and the bike started up again with no problem. She let the bike pick up some actual speed for a short while after that, and the trees whipped by in flashes of green and brown. The sense of freedom slipped back in, and it wasn't until the foliage thinned out again that Elle slowed, then came to a halt and cut the engine. When she pulled off her helmet and lifted her gaze, she could just catch the peaked roof of Trey's cabin over the line of shrubs surrounding his yard.

Almost there.

Despite the fact that she was sure she was too far away to have been either seen or heard, Elle took a moment to listen for sounds of an alert. She held her breath and ignored the nervous beat of her heart. But the only noises were the odd chirp of a bird, and the breeze rustling the branches overhead. She moved with caution anyway. Crouching low, she used varying objects for cover. She slunk from the trees to an enormous rotted-out stump. She did an awkward jog from the stump to a clump of salmonberry bushes. From there, she darted to a chopped woodpile, then to the woodshed itself. Next, she made a bold run to the manicured shrubs nearer to the house, and she pressed herself into their thick cover. She took a moment to catch her breath, then squeezed between the cedar-scented branches, took three steps, and pressed her body to the six-foot privacy fence. On her tiptoes, she peeked through the lattice at the top. When she found the area clear, she moved again—this time to inch along with painstaking slowness. At last, she reached the gate that would lead to the rear of the yard. She knew her new position placed her just two dozen feet from the back door. If she craned her neck, she'd even be able to see the bedroom window. And Katie was in there waiting.

Using that thought to propel herself to take the final steps, Elle lifted a hand and flicked open the gate. She took a breath and moved through. And just about tripped straight into a man who crouched right below the gate. He was on his knees. He held a weapon in his hands. And it was aimed at her chest. But that wasn't the worst part. What made the fact that she'd been duped far more terrifying was the familiar, falsely sweet voice that called out to her.

"Oh, Mirabella," said Trey. "Did you really think it would be so easy?"

Slowly—so, so slowly—Elle made herself turn toward him. He stood just inside the door frame that led from the porch into the house. The sight of him tried to bring in a thousand bad memories. But Elle had had nearly a decade to fight them. To cope with them. To live with them. To overcome them. And it was startlingly easy to sidestep them now, in favor of assessing the concrete details.

As always, Trey's hair was perfectly in place. Maybe he had an extra line or two around his eyes, but otherwise, he was nearly the same as Elle remembered. He wore a carefully tailored suit, immaculate shoes and an oversized watch. When she was a kid, Elle had thought of his manner of dressing as his uniform. Later on, as a teenager, she'd speculated—only to herself, of course—that the outfit was designed to tell people exactly what Trey Charger could afford. She hadn't liked it then. And it filled her with loathing now, too.

But there was an important new detail that overshadowed the old ones. The fact that Trey looked smaller than Elle had always thought. Narrower shoulders. Not much taller than she was herself, really. And for a second, she actually wondered what she'd ever found so intimidating about him. When he spoke again, though, she recognized that what mattered wasn't so much the control he'd had over her in the past; it was what he could do to her now.

"This is an interesting little turn of events," he said, pulling out Katie's shoe from his pocket, then tossing it from hand to hand. "Where is she?"

Elle watched the shoe. He was practically a caricature. Still just a picture of how he wanted others to see him.

Rich. Dangerous. Deadly. But there was nothing amusing about his display at all.

Elle yanked her eyes to his face and spat out a one-word lie. "Gone."

He cocked his head, still comical but not. "You went to an awful lot of trouble to leave here, and even more trouble to come back. And you expect me to believe that my daughter is just gone? Wherever Katie is, she'll want you. Sooner rather than later, I think."

Elle pressed her lips together. Because what he said was truer than he could know. How long would Katie stay in the closet? How long could she stay there? And how much time would Elle allow to go by before she had to give in and tell him the truth?

She breathed out and made herself maintain an even tone. "I had another, perfectly good reason for coming back."

"What could possibly be more important than escaping from me?"

"Just one thing. Killing you." As she said it, she yanked the stolen gun from the back of her waistband and took clumsy aim.

She knew she wouldn't have time to fire accurately. But she also knew that Trey wouldn't let his lackeys shoot her with deadly force. Because if that had been his aim, she'd be lying on the ground already. All she needed was enough chaos that she could flee once more, then give herself enough time to come up with a new plan to save Katie. Taking the shot was worth it, and it might be her only opportunity to escape. So she squeezed the trigger and hoped for the best.

The crack echoed through the air. Trey dived sideways. His armed guard—the one who'd trained his weapon on Elle to start with—came leaping forward, and two more men exploded out the backdoor. But aside from taking a moment to appreciate the look of shock and fear on Trey's face, Elle didn't pause. She fled.

Her feet tore over the grass as she ran toward the side of the house. She slammed though the spring-loaded gate that led to the front, ignoring the way the wood panels drove splinters into her forearm. Her mind was on Katie. On whether or not the little girl had been frightened by the commotion. On whether or not she would stay put as instructed. Briefly—for no more than a flash—Elle considered changing her path and heading back into the house. As quickly as the wishful thought came, though, it also retreated. She wanted Katie in her arms. But trying to carry her to safety was a ridiculous notion. And even if she'd been strong enough, the option itself was far-fetched. Trey's men would recover from their surprise quickly, and Elle wouldn't even have time to get up to the bedroom before getting captured all over again. She could already hear their shouts and the pounds of their feet as they began their chase.

You need Noah.

The thought almost made her falter. But as she veered from the driveway back toward the woods and the dirt bike, she couldn't help but wonder why in God's name she'd sent him away. The one man who would undoubtedly have helped her. A man who wanted to help her. Whom she could trust. Whom she felt connected to. Whom she cared about too much to let him sacrifice himself. And who she wished was there now, so badly that it hurt.

She pressed on in spite of the sudden burn of tears. She made it to the trees, and past. Her chest heaved with the exertion. Her muscles throbbed. Sweat slid down her forehead and into her eyes with a blinding sting. Despite that, in the end, her efforts weren't enough. She no sooner spied the handles of the dirt bike sticking out from the spot where she'd abandoned it than a bullet hit the ground just in front of her feet. Elle was certain the shooter wasn't aiming to kill. That didn't mean that logic could overrule her body's reaction to the shot. She leaped sideways to avoid it. She stumbled. She hit the ground, arms flailing uselessly as her chin smashed against the rough terrain. Stars sparkled behind her eyelids. And before she could recover enough to even get up to her knees, a rough hand landed on her shoulder and a knee pressed to her back, forcing her flat down. Then Trey's voice filled the air, making things impossibly worse.

"Get the hell off her," he ordered. "You guys have screwed this up enough times over the last six years. I'll take it from here."

For a moment, the physical pressure eased. But the reprieve was an illusion. And a short one, at that.

Trey roughly took hold of her elbow and yanked her up hard. The world spun, but Elle still tried to pull herself from his grasp. And his grip only tightened.

"You owe me a debt, Mirabella," he said coldly. "You forced me to go back on my word, and I'm tired of chasing you down. So you know what? We're going to take care of that issue right now. Then you can be someone else's problem."

She spat out a mouthful of dirt. "It's Elle."

He rolled his eyes, barked out a command to his men, then dragged her across the yard without heed for her dizziness, her stumbles or the occasional cry that left her mouth. He didn't pause until they'd reached the driveway. And there, he stopped only long enough to yell something else to his thugs—this time, a nonsensical order about finding a suit—and then he shoved her into the back seat of the car and slammed the door so quickly that she barely had time to slide into the seat.

Holding her undoubtedly bruised arms close to her body, Elle closed her eyes. She knew there was no point in trying to get out. This was Trey's personal vehicle. And past experience had taught her that he had police-issue locks—the kind that opened only from the outside—installed in every car he owned. She had to bide her time. Come up with some workable solution. But it was hard. Her head was fuzzy from her fall, and her body ached all over. She could feel desperation and hopelessness hovering on the periphery of her heart and her mind.

When the creak of the door announced that someone was climbing in, Elle opened her eyes just enough to see that one of the bodyguards had taken the driver's seat, while Trey himself buckled into the passenger seat. Both men were silent, as the oversized driver started the engine. Neither said a thing as they pulled a U-turn and headed down the driveway. The wordlessness gave Elle's mind too much space to wander. And it didn't go in the direction she would've liked. What was Trey thinking? Planning? Where was he taking her? What nefarious plot did he have in store? She knew what he'd wanted her to do—what he'd been going to force her to do—when she was eighteen. Yet he couldn't still be thinking of making his plot into reality, could he? Not after this long.

The quiet moments dragged into minutes, and the only sound was the crunch of the tires rolling over the road.

Elle fought a renewed round of tears. Every second pulled her farther away from Katie. She focused her attention out the window and tried to steer her brain to a more positive, more solution-oriented place. She'd escaped from Trey in the past. She'd rescued Katie right out from under him before, too. So there was still hope, even if it seemed far away right then.

Holding tight to that small bit of reassurance because it was really all she had, Elle started to make a mental list of any and every idea she could come up with. But she didn't get any further than imagining herself giving both men a simultaneous blackout-inducing crack on the head—somehow, anyhow—before the driver's voice interrupted her.

"Boss," he said, low and urgent. "We got a tail."

"A tail?" Trey repeated. "How in the hell did we—" He cut himself off. "Can you see who's driving the vehicle?"

"Not quite close enough. A blond, maybe?"

Trey turned around and flashed an icily furious look at Elle, "Your boyfriend's not too smart, is he? But I guess his brains don't matter anymore anyway. He's a dead man."

Noah.

Elle bit her lip but said nothing back. She didn't dare glance in the direction of whoever was following them, either. She was afraid he was right. And she was afraid he was wrong, too. Was it really him? Had he tracked her down? Put his life on the line and disregarded their last conversation?

After another second of silence, Trey spun back to his driver. "Bait him."

"Bait him, boss? You mean lose him?"

"No, you bag of rocks, bait him. Guide him somewhere off the main road, but make it look like you're trying to get away."

"You got it, boss."

The car jolted forward then picked up speed. The rhythmic roll of the tires became an urgent spin, and as much as she didn't want to react, Elle had little choice but to hold on. The vehicle whipped around corners. Scenery flashed

by faster than Elle could even note it. They tore past the
turnoff into the main part of town, and they kept going.
For a minute, they cut onto the highway. Then they made
a sharp exit onto a warren of bumpy side roads.

"Still on us," announced the driver after a particularly
sharp turn.

"Good," replied Trey.

The vehicle picked up speed once again, and the fuzziness in Elle's head amplified. The road was growing narrower, the trees thicker. Silently, she prayed that if it was
Noah following them, then he'd have enough sense to realize he was being duped. But she kept her eyes straight
ahead and refused to give in and look. And on they went.
Up a hill. Down another. Then Trey's driver made another quick turn, and quite abruptly, they were back on
the highway. Elle spied the sign that thanked visitors for
coming to Wavers Hollow right before the car veered off
the road, dipped down a short embankment and came to
a shuddering halt on a patch of gravel. They were well
shielded from the main road, and as the driver turned off
the engine, and the sound of an approaching vehicle carried on, Elle's heart thumped a frightened beat. Tension
rolled through the small space.

Her internal voice was all but sobbing. *Noah. What you
were thinking?*

But just a moment later, her worry changed to confusion.

"Boss," said the big man in the driver's seat. "It's not
him."

Now Elle did twist around for a look. And the driver
was right. It wasn't Noah, climbing out of a silver SUV. It
wasn't a man at all. It was a statuesque woman, dressed
in jeans and a T-shirt. Her blond hair was piled on her

head in a haphazard bun, and she had a slightly harried expression on her face. And for a second, Elle thought she knew the woman from somewhere. There was something familiar about her features. But Elle's vague recognition quickly took a back seat to the fact that the woman was hurrying toward them.

This isn't going to end well, Elle thought.

As if to confirm the thought, Trey swung another chilling stare in her direction. "One move. One flick of your eyes. If you do anything that makes her think you need help, I'll have Jake kill her on the spot." He brought his attention back to the driver. "Get out with me," he ordered. "And keep your gun handy in case Mirabella doesn't believe me."

Elle held her breath as the two men exited the vehicle. Even though she knew she probably shouldn't, because it might put the unknown woman at risk, she couldn't quite stop herself from watching the interaction. The blonde made it all the way to the car's rear bumper before Trey and his driver—Jake—intercepted her. And thankfully, Trey had left his door open just wide enough that Elle could hear everything being said.

The blonde let out a breathless laugh. "Oh, thank goodness. I was starting to think you were deliberately leading me on some wild chase!"

"No, ma'am," Trey replied, his voice dripping with false charm.

"Bit of vehicle trouble," Jake added. "Just trying to figure out what the problem is."

"Well, that makes a little more sense." The woman laughed again. "But speaking of problems…you guys totally dropped this back there. I think it fell off your roof."

Elle watched as the woman held out the small, black object in her hands.

"What is it?" the driver asked. "Some kind of purse?"

"An expensive one," the blonde agreed.

"I afraid you've wasted your time," Trey told her. "It's not ours."

The woman released a third laugh. "Well of course it's not yours, specifically. But I thought it might belong to the lady in your back seat?"

"Not hers, either," said Jake with a grunt.

"Don't you want to ask her?" the woman wondered aloud, sounding both perplexed and uncertain at the same time. "Because I'd really kick myself if I lost one like this. Not that I could afford it in the first place. But it's designer, so…she might want it back, if it is hers?"

As all three turned their attention to Elle, her body went so stiff that her aches and pains doubled. She willed the unknown woman to just accept that she'd made a mistake and drive off. Instead, she took a small step toward the car. And as she moved, Jake's fingers came up to his belt, undoubtedly reaching for his weapon.

Go away, Elle begged silently. *Please, please.*

But she didn't. In fact, Trey put a hand on her elbow and propelled her even closer, speaking as he did.

"You know what?" he said. "You're right. We probably should ask her."

Elle cringed as he took hold of the door handle and pulled it open. She waited for a shot to be fired. But Trey just smiled.

"Pardon my daughter's appearance," he stated. "She and her dirt bike don't get along all that well."

Elle clenched her teeth into a smile to stop herself from protesting against the familial label, and she forced what she hoped was a pleasant greeting. "Hi, there. Thanks for chasing us down, but it really isn't my purse."

For the briefest second—so quick it almost seemed

imaginary—deep concern flashed across the other woman's face. Then it was gone, and she smiled and bent forward.

"Wow!" she exclaimed. "You and that dirt bike really don't get along, do you?"

Elle swallowed, unable to add anything for fear of giving away the truth about her situation. But even if she *had* been able to form the words, she would've halted them in surprise a moment later anyway. Unexpectedly and with a swift and sure amount of stealth, the strange woman's hand slipped into the car, pressed something into Elle's hand, then dropped away again.

"All right," said the blonde. "Sorry to have gone all crazy on all of you. Guess I'll just put up a lost and found ad in the Wavers Hollow library, or something."

"No worries," Trey told her, all smoothness again. "Let me walk you back to the car."

Elle missed the specifics of the rest of whatever happened. She was vaguely aware that the woman pulled away unharmed, and she half heard Trey bark something at Jake. But everything else was lost. Because the object that Elle now clutched tightly to her thigh—out of sight—was a cell phone. And not only was the object a secret lifeline, it was also connected to a live call. One that flashed with the name Little Bro Noah across the screen.

Chapter 21

Noah pressed his phone to his ear, straining to hear Elle's voice. He was desperate for it. But the only sound that carried through was the staticky rub of something on the receiver. It crackled unpleasantly, making him grit his teeth. He still didn't pull the phone away. Instead, he tried to picture it—to picture where and how Elle held it. Had she shoved it into her pocket? Stuffed it down her shirt? Was she holding onto it for dear life, like Noah was holding his? His heart burned with the worry of it.

His position in the back of Norah's car—covered in a blanket, hidden against the floor where the seats had been removed—made him feel helpless. He didn't like it one bit. Of course, he'd been poised to react if things went south with phase one of their plan. Hell. A part of him had hoped the situation would take a turn for the worse. He wanted to act. Except he knew better than to jeopardize his sister's life, Elle's life and his own, too. It was the exact reason why he and Norah had come up with their plan in the first place.

Infiltrate the enemy. Take stock of their arsenal. Plant a tracking device. Create a viable retrieval.

It had seemed much more aggressive before Noah had been forced to hide out like a coward. So when he felt his sister's vehicle come to a rolling halt for the second time in five minutes, it took a great deal of self-restraint to keep from jumping out and demanding some answers. He forced himself to wait until Norah spoke, giving him the all clear. Then he tossed away the blanket, pushing himself to a sitting position, the questions rolling from his mouth.

"How'd she seem? How does she look?"

His sister's expression said it all.

He growled and violently swiped his too-long hair away from his face. "You couldn't just fake it for me?"

"Noah—"

Without waiting for her to finish, he forced open the rear gate of the SUV, then jumped out. He saw that Norah had pulled them into a highway rest stop, but the only reason he cared was because it gave him room to pace. His foot throbbed with each step, but the pain was cathartic.

What was I thinking? he demanded silently of himself. *Why didn't I go after her when I had the chance? Why do I feel like I keep making the same damn mistake at every turn, and why do I—*

His sister's voice—soft and concerned—cut off his angry mental rant as she said his name again. "Noah."

He stopped walking and turned to face her. "Yeah. I know. I'm being ridiculous. And we have to stick to the plan. We have to get on that stupid tablet of yours and see if we can figure out where they're headed. I know all that, too. I just…" He sighed and scrubbed at his stubble. "You were right. I care about Elle far more than is reasonable after knowing her for so short a time. I care about the kid, too, even though I've never met her."

"That doesn't seem ridiculous to me at all, little bro."

"So, please. Indulge me for five seconds, and tell me what you saw. Don't leave anything out."

His sister's reply was laced with reluctance. "She had a scrape on her chin, and a big bruise on her cheek. There was a small split in her lip. Her legs were bare, and they were too dirty for me to see if they were banged up or not, but I suspect they were."

Sickness roiled in his gut. "How many?"

"Just the two of them and Elle."

"So we could've just taken them out."

"No. There would've been too much risk to Elle."

"There are two of us and two of them," Noah pointed out. "Pretty good odds."

His sister shook her head. "I'm not an experienced fighter. I'm a mediocre shot at best, and I win most of my battles with words. On top of which, you're trying to ignore the fact that you got shot in the foot, but I saw the way you were limping just a second ago. And then you have to factor in the hostage element, Noah. It would've been far too risky."

His shoulders sagged, but the fury still broiled underneath. "I'm going to kill him. I swear to you, Norah."

"You're not going to kill him, Noah. You're going to save Elle and Katie, and you're going to make sure Trey Charger is behind bars for good." She put her hand on his elbow. "You're a good man, little bro. So you're going to do this the right way."

He sighed. "Do you always have to be right?"

She smiled. "As a matter of fact…"

"All right. Fine. No killing. Just three hundred years behind bars." He gestured to the SUV. "Show me the damn tablet and its magic."

"C'mon, then."

His sister led him back to the vehicle, this time letting him into the front seat rather than burying him in the back. Once they were both inside, she pulled the tablet from her oversized purse, tapped the screen a few times and pulled up a map. Immediately, a moving, flashing red dot appeared on top.

"Obviously, that's them," she said, then pointed a little lower down on the map. "And we're here." She moved her finger again, this time to press and hold down one corner of the screen until a small menu popped up. "These are the available options," she explained. "If you tap the distance button, it will bring up a green dot to show our position— the tablet's position, really—and an onscreen display of the kilometers between us." She demonstrated the tool, showing that they were now about five clicks from Elle, then moved on. "This other one here is the one we want, I think. What it does is provide a list of popular nearby locations. Like this." She tapped once more, and a series of dotted lines appeared between Trey's red marker and several highlighted spots on the map. "All you have to do is tap one of them, and it will tell you what it is. Try it."

Noah selected one at random, tapping the spot with his index finger, and a robotic voice came to life. "Wavers Hollow Community Center. Get directions?"

His sister swiped her thumb over the screen, and the prompt to accept disappeared. "All we have to do is watch their red dot for a few more minutes, and we should be able to figure out where they're headed."

"Unless they're making a run for China, or something," Noah muttered.

Norah rolled her eyes. "You're the one who pointed out that they must've come to Wavers Hollow for a reason."

He let out another frustrated sigh. "Yeah. I just wish I knew what it was. And I wish I didn't feel like it was something—"

"Hang on," his sister interrupted.

"What?"

"Look at the dot."

He turned his attention back to the screen. The blinking locator had abruptly switched direction, and it was no longer headed directly into town. For a second, Noah thought his sarcastic comment might actually have been true—maybe they were leaving Wavers Hollow. Then his sister spoke up, her tone puzzled.

"It looks like they're moving toward the private docks off Wavers Lake," she said. "But why would they go down there? The lake doesn't go anywhere. I mean…if they head out into the water, they'll just be giving life to the expression 'sitting ducks.'"

As soon she'd finished speaking, though, an image flashed into Noah's mind. It was something he'd seen as the doctor drove into Wavers Hollow. Something he'd barely noticed because it hadn't seemed at all relevant when he'd spied it. It was a sign. One that announced that Wavers Hollow and Wavers Lake were the proud provider of a unique wedding venue—a small island in the middle of the lake, complete with utilities, a chapel, amenities…everything required to make an already special day incredible. And with the recall of the sign came something else. A part of Elle's explanation of what kind of man Trey was. The kind who forced a girl to get married against her will.

The anger and frustration that pricked at Noah became a cold stab.

It was the perfect explanation for her sudden flight from

Trey Charger those eight years earlier. The pull of the lynchpin.

He had no idea whom Trey wanted her to marry, or how he planned to make her do it. But whatever it was, it could be nothing less than sinister.

"Noah!"

He jerked his attention to his sister. Her voice was urgent, and he had a feeling she'd said his name several times with no response. He didn't have time to ask or to apologize.

"We need to get down to those docks," he said grimly. "Now."

And thankfully, Norah didn't argue or even ask for an explanation. She just turned the key in the ignition and started to drive.

The nearer they got to the lake, the antsier Elle became. The increasing flickers of deep blue were too still. Too boundless. They didn't match the quick jump of her heart, and they didn't line up with her growing belief that she was nearing an ending of some sort. Whether it was literally her life, or just the life she knew, she wasn't sure. But either way, no serenity was coming her way. And it grew worse when they took the final turn and headed down toward the dock. Not because Elle knew the spot well enough to know it meant they were headed for Trey's private boat launch. And not even because the thought of being alone with the men, somewhere in the middle of the lake scared her. But because Trey dropped the first smug hint at what he had planned.

"What's your dress size, Elle?" he asked. "About a four?" His eyes met hers in the rearview mirror, and she didn't quite look away quickly enough before he spoke again, a smile exposing far too many teeth to look natural. "I guess it doesn't really matter. You won't have the dress on for long anyway."

Elle's heart didn't just drop. It slithered down the inside of her body, then sank through the floorboards. Her mind whipped unwillingly back to the day Trey had told her his plans. He'd started it by saying her time living off him was done. And even though the implication was that she was a freeloading sponge rather than his DNA-provable offspring—who would really rather have had anyone else as her father—Elle had still been a little excited. A little hopeful. Of course, it hadn't been that easy. Trey'd had no intention of letting her go anywhere. She owed him a debt. Years of food. Lodging. Clothes. All the things that a normal parent would give freely. But Elle had learned early on that Trey wasn't normal. So at the announcement that she would be paying her debt by marrying a man more than twice her age, she hadn't been surprised. Just scared. And certain that she wouldn't be able to escape that inevitable fate.

But things are different now, she reminded herself. *I did escape. And I've spent eight years not being powerless.*

Elle lifted her eyes to the rearview again, and she channeled some inner strength. "I won't do it."

"Won't you?" Trey's reply was infused with casual—almost indifferent—disbelief.

And a moment later, they rounded the final corner before they hit their destination, and Elle spied the reason for his tone. Just ahead, on the dock, stood a small group of people.

The gathering included two more of Trey's thugs, each of whom had his hand on his weapon.

It included a nervous-looking man whose eyes kept darting around like he was wishing he were anywhere else.

It included Detective Stanley, looking decidedly ill in spite of his fresh suit and bow tie.

And it included Katie, hair askew, face ashen and clad in a frilly pink dress about a size too big.

No!

"You have a choice here," Trey said, his voice low and dangerous. "You. Or her."

This time, Elle gasped the word aloud. "No!"

"I'm afraid it's all you've left me with," Trey told her. "I owe Jimmy. I've owed him for over twenty-six years. I promised him I'd make it up to him for taking Tawney from him. And what could be closer to the real thing than her daughter? But the truth is, I'm tired of feeling like I'm indebted. And I think Jimmy's a little cracked now, too. So he'll take the substitute, I think. Then we can finally close this chapter of our lives."

The car slowed, then came to an ominous-feeling stop.

"There are two white dresses in my trunk," Trey stated. "One is a ladies' size four. The other will fit Kaitlyn perfectly. It's up to you which one we use. Decide, Elle. Quickly."

But it wasn't really a decision at all, of course.

Chapter 22

Noah was about four seconds shy of sliding his injured foot across the floorboards of the SUV and slamming his borrowed boot into the gas pedal. He knew his sister was traveling as fast as she dared. As fast as wouldn't get them both killed. But—in spite of the fact that the lake flashed in and out of sight now—it still wasn't fast enough.

Go, go, go! he urged silently.

Instead, Norah braked. In response, a furious yell of protest and frustration nearly escaped Noah's throat. Then he clued in. They'd reached their destination. A short distance ahead, a luxury boat—a forty-footer, it looked like—was pulling away from a custom-built dock. Sitting in sight at the stern was a blond head, sticking out of a puffy white dress.

Elle.

"I have to get to her," Noah said under his breath, scanning the area for a means of doing it that didn't involve leaping into the water and swimming out.

Reading his mind as usual, his sister pointed to a small outbuilding that sat a few dozen feet away. "There," she said. "I'd bet your wrecked foot they keep some nonmotorized watercraft in there."

"I love it when you bet away my damaged appendages," Noah replied as he opened the door and hopped out, leaving Norah to scramble to catch up.

Truth be told, his foot really was starting to throb harder. He wasn't sure how much longer he'd be able to pretend it wasn't happening. Right then, though, he had no choice but to use the pain to motivate himself to move faster. He hurriedly limped to the building, paused at the door and glared down at the padlock that held it shut. He gave it a hard tug, but of course it didn't budge. His patience was at an all-time low. Not bothering to waste any time, he yanked his weapon from his side and started to take aim. His sister stopped him, though, before he could actually fire.

"Hang on," she said, touching his elbow.

"Not enthused about waiting," Noah muttered.

His sister lifted an eyebrow, pulled a pin from her hair and turned her attention to the lock. In fifteen seconds flat, she was clicking it open.

"Brains not bombs," she said, stepping back.

"Funny."

But he was already moving again. Sliding the wide doors open. Flicking on the light and scanning the fuel-scented space for an option. He found one right away in the form of a single-man, sit-on-top kayak. Norah had clearly spied it, too.

She pointed. "If you grab a pair of those goggles from the shelf, they'll have no idea it's you until you're right on top of them. If you can call chasing down a luxury boat with a kayak being 'right on top of them,' that is."

Noah nodded, hurrying yet again. He limped to the shelf in question and snagged a pair of goggles at random. He grabbed a life jacket, too, and slipped it on and fastened the zipper and clasps. Next, he turned to the kayak itself. It wasn't his first time using one, and he knew it was light enough for him to carry on his own, if a little awkwardly. He didn't protest, though, as he grabbed one end, and Norah grabbed the other. It was more about solidarity than assistance. Together, in unspoken agreement, they lifted it from its stand and carried the watercraft out of the building, away from the exposed dock, then down a side path. In under two minutes, they were beachside, and the kayak was bobbing halfway in, halfway out of the water.

"I'm going to try to find a way over to the island too," Norah said, giving him a quick squeeze.

Noah didn't bother to argue or even shake his head. There was no point. She'd do whatever she could to help him. He knew, because he'd do the same for her.

"Be safe," he said instead.

"Ditto," she replied.

He stole another little hug, then turned his attention to the task at hand. In moments, he was on the water, arms pumping in a steady rhythm. At first, he envisioned himself actually overtaking the luxury boat, like his sister had half-jokingly suggested. He quickly realized it wasn't just an overzealous idea; it was utterly unfeasible. His manpower couldn't come close to the thrust of the boat's engine. By the time Noah was halfway out on the lake, he could see that Trey and his crew were already nearing the island. He pushed on anyway, forming a new plan.

Cutting to the east, Noah guided the kayak out wide and well out of attention-grabbing distance. Soon, his arms ached with the effort, but he ignored the burn and pushed on. Still paddling hard and straight—as though he were headed anywhere but to the island—he pushed on for another minute or two. At last, when he'd brought himself to an angle that took Trey's boat out of view, he cut west again. His sharp turn brought the kayak to a rocky halt, and he let himself take a moment to recover from the energy-sucking ride.

Through the picturesque tree line, he could see the outline of the chapel. It was white and hung with twinkling lights that still shone brightly, even in the sun. It was a beautiful location. Noah fully understood the appeal of it. Right then, though, it made him taste bile.

Drawing a breath, he plunged the paddle into the water again. The bow parted the smooth surface of the lake, and the hull glided along with power and precision. Another couple of minutes of hard work brought him to the pebbled shore, and he guided the kayak along the edge to a small cove. There, he disembarked, stowed the boat and immediately began his hike in toward the chapel.

The going wasn't easy, and the farther in he got, the more his foot burned. Before long, the pain extended up to his calf. His pants were damp and chafed uncomfortably. Sweat—more from the fight against the pain than from exertion—slid down his forehead and stung his eyes. At one point, he tripped over an unseen rock and smacked his injured foot against a partially buried tree stump, and it took everything he had to keep from hollering every curse word he knew. By the time he'd pushed through the forested area to the edge of the cleared property, Noah was questioning his sanity. Why hadn't he taken a chance that someone at the local RCMP detachment would be untouched by Trey's taint? Why hadn't he let his sister call one of her out-of-town contacts? What had made him assume that coming alone was the best, most efficient method of rescuing Elle and Katie? The questions tumbled through his head on repeat. But when he finally reached a spot close enough to the chapel to stop to assess his surroundings, all of the questions—all of *everything*—slipped away.

Elle sat alone on a bench in the clearing just outside of the chapel. Her head was down, her eyes on the hands she had laced together in her lap. The wedding dress was a mess of lace and puffy fabric and Noah was one hundred percent sure she would never have chosen something so flamboyant on her own. But in spite of that, and despite her heartbreaking pose, too, her beauty was undeniable.

Noah wanted to go to her. To sweep her into his arms and put the dress to real use. He had a desperate need to tell her that he thought they should join their lives together right there, right then. That they could work backward. A quick marriage to a languorous courtship. It made utter sense in his head. The hours they'd spent apart had shown him that what he wanted most was more hours together.

As if she could feel the way Noah's thoughts were projecting, Elle lifted her eyes and looked right at the spot where he stood hidden. A voice in his head screamed at him to not move. It pointed out that it made no sense that she was alone, and it warned that exposing himself before he meant to could equal death for both of them. He took the tiniest step backward. He might've gone farther, too. Except he couldn't. A cold metal barrel pressed to his head and a voice he'd already committed to memory stopped him.

"Don't move unless I say to," ordered Trey Charger. "If you do anything other than what I told my guys would happen, then my man over near the chapel is authorized to shoot without warning."

On cue, a red dot appeared on Noah's hand, then slowly slid up his arm and came to rest on his chest. And he did as he was told.

* * *

It took Elle a long, slow-blink moment to clue in that she wasn't seeing a mirage. Noah really was stepping into the spot where Trey had instructed her to wait.

Noah.

Elation soared through her. His handsome face filled her heart with hope and warmth. Elle pushed to her feet, fully prepared to throw herself into his arms. But then—before she could really process the fact that only Katie had ever infused her with that kind of joy—all the good feelings rushed out. Because Noah wasn't alone. Trey stood behind him. And judging from the two men's stances, Trey had a weapon pressed to Noah's back. A second later, they were close enough that she could see that her assumption was correct. And she realized something else—she'd been used as bait. Trey had told her she was awaiting her "man." Now she knew he'd used the word deliberately. Not as a jibe, but as a means of showing his cleverness. His wide smile right at her proved it.

"Isn't it nice that Mr. Loblaw decided to join us? If he'd given us a little more notice, we might even have been able to provide him with some proper attire," he said with an exaggerated sigh. "But since he paddled all the way in from the mainland, the least we can do is let him enjoy the festivities. Maybe even walk you down the aisle?"

Noah cut in, his voice a growl. "You really are a special kind of despicable, aren't you?"

Elle's eyes burned, but she refused to cry, and instead lifted her chin and replied, "It's fine, Noah. God knows he didn't earn the privilege of giving me away."

The narrowing of his eyes was the only sign of Trey's irritation. Other than that, he maintained his unnatural politeness. He stepped back a little from Noah and gestured toward the bench that Elle had just abandoned.

"Have a seat," he suggested. "If you're not going to participate, you might as well have a good view."

Elle could see the pinch around Noah's eyes. The even line of his mouth. And for the first time, she really noticed his appearance. He looked unimpressed, yes. But also injured. His face was covered in little scrapes, his shirt torn. The spot in his neck where one of Trey's lackeys had jabbed him with the needle was bright red, the hole a crimson speck in the middle. He looked like he was soaking wet, too.

Before she could stop herself, Elle swung to Trey. "You gave me your word that you wouldn't hurt him."

He shook his head. "Uh-uh. I gave you my word that I wouldn't kill him. And that promise was contingent upon him staying away. Apparently, even telling him you're a murderer wasn't enough."

"Because I'm not a murderer."

"It doesn't matter, anyway, does it? He's just lucky I haven't killed him already. But now that you've brought it to my attention, all this waiting does is create friction, so..."

As he trailed off, he reached for the gun at his side. But before he could get a grip on the handle and drag it from its holster, another voice drew everyone's attention.

"I always thought she could love me."

The statement came from the shadows near the chapel, and they were followed by the appearance of Detective Stanley. He stepped into view, and Elle couldn't quite stifle a gasp. The detective's usual, intense look had turned wild-eyed. That hint of crazy that Elle had always sworn was there had boiled over. His hair was disheveled, his tie askew. And though he still wore the suit Trey had provided, the jacket hung open, revealing something even more terrifying than Trey and his men—a mishmash of wires and canisters that could only be a bomb. And if there were any doubt about it, it was swept away by the cord leading from the device straight up to the detective's hand.

For a moment, silence hung heavily in the air. The stillness was as subtle as a hammer hitting an anvil, and just as jarring. Finally, Trey spoke up.

"What the hell are you doing, Jimmy?" he demanded, the worry in his voice only just sneaking out from behind his authoritarian tone.

The other man shook his head and repeated his first statement. "I always thought she could love me."

"She can," Trey replied. "That's why we're here, isn't it? So you can marry Mirabella?"

"Not Mirabella," the detective said.

"He means Tawney," Noah interjected, adjusting the angle of his body so that he all but covered Elle. "Don't you, Detective?"

Detective Stanley swung his glassy eyes toward Noah, nodding. "I can't live like this anymore. Trying to pretend Tawney's daughter could fill her shoes."

Elle's heart skipped about three terrified beats as his grip on the detonator visibly tightened, and her mind shifted to Katie. Where was she now? Trey had left her with the detective and his men. And if the men hadn't stopped Stanley from coming out…

Dear God…please let her be alive.

The detective flipped his attention back to Trey. "Tell them."

"There's nothing to tell," the corrupt businessman said.

Detective Stanley lifted the detonator higher. "We can't live like this anymore, Trey. You've been ruining lives for too long. Framing Mirabella for that nanny's murder. Making me cover your tracks. All of it. But I want someone to know why it has to be this way."

Trey refused to budge. "You're unstable, Jimmy. You were always a little off, but this…"

The other man's face reddened with fury, and his next words were a scream. "Tell them!"

Elle jumped back, startled by the vehemence. Her slight stumble drew both Detective Stanley's attention and his ire.

"You aren't her," he spat. "In the dark, maybe you'd pass. But it's like putting cheap wine in a nice glass. No matter what, the taste will always be sour." He spun back to Trey. "Tell them now, or I'll lift my finger, and we'll all blow to hell."

Trey's jaw ticked. "I don't know—"

Detective Stanley swung the detonator hard, and his snarl was more vicious than a wolf's howl, and he began a wild pace of the cleared area. "We killed him. That day on the mountain. We killed him, and we buried him, and we swore not to tell anyone. Trey made us promise." He stopped dead, fixing the other man with another stare. "Tell them."

At last, Trey seemed to relent, at least a bit. "You're remembering it wrong, my friend. Tawney and I helped you with the body, yes. But you killed him. We only ever wanted to help."

Detective Stanley blinked like he was trying to process the claim, shook his head, then scratched it, and rambled on, almost under his breath. "No. No, that's not how it happened. I've been dreaming about it every night for twenty-six years. I remember every detail. Every minute. Every damn second. I told Tawney I loved her. She looked at me like she pitied me. She told me she was going to marry you. My best friend."

"That's right," Trey agreed. "All of it. And then you attacked me. And the hiker turned up and tried to pull you off me, and—"

"You killed him!"

"No."

"Yes. Yes, you did. Tawney was screaming for you to stop. Begging you. But you were so angry, and…" The detective trailed off and gave his head another shake, his words coming more surely. "You told me it was my fault, because you were trying to hit *me*." Still gripping the detonator in his left palm, he freed his weapon using his right hand. He aimed it at Trey's head. "Last chance," he said, his voice suddenly quieter than it was crazy. "Tell. Them. Now."

For a second, Trey's eyes closed. Then they opened, and slipped to Elle, then Noah, then came to rest on Detective Stanley. And even if he hadn't spoken, the truth was obvious in that brief glance. Insane or not, every word that the detective had said was real.

"Yes," Trey said. "You're right. I gave him the final hit. I stopped you from calling the police. I refused to have anything to do with Tawney after she told me she was pregnant."

"And then what?" Detective Stanley prodded.

"When she died and the lawyers brought the sniveling kid to my door, I thought I saw a way out. She looked so much like Tawney. And that was all you ever wanted, so…" Trey shrugged. "Fair substitute."

"I was never looking for a substitute. That's never what I wanted. I loved her, Trey."

"You've been half-crazy since that weekend in the mountains, Jimmy. You don't know what you want. Look at you now. Are you really going to blow yourself and all of us up just for the sake of being right? If you wanted to die, you should've just said so years ago. You have to know that the only reason I never killed you or Mirabella was because you stole that map of where we hid the hiker's body from me and promised it would go public if you died."

A triumphant smile broke on the detective's face. "That, my friend, was the best lie I ever told you. I didn't keep that map. I burned it the very next day."

For the first time in all the years that she'd found out that Trey Charger was her biological father, his facade truly broke apart. He was furious. Embarrassed. Humiliated. Each emotion played across his face with absolute clarity. He lunged forward. But as he did, Detective Stanley lifted his thumb from the detonator. Simultaneously, Elle felt the air leave her lungs and the weight of Noah's body hit her as he knocked her to the ground, shielding her from the oncoming blast.

But it never came.

Instead of an explosion, it was a simple shot that rang out. And when Elle lifted her head out from under Noah's arm, she saw why. The "bomb" remained intact. It was a fake. A decoy. But Trey Charger lay on the ground, eyes open and sightless, blood seeping from a bullet hole in the center of his forehead.

"Couldn't stop me from calling the police this time, could he?" said Detective Stanley, and he collapsed to the ground and put his hands on his head.

Epilogue

Six months later...

Elle stared out at the bright water, basking in the sunshine as she watched Katie bounce along on her inflatable unicorn. Her daughter—officially, now that all of the proper paperwork had at last been processed—was always like this. Laughing and smiling. Like the first six years of her life hadn't been spent in hiding. Like the man who was her biological father had never kidnapped her. It was everything Elle had ever wanted. And she had no complaints. Especially not since they were spending Katie's seventh birthday on a Hawaiian beach. There was only one small piece missing. And a glance down at her phone told her that he'd be finished talking to his twin sister any second, then joining her on the colorful blanket to soak up some more sun together.

As if on cue, a pair of warm lips landed on her shoulder,

and a set of equally warm hands slid down her arms. And Elle automatically smiled in response. She didn't flinch. She didn't have a moment of panic where she worried that it might not be Noah as he slid in behind her and pulled her against his chest. Belatedly—and with a great deal of surprise—she realized that she was much like Katie in that regard. She'd somehow managed to acclimatize to the idea that she was safe. Her brain and her body made the assumption that no one was out to get her, whereas before, she assumed danger lurked around every corner. It was remarkable, really, to think about it.

With Detective Stanley's confession had come a deeper police investigation. The remains of a long-missing hiker were uncovered on the mountain, right where he'd said they would be.

Closure, she thought. *This is what closure feels like.*

She opened her mouth to comment on it all to Noah, but he spoke before she could. "So… I've been thinking…"

"Oh, you have, have you?" Elle teased.

"Mmm. Hear me out."

"I'm listening."

He pulled his arm away, shuffled a little behind her, then dropped something onto her lap. She looked down at the pink velvet box and opened her mouth. But Noah was faster again.

"I know I've asked you ninety-nine times before…" he said.

"Thirty-two," Elle corrected.

He chuckled and kissed the back of her neck. "And each time you've turned me down because it was 'too soon,' as you put it."

"Marrying someone after knowing them for one day is too soon by anyone's standards," she pointed out.

"So you say."

"So I *know*."

"Fine. But you still have to listen to my spiel."

"I did say I was listening," Elle teased.

"Okay. I've made a little list." He shifted again, this time so she had a view of his fingers as he counted off. "One. Your paperwork for Katie came through."

"Yes, it did."

"Two. Sentencing came down for James Stanley."

"Also true."

"Three. The government lawyers finally went through Trey's stuff, and you're more or less sorted for life."

"I still don't like it. But yes."

"All of that's led me to the only thing that makes sense."

Elle fought a smile. "Which is?"

"You can pay me back what you owe me," he announced.

"Noah, you know I'm— Wait. What?"

"You owe me twenty grand."

She waited for the punchline, and when he said nothing else, she turned to look at him. "Seriously?"

He nodded. "Yep."

"Okay, putting aside everything else…twenty grand? I thought I was at thirteen-thousand and something."

"Yeah, well. Our time apart added a doctor's bill, a cab ride…some stolen property. Oh. And some serious heartache."

"I paid for this trip!" she protested.

"The trip came post-relationship," he pointed out.

With a weird stab of disappointment pricking at her, Elle swiveled to face Katie again. Noah swept her hair away from her shoulder and gave her ear a little nip.

"But lucky for you," he said, "I've come up with a solution. Open the box."

She wrinkled her nose, but did as she was told, noticing for the first time that the box was different than the one he'd pressed into her hands thirty-two times before.

"Did you pick a new ring?" she asked.

"Only one way to find out."

Her heart fluttered. She was inexplicably more nervous than she'd been with his clockwork proposals. But when she lifted the velvet lid, all she found was emptiness.

"I don't get it," she confessed.

Noah laughed against her skin. "That's because this time, the ring wasn't for you."

"Who was it…" Elle trailed off, and her eyes found Katie.

She realized abruptly that the little girl had been unusually quiet all morning. And that she'd spent an awfully long amount of time out of chatting distance, too. And now, Elle could swear she saw a sparkly flash on Katie's finger. And it pleased her immensely.

"What did you tell her?" she asked.

"The same thing I tell you every day," he replied easily. "That I love her. That each day, I love her more. That I want to keep loving her for the rest of my life."

"And what did she say?"

"That I should probably marry her momma."

"And?"

His mouth made a pleasant heated path from her ear to her chin. "I said I'd ask. Again."

"And?" Elle repeated, keeping her eyes on her daughter, but leaning into Noah at the same time.

A second little box plopped into her lap—the same one she'd seen thirty-two times before. "Please, Elle. I'm pretty sure I've loved you since the second I saw you there in that park. Be my wife?"

"All right, Noah. I guess thirty-three is your lucky number."

"Yeah?"

"Yes."

There was this briefest pause, and then Noah added, "Well. This takes care of the money you owe me. But I think it's going to create some more paperwork."

"What? Why?"

"All the legal stuff it'll take to make Katie my daughter, too."

Elle's mouth opened, but whatever she was about to say was cut off by Noah's lips. They pressed to hers in an unhurried kiss. Tender and slow. Familiar and wondrous. A touch that let her know that she was his, and he was hers. Then he pulled away, touched her cheek, and jumped to his feet. He cast her a quick, sexy wink before loping off toward Katie. And as Elle watched him go, she couldn't help but think how good it was to be thinking about a beginning instead of an ending.

* * * * *

Don't miss Noah's sister's book, coming in May 2021 wherever Harlequin Romantic Suspense books and ebooks are sold!

**WE HOPE YOU ENJOYED
THIS BOOK FROM**

**HARLEQUIN
ROMANTIC
SUSPENSE**

Danger. Passion. Drama.

These heart-racing page-turners will keep you guessing
to the very end. Experience the thrill of unexpected
plot twists and irresistible chemistry.

4 NEW BOOKS AVAILABLE EVERY MONTH!

She shivered next to him, clearly upset as she spoke. He put his arm around her and pressed a kiss to the top of her head.

"It's okay," he soothed, stroking her upper arm. "I'm here now. I won't let anyone hurt you or Ben."

"I think he has a key."

That got his attention. He paused midstroke, digesting this bit of news. "What makes you say that?"

She told him about Jake Porter, the man who claimed to be Will's grandson. The way he'd visited her earlier, his displeasure at finding her in the house.

"We'll change all the locks," Carter declared. "I'll go first thing in the morning, as soon as the hardware stores open. We can even put some extra locks on, as additional deterrent. And I want you and Ben to stay with me until he's apprehended." His apartment wasn't large, but they would make it work. She could have his bed and he'd take the couch. The discomfort was a small price to pay for knowing she and the baby were safe.

"Oh, no," she said. "We can't do that."

Carter drew back and stared at her, blinking in confusion. This was a no-brainer. Someone was out there with an agenda, and it was clear they were after something inside this house. Changing the locks was a good first step, but he doubted the intruder was going to be put off so easily. Unless he missed his guess, this guy was going to come back. And the next time, he might not be content to simply ransack a few rooms.

Carter took her hand. "I'm not trying to be alarmist here, but he's probably going to try again."

"But the locks," she said weakly.

"I doubt he'll let new locks stop him," Carter replied. "And given the way he acted with you before, it's probably only going to escalate. If he finds you here, he might hurt you."

Get 4 FREE REWARDS!

We'll send you 2 FREE Books plus 2 FREE Mystery Gifts.

Harlequin Romantic Suspense books are heart-racing page-turners with unexpected plot twists and irresistible chemistry that will keep you guessing to the very end.

FREE Value Over **$20**

YES! Please send me 2 FREE Harlequin Romantic Suspense novels and my 2 FREE gifts (gifts are worth about $10 retail). After receiving them, if I don't wish to receive any more books, I can return the shipping statement marked "cancel." If I don't cancel, I will receive 4 brand-new novels every month and be billed just $4.99 per book in the U.S. or $5.74 per book in Canada. That's a savings of at least 13% off the cover price! It's quite a bargain! Shipping and handling is just 50¢ per book in the U.S. and $1.25 per book in Canada.* I understand that accepting the 2 free books and gifts places me under no obligation to buy anything. I can always return a shipment and cancel at any time. The free books and gifts are mine to keep no matter what I decide.

240/340 HDN GNMZ

Name (please print)

Address   Apt. #

City   State/Province   Zip/Postal Code

Email: Please check this box ☐ if you would like to receive newsletters and promotional emails from Harlequin Enterprises ULC and its affiliates. You can unsubscribe anytime.

Mail to the Reader Service:
IN U.S.A.: P.O. Box 1341, Buffalo, NY 14240-8531
IN CANADA: P.O. Box 603, Fort Erie, Ontario L2A 5X3

Want to try 2 free books from another series! Call 1-800-873-8635 or visit www.ReaderService.com.

---

*Terms and prices subject to change without notice. Prices do not include sales taxes, which will be charged (if applicable) based on your state or country of residence. Canadian residents will be charged applicable taxes. Offer not valid in Quebec. This offer is limited to one order per household. Books received may not be as shown. Not valid for current subscribers to Harlequin Romantic Suspense books. All orders subject to approval. Credit or debit balances in a customer's account(s) may be offset by any other outstanding balance owed by or to the customer. Please allow 4 to 6 weeks for delivery. Offer available while quantities last.

Your Privacy—Your information is being collected by Harlequin Enterprises ULC, operating as Reader Service. For a complete summary of the information we collect, how we use this information and to whom it is disclosed, please visit our privacy notice located at corporate.harlequin.com/privacy-notice. From time to time we may also exchange your personal information with reputable third parties. If you wish to opt out of this sharing of your personal information, please visit readerservice.com/consumerschoice or call 1-800-873-8635. **Notice to California Residents**—Under California law, you have specific rights to control and access your data. For more information on these rights and how to exercise them, visit corporate.harlequin.com/california-privacy.

HRS20R2

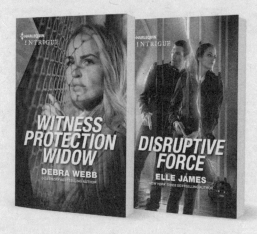

Love Harlequin romance?

DISCOVER.

Be the first to find out about promotions,
news and exclusive content!

Facebook.com/HarlequinBooks

Twitter.com/HarlequinBooks

Instagram.com/HarlequinBooks

Pinterest.com/HarlequinBooks

ReaderService.com

EXPLORE.

Sign up for the Harlequin e-newsletter and
download a free book from any series at
TryHarlequin.com

CONNECT.

Join our Harlequin community to
share your thoughts and connect
with other romance readers!
Facebook.com/groups/HarlequinConnection

HARLEQUIN

Heartfelt or suspenseful, inspiring or passionate, Harlequin has your happily-ever-after.

With new books published
every month, you are sure to find the
satisfying escape you know you deserve.